HUNKS OF HOCKEY

HUNKS OF HOCKEY

They're the bad boys of the ice—the men of the Dallas Blaze hockey club who take to the cold, hard surface on a regular basis to do battle over a small, black disc of vulcanized rubber. Meanwhile, off the ice, these hunks wage a more subtle and seductive battle to win the hearts, minds and bodies of their ladies.

Previously available only in electronic format, these steamy novellas have now been combined for a paperback edition! Included are the tales...

In The Crease

Faced with a career-ending injury, superstar goalie Adam Cryder, finds his mind and libido snared by strong and sexy physical therapist Susannah Robers...

"Erica DeQuaya did it again with this remarkable story about letting the past go and learning to love again, not an easy task when it comes to two people afraid to love. If there is one book of Ms. DeQuaya's to start the New Year, [this] is it...great to read, but also the power of healing is strong in this book."

—Lena C.
Fallen Angel Reviews

"The chemistry between (Susannah and Adam) is hot, but there is more to their relationship than lust. If you're looking for a quick but enjoyable read, look no further than *In the Crease*."

—Mary E
Coffee Time Romance

Two On One

Hockey forward Gary Jacobsen's past shame means he'll do anything to win back the love of his wife, Jeanne Bradley-Jacobsen, even if it means sharing her with another man...

Penalty Kill

Adrian Donelson, passionate defenseman, learns that giving up hard-earned control to best friend and dominatrix Daria DeCarlo creates a night to remember and regrets the morning after...

Welcome to the world of professional hockey, where the hits are hard...the games intense...and where anything is possible in the bedroom.

"Recommended Read!...Erica DeQuaya's writing skill is evident as she takes Adrian and Daria from friendship to lovers and never misses a beat. If you are looking for a quick read to warm the night, *Penalty Kill* delivers."

—Barb
TwoLips Reviews

HUNKS OF HOCKEY

BY

ERICA DEQUAYA

AMBER QUILL PRESS, LLC
http://www.amberquill.com

HUNKS OF HOCKEY
AN AMBER QUILL PRESS BOOK

Amber Quill Press, LLC
http://www.amberquill.com

Copyright © 2007 by Erica DeQuaya
ISBN 978-1-60272-939-1
Cover Art © 2007 Trace Edward Zaber

Layout and Formatting provided by: ElementalAlchemy.com

PUBLISHED IN THE UNITED STATES OF AMERICA

TABLE OF CONTENTS

IN THE CREASE

HUNKS OF HOCKEY

CHAPTER 1

Susannah hesitated a moment outside the office door, gathering her thoughts. She was about to meet with Mr. and Mrs. Hockey, as they'd been dubbed more often than once by the Dallas-Fort Worth media, and she'd need to have all her wits about her.

The couple's prized possession, one Adam Cryder, goalie extraordinaire, nicknamed "Crate," was injured. And she, Susannah Robers, was the lucky one who would have to break the news that his injury would keep him off-ice for a few more weeks, if not longer. His recovery time had been grossly underestimated by the team physician, and she cursed him. Nothing new about that. She'd been cursing the team doctor on a regular basis since having this case dropped in her lap some weeks ago.

Susannah leaned on her cane for a moment, trying to postpone the inevitable. Her leg ached. Stress did that sometimes, but she forced herself to ignore the pain as she reviewed, in her head, the information about Adam's case.

A rookie's skate had moved over the goalie's somehow exposed wrist during a heated game, opening the skin, nicking the artery and slicing a few tendons for good measure. What Susannah didn't know, what none of the medical staff knew right now, was potential damage done to the ulnar nerve. Depending on the extent of that nerve damage, it could be bye-bye hockey career for the Dallas Blaze's starting goalie.

"Well, may as well get this over with," Susannah muttered to herself. "They're not going to be any less pissed with a delay."

3

She raised her cane and rapped sharply on the door. She'd seen people do the cane-rap-on-the-door routine in movies and thought it looked kind of cool. Suave and debonair. Unfortunately, it didn't work for her as she almost lost her balance and fell against the door. Susannah restrained a laugh as she set the cane back down on the floor.

Susannah, Queen of Grace, strikes again.

She was told to enter, and stomping on her wry amusement, Susannah did just that.

Brian Corrigan, owner of the Dallas Blaze and part owner of its minor league affiliate, North Texas Panthers, sat at his desk, his chair cocked back, legs on his desk. Kristin DuChein, Brian's wife and co-owner of the Panthers, stood at the window, examining the view of the Dallas skyline, arms folded. Both seemed relaxed, but Susannah could sense tension in them. They craved good news about Cryder and Susannah swore to herself. The news she had was anything but good.

"Have a seat, Susannah." Brian's voice was polite. Taking him up on it, Susannah sat on one of the many comfortable chairs littering the huge office. She put Cryder's file on her lap, cursing the fact she was too damn good at her job. If she'd been a quack, Kristen never would have sought her out in the first place. Susannah would be in her Far North Dallas clinic, happily rotating shoulders, flexing ankles and using acupressure on sore joints.

But she was here, so nothing could be done about it. Before she could start talking, though, Kristen turned, regarded her and sighed.

"It's pretty bad, isn't it, Anna?" Kristen asked.

"It's—" Susannah groped for the right words to soften what she was about to say, then gave up. There were no right words. Not for this one.

"Right now, the goal is to get his arm and hand moving again," Susannah said, slowly. "Outside of that, I can't make any promises about his future."

The uncomfortable pause following her words made Susannah sorry she'd been so blunt.

"What, exactly, is wrong?" Brian spoke shortly. "Leaving out the medicalese. I swear to God if I have to listen to one more doctor spout nonsense about carpals and nerves and tendons, I'm going to punch someone out."

"Brian." Kristen spoke softly and he looked away, clearly trying to control his anger. Then Kristen nodded for her to proceed.

Susannah cleared her throat and glanced warily at Brian. He seemed like a panther, ready to strike. Kristen, following her glance, frowned at her husband. "And we'll both keep quiet until she's finished, won't we?"

Brian shot a glare at Kristen for a moment, then looked away, mulishly pressing his lips together.

Susannah restrained her laughter, with an effort. The battles these two had were legendary in the hockey world. Even Susannah, who was only on the periphery, had heard the gossip about their torrid relationship which, apparently, was carried into the bedroom.

But she wasn't here to speculate on Brian and Kristen's sex life. "Okay, Brian. I'll explain this as simply as I can, without the medicalese," Susannah said, flashing a grin at the Blaze's owner. Brian responded with a grimace of his own that Susannah believed was suspiciously close to a smile.

"Anyway. When the blade moved over Cryder's arm, it made a mess. A cut artery, which is why he bled so much. Six tendons were slashed. And the ulnar nerve." Susannah paused, waiting for another outburst, but apparently Kristen's words were doing their job. The man nodded at her to continue, and Susannah cleared her throat.

"The tendons will heal; he's in pretty good physical shape. They repaired the artery, too, so nothing wrong there. From what I can tell, it seems to be healing fine. He's afraid to move his hand, but we can get him over that." She swallowed. Now she was getting to the part she didn't want to talk about. "My concern is the nerve. They've managed to repair it, but it takes time to heal—"

"How long will it take? What happens after it heals?" Brian's words cut across her spiel, and Susannah sat on a sudden burst of anger.

So much for keeping him calm and rational.

"I don't know. But if it doesn't heal correctly, he won't be able to grip his stick." Susannah decided on bluntness again. She was tired of tip-toeing around this whole thing. If Brian was going to fly into a temper tantrum, so be it.

"He can't play if he can't grip his stick," Kristen said.

"Really?" Brian's voice was loaded with sarcasm and Kristen faced him, hands on her hips, her eyes flashing.

"Don't be a jackass."

Susannah cleared her throat. She was concerned enough about Cryder without dropping The Needlers, the constantly bickering couple from "Saturday Night Live," into the mix.

"It's not a death sentence," Susannah said firmly. "Adam can undergo occupational therapy to get everything moving again. It's not hopeless. Some nerve injuries do pretty well. But some of this is psychological. Would he be able to get out on the ice to skate again? I don't know. A lot depends on how this accident might have spooked him."

"Could you help him out?" Kristen asked.

There it was. The $64,000 question. "Well, I'm a physical therapist, not an occupational therapist," Susannah said slowly. "I'm also not a psychiatrist or anything. This type of thing is probably better—"

"I trust you," Kristen said. She nodded at Brian. "We both want Adam to be with someone we trust. Someone we know. You've worked with our guys."

Sure, she had. But she didn't have crushes on those guys. Not like the crush she'd had on Adam Cryder for years. Despite that, and despite Susannah's work with the team, the first time she and Adam had met face-to-face was following his emergence from the three-hour surgery to repair his wrist. Problem was, his reaction hadn't been very positive when he'd set eyes on her.

"Shit," was his comment. Not that Susannah had blamed him. The prognosis was rarely good if they had to call in the "Angel of Pain" as some of the other Blaze players sarcastically dubbed her.

"You're one of the few PTs in the area who works with extremities," Kristen said now.

That's the problem, Kristen. There's only one extremity of Adam's I'm interested in...

"I don't know much about sports injuries," Susannah said, pushing sex-soaked thoughts about the Blaze's goalie out of her brain.

"Bullshit." Kristen's eyes shot violet fire and Susannah wondered if she should be more afraid of Kristen or her husband. "You treat the Blaze on a regular basis. You've treated the Panthers and the Wildcats—"

"Sure. Sprains and strains." Susannah looked at them both soberly. "Okay, I'll be honest. I've dealt with a lot of carpel tunnel syndrome. And yeah, I've loosened up hands and wrists when they've been immobilized in casts. But this goes way beyond any of that. And if I can't do it and he doesn't get better, guess who gets blamed? I'm not going to be the scapegoat if Adam Cryder finds he can't hold a hockey stick again."

"No one would blame you," Kristen said.

Susannah looked at her, steadily. They both knew it was bullshit. If she was charged with getting Adam's hand moving again and it didn't work, she'd be blamed for not pulling a miracle out of the hat. Conversely, if she succeeded, she wouldn't be thanked. Welcome to the world of sports medicine. You're damned if you don't, not thanked if you do.

"Okay." Susannah wasn't in the mood to argue. She'd delivered her news and they could do whatever they wanted with the prognosis. "My recommendation is some sessions of therapy. Get the hand and wrist moving again. Once he's there, you can determine the next step—"

"I'd like you on the case," Brian said, interrupting her once again. "But you don't want to do it. I thought you therapists adored challenges."

Susannah considered Brian's words. He was right; she was almost salivating at the challenge of getting Adam Cryder back on the ice. But another part of her, the one that ruled her libido, relished the challenge of getting Cryder into her bed. If her libido overruled her good sense— even supposing Cryder enjoyed balling tall, somewhat overweight women with limps who wore glasses—it could get her into huge trouble with the Texas Physical Therapist Association. Most of the folks in that organization frowned on consensual sex between client and therapist.

Besides. He was a jock. Automatically off-limits. 'Nuff said.

"We'll pay well." Brian sensed some of her reluctance, but misjudged the reason.

"It's not the money," Susannah said. "There's the commute from North Dallas to downtown. Cryder's not my only patient, and I'd have to arrange for my caseload to be taken over. Also, I'm just not sure I'm the one he needs. I'm not one to coddle my patients."

"That's exactly what he doesn't need," Brian said. "I don't want Crate feeling sorry for himself."

"Please." Kristen's eyes met hers again, pleadingly. "Crate's special to this organization. Even if he can never block a goal again, or anything like that, he might fit in as a coach…"

Susannah sighed, melting under the other woman's pleas. *What a fucking marshmallow I am.*

"All right," she said. "I'll do my best."

CHAPTER 2

Adam saw her as he stepped into the Blaze's training room. He had the advantage, as her back was to him. She sat at one of the desks next to the wall, and her head, with its short blonde hair, was bent over paperwork.

He took advantage of her absorption in work to study her. Susannah Robers, nicknamed the Angel of Pain by a lot of his teammates and others in the Dallas sports world. Susannah had the reputation for providing cures to injuries that, many times, were worse than the injuries themselves. A lot of his teammates discussed her in tones of almost reverential fear, but until now, Adam'd never had the pleasure of her skills. He knew she had little patience for whining or excuses. But her bullying and prodding got injured players back in the game. For better or worse, she had the ruthless, yet disciplined hands of a healer.

Adam's problem was that he wished those hands would be doing something else on his body, another type of healing. Angrily, he swatted Marvin Gaye's "Sexual Healing" out of his mind. No way was Susannah his type. She was too large, she swore like a sailor in a whorehouse, and she made it abundantly clear that she never dated jocks. *Never.* He had nothing against women in glasses who limped and who steered clear of romantic entanglements with sports guys. He just didn't relish the idea of taking them to bed. Nor did he need to. Since taking the hockey world by storm some two decades before, Adam had never lacked for female companionship in or out of the sack.

Under normal circumstances, he wouldn't have looked twice at

Susannah. Yet since he'd swum up to consciousness from surgery some weeks back to see her standing by his bedside, talking quietly with a nurse, he'd felt a sudden and inexplicable primal lust for this woman that hadn't abated with time. At first he'd thought it was the drugs that put his brain on high-erotica. But that hadn't washed. Since then, and on a regular basis, Susannah had trotted through his sexual fantasies, leading him to beat off with his good hand.

Thinking about his good hand made him think about his left hand, the one attached to the wrist he'd injured. Adam sighed, looking down at the brace covering his little problem. He remembered falling on the ice from a blocked shot. He remembered, somehow, that his sleeve had slid up his wrist, making the sensitive flesh vulnerable to a skate. And the skate that had cut him had belonged to some numb-nuts rookie from his own goddam team, who wasn't looking where he was going. The result was a wrapped hand which was useless to him. Adam hung on to his anger at the rookie. It did a decent job of dousing his outright fear that he'd never play again, not to mention the unreasonable lust for the woman who would hopefully help him get back to the ice. He wanted nothing more than to be guarding his crease, that area in front of the net. He forcefully put out of his mind another crease he'd like to be playing around with—the moist crease between Susannah's legs.

Squaring his shoulders and ordering his libido to calm down, Adam cleared his throat. Susannah swiveled around in her chair, and examined him carefully with turquoise eyes through gold-rimmed glasses. Then she smiled and got to her feet.

"I'm glad to see you on your feet, Adam Cryder. The last time I saw you, you were a little out of it." Her voice was low and sexy, curling seductively in his ears, stroking his brain. She held out her hand and he took it with his good one, trying to ignore the erotic heat the touch created. She wasn't trying to be coy or alluring, but his body was sure reacting as though she were.

"Yeah, 'a little out of it' describes it pretty well," Adam said, forcing himself to respond to her comment with an easy manner. He dropped her hand. "It's nice to see you again, Susannah."

Her eyes twinkled at him, though her face was solemn. "I'll remind you of that in about a week or so, when you're ready to swear at me. Take a seat." She motioned to one of the therapy tables. Adam chose one, hooked a stool with his leg and sat. Susannah pulled her own stool forward and perched on it. "Let's see what's going on here. Take off your brace."

Trying to keep his mind off her citrus scent and the funky things it was doing to his body, Adam reluctantly removed the brace and stocking covering his arm. As he always did, he had to turn his head away from the ugly scar forming there. God, he hated that thing and everything it represented. The pain. The frustration of being so helpless. The fact it was keeping him from the ice.

Susannah said nothing, but studied his hand and wrist carefully. Despite it all, he felt himself tensing. She caught his eye and grinned, reassuringly. "Relax, Cryder. It's not going to hurt. Not yet, at any rate."

"It hasn't stopped hurting," Adam told her, then regretted the complaint. As a goalie, he'd learned to keep his aches and pains to himself. Force of habit—none of his teammates sympathized when he'd get hammered in a game, not that he could blame them. He supposed a person had to have a masochistic streak to stand in a net and willingly have pucks shot at him. He laughed suddenly and Susannah regarded him with a smile.

"Share the joke?"

"I must be insane to be a goalie."

She shrugged and went back to studying his hand. "Well, maybe not, maybe so. But you're damned good at it. Leading the Blaze to the Tannen Trophy last year. Winning the Gustav Trophy for lowest GAA." She shook her head, marveling. "You deserved it, Cryder. I saw how close those games were in the finals. It comes down to the goal-keeping during playoff time. You were all over the crease; at times, I thought there were two of you in front of the goal. Amazing."

Adam stared at her, astounded she'd followed it all so closely. He knew she dealt with sports players on a regular basis, but didn't realize how deeply she was into it. "You know a lot about hockey."

She shrugged. "I like hockey. I follow it. Try to move your fingers, will you?"

Adam wondered about her reluctance to talk about hockey. Typical hockey fans bent his ear, on and on, until he wanted to scream at them to shut up.

"Wiggle your fingers," she said again.

He swallowed, his gut clenching in fear. "I—can't." The panic was back, the panic that he couldn't move his hand and never would.

Susannah nodded and her eyes softened. "Okay. Calm down. This is normal. When the arm and hand have been immobilized like yours has been for weeks, it'll be stiff. That's why you're here. That's why I've been brought in."

Yeah, right. And speaking of stiff...

Adam realized, to his grim astonishment, that his close proximity to the woman was getting him hard. But he thought he had it figured out. Her demeanor and posture reminded him of some fierce Brünnhilde, off to protect Siegfried, despite the fact she'd lose out on immortality for doing so. He'd always appreciated Brünnhilde's bravery in Richard Wagner's operatic ring cycle. Now here she was, in the flesh, in the form of Susanna Robers.

I could be Siegfried to her Brünnhilde.

Good God. Adam shook his brain free from the wacko love story and accompanying erotic images his mind was creating, with himself as the powerful Siegfried kissing awake the sleeping Brünnhilde. And doing other things to her that weren't in the opera.

"I'm good at my job," Susannah was saying, and Adam focused on her words. "I'll do my best by you." She adjusted her glasses, and looked at him.

"But it will heal?" He wondered at the pensive look on her face.

"Nerve injuries depend on a lot of things. The age and physical condition of the person. But you're young, you're in good shape, so yeah. It should heal if"—she glared at him—"you follow my instructions to the letter."

"Yes, ma'am!" He gave her a mock salute and she laughed.

"For the time being, let's see if we can get some of those joints loosened with a paraffin bath. Come on."

She stood up, picked up her cane, and limped to one of the counters where a small container sat. As he followed her, Adam looked at it hesitantly. It reminded him of a crock pot. When Susannah opened it up and Adam peeked inside, he saw something that looked like liquid wax. Hot liquid wax.

"What is that?" he asked.

"Liquid wax."

"Uh—" He pulled away slightly. "Wax is for candles where I come from, sweetheart. No way am I burning my hand with that shit."

Susannah crossed her arms and he could tell she was restraining her laughter with an effort.

"Jeez, for a guy who blocks hard rubber for a living, you're such a marshmallow. Trust me, Cryder. This isn't going to hurt. It'll help, if you let it. Now sit, and let me dip."

He flushed at her implied challenge, then wordlessly gave his hand.

Brünnhilde and a ball-breaker in the bargain. Not a good combination. He forced the sudden picture out of his head of Susannah touching his balls, licking them. Adam shifted, hoping to hide his erection.

Seemingly oblivious to his lust, Susannah took his hand gently and dipped it once, twice, three times into the liquid paraffin. Adam was relieved and amazed to realize it wasn't hot at all. Even more amazed to realize the warmth felt good on his sore tendons. She wrapped his hand in foil and laid it gently on the counter.

"Did you bring a book?" she wanted to know. "You're going to be doing nothing for fifteen minutes so I hope you can amuse yourself."

"So you warned me on the phone yesterday. Book's in my backpack."

"I'll get it."

Suiting action to words, Susannah was on her feet and moving to his pack. Her limp seemed fairly pronounced, but before he could ask her about it, she had the book in her hands and was staring at it with interest. She came back to him and handed the book to him.

"Janet Evanovich?"

Adam looked up and grinned, almost sheepishly. "Yeah. Good mind candy."

"Pretty accurate, too." Susannah sat down with her files and continued. "My mom is from Jersey, from the part Evanovich writes about, so she knows a lot of those characters."

"They're all like that in the 'Burg,' huh?"

Susannah grinned at him. He'd just about wrestled his hard-on to a manageable level, but her smile brought it raging up again. Welcome to the land of blue-balls.

"Actually, Evanovich was being kind," Susannah said, in response to his question. "They're pretty clannish there. They believe the world begins and ends in that little patch near Trenton. It's not surprising that my mom's family was appalled when she married my dad, a bonafide Texan. *His* family had settled in New Braunfels."

A shadow crossed her face for a moment, then it was gone.

"Mom told me she'd been afraid to move down here because of the Texan attitude toward Yankees; leastwise, that's what her charming family told her," Susannah went on. "Well, they were very welcoming and all. Dad had the problems, though, the other way around. The Jersey folks refused to accept him."

"How about you? Did they embrace you as the prodigal daughter?"

She snorted. "Hell, no. I'm too much my dad's daughter. Too much

Texan. I even look like him—blonde hair, blue eyes; a descendent of all those Germans who settled around New Braunfels in the distant past."

Adam listened closely. He could discern a faint Southern accent, but nothing major. When he commented on it, she smiled.

"I went north to college and physical therapy school. I made myself lose it. But"—her voice suddenly took on a Texan lilt, thick as honey and as sweet—"there are times when a lil ole accent comes in handy, don't you think, darlin'?"

She fluttered her eyes at him. He knew she was teasing, but the accent, combined with the fluttering eyelashes did it. Forget about blue balls. Dancing before him was the image of her stripped naked and himself buried deeply inside her moist heat...

"Are you native, Cryder?" Her comment jolted him from his sensual reverie. He took a deep breath and told his hormones to calm down.

"From Minnesota," he said.

She looked at him appraisingly. "Well, that makes sense. You have that Nordic-Viking look about you. Red hair, green eyes, tall. Too tall for a goalie, as I think about it."

"You got that right. One benefit of this"—Adam motioned to his hand—"is that my back isn't hurting anymore. I have to crouch too much around that damned goal. There's a reason why most goalies top out at five-foot-nine or so."

"I bet." Susannah looked at his foil-wrapped hand. "How's that doing?"

Adam tried flexing his fingers and realized, to his surprise, that the heat had loosened them a little. "Good. Better than it has in awhile."

Susannah nodded. "Okay, read your book. You're stopping me from my paperwork, and while I'm glad to have an excuse, I gotta get it done."

She smiled at him to take the sting from her words and returned to her desk. Adam cracked open his book, but his mind wasn't on Evanovich's scattered hero, bond agent Stephanie Plum. His mind was on Susannah Robers, physical therapist extraordinaire. He wondered about her. Wondered why she was so good at her job. Wondered why she limped.

Wondered why she was getting him so aroused.

No answer to that one, he realized grimly. With an effort, he turned his attention to the book.

Some time later—approximately two chapters, in Adam's estimation—Susannah returned to his side, unwrapped his hand and gently flexed his wrist.

"It's stiff," she told him.

Well, yeah. She was right about that.

"That's the understatement of the year," he said out loud, assuming she was talking about his hand, rather than his cock.

"What painkiller are you on?"

"Vicodan."

"You're not driving on that shit, are you?" She looked at him narrowly and he shrugged.

"Take a cab," she suggested. "Bill it to the team. You're going to need to be on that painkiller before you come see me. Your team doctor and Brian Corrigan gave me a deadline to get you out on the ice, and if this is going to work, I have to push you."

She gently began manipulating his fingers. While the touch wasn't painful, he felt his groin begin to throb. Gritting his teeth, Adam willed away his hard-on, but the more he tried, the harder he got.

"I'm sorry if I'm hurting you," she said softly.

"It's okay." Adam craved the pain, actually, hoping it would get his mind off his penis. At his words Susannah proceeded to slowly straighten his knuckles out. Forget about blue balls now; the pain was exquisite from joints held immobile for weeks and stretched to the maximum. His hard-on forgotten in a sudden wash of agony, Adam fought the pain with a will. He'd been a goalie for most of his life and had endured various aches. Never before had he realized how excruciating this particular pain could be. But he'd swallow knives before telling her.

But Susannah stopped her ministrations and glared at him. "Adam, you need to tell me if it's too much."

"It's fine." His voice was a wince through gritted teeth.

"Bullshit. You're not helping anyone here."

"I'm a goalie. I can deal with it."

"You're a macho idiot. All you jocks are alike; can't admit it when you're in pain. It doesn't do you, or me, any good if you're in pain when you leave here. You won't want to come back."

Adam shook his head. "Not true. I want to get back to the ice. More than anything."

She looked at him, her face set, then bent to his hand and wrist again. This time, her touch was gentle and Adam let out a small sigh of relief. It still hurt, but it wasn't the burning agony of a few seconds before.

"Okay. I think we're done here," she said. "I don't want to strain this too much. But please remember to take that painkiller, Cryder."

"Sure. Thanks." Adam put his brace back on and watched as she stood and stretched. She looked sexy; the green turtleneck she wore set off her blonde hair and pale complexion well, while emphasizing her full breasts.

"Have you ever thought about not wearing glasses?" he asked.

Susannah looked at him, startled at the question. Then she smiled. "Are you kidding? I'd be as blind as a bat. I thought about contacts, but with the four allergy seasons here in Texas, it would be impossible."

"Take them off for a minute, will you?"

Susannah looked at him, frowning, suspicious. Then, shrugging, she removed them. Adam hadn't realized she had such an attractive face; rounded at the bottom, with a firm chin and high cheekbones. Not to mention those wonderful eyes, which were soft, unfocused.

"Well, you haven't run from the room screaming, so I'm assuming I haven't grown three noses or anything," Susannah said.

"You look good either way," he said noncommittally, though his heart was thumping. He hadn't expected her to be so pretty. She had an attractive quality with her glasses; without them, she was downright appealing.

Susannah put her glasses back on and regarded him. "What were you trying to pull there? What trick?"

"Trick?"

She put her hands on her hips. "Don't play innocent with me, Adam Cryder. I hear rumors of you. All those pranks you play. The trouble you get into."

Adam smiled, disarmingly. "All rumors. Of course."

"Of course." Her voice gently mocked him.

"I wouldn't do it to you, Anna," he said. "It's called payback. You can inflict pain on me. I know better."

"Ah, so you're learning, aren't you?" She grinned at him and, to his surprise, he felt his heart flip over. This woman was the furthest thing ever from his type in terms of looks, but he found her challenge of him enormously appealing.

He found himself wondering if she'd be as challenging in bed.

He quashed that thought instantly, telling himself once and for all to get her out of his mind. Susannah Robers was his physical therapist.

She'd been charged to get him back on the ice. If she failed because of his ham-handed attempt to get into her pants, she'd be the one to pay. Not him.

Adam cleared his throat and got to his feet. "Well, thanks for the—uh—session." He held out his right hand and she took it in both of hers. The soft feel of her flesh against his sent an unwelcome and unexpected wave of lust through him and he clenched his teeth.

Her hand tightened on his. To his surprise, he detected a momentary flash of desire flowing across her face. There, then gone.

She dropped his hand almost as if it burned.

"Adam, I'm going to be honest with you. If you're upset at the pace at which this is going, you can yell at me and curse me out all you want. I won't mind—I'm used to it. The lot of a physical therapist. But tell me if I'm doing something wrong, or if something is truly hurting. I can't read minds."

"Okay."

She touched his cheek gently and smiled then.

"Thanks," she said quietly. Before he could respond, she turned and left.

CHAPTER 3

Susannah awoke, a startled cry on her lips. She stared at the ceiling for a long moment, still in the grip of a vividly erotic dream about Adam Cryder. Ten days of intense therapy with Adam the patient, trying to get his stubborn hand and wrist to move. Followed by ten nights of sweaty, panting dreams in which Adam, the lover, took her in various positions, numerous times.

Susannah sat up and turned on the light, trying to still the eager trembling of her body and chewing over the same thought she'd had since agreeing to be Cryder's PT.

The whole thing had been a mistake.

She never, ever, should have agreed to help Adam, especially given her attraction to him. Even if that attraction was returned, it would never work. First, he was her client. Second, he was a jock. Third, he was a jock. Sure, a good-looking jock with longish red hair, dark green eyes and a tall body, complete with broad chest, slender waist and muscular legs. She shivered, remembering one dream when those legs were wrapped around her, imprisoning her as he did other things to her with his hands and mouth.

But Adam was more than the sum of his physical parts, as Susannah was learning daily. For one thing, there was his wacko sense of humor. He was the stuff of urban legends in the hockey world. A lot of the Blaze's players came to her clinic and, through them, she'd heard about Cryder's practical jokes. How he showed up at one game with a target on his chest, daring the other team to hit it. How he superglued pucks to the ice one day before practice and laughed as the players hacked away at them. How, when brought up to the Blaze from its minor league affiliate, he'd changed all the screensavers in the corporate offices to read "Goalies Rule, Defensemen Drool." The Blaze defensemen had gotten back at him by refusing to help him on his first game, giving the opponent a spectacular 7-0 victory. Not an auspicious start for the goalie, and Susannah heard that Corrigan had given him a tongue lashing on that one. But it hadn't stopped Cryder from his pranks.

Today, she'd been the brunt of one. She'd gone to the training room to see a grim-faced Adam, his left arm and hand wrapped in about three miles of gauze.

"You've fucked me up for good now, Robers," he'd said. "Thanks to one of your goddam exercises, my fingers are wracked up. Team doctor put me in a brace."

Heart pounding, Susannah had unwrapped the gauze from his arm, frantically digging in her mind what she might have done or if he might have misinterpreted one of her exercises. What seemed like hours later, when she'd uncovered the hand, her first reaction was to let out a sigh of relief. The hand was fine. Unmoving, as usual. But fine. Her second reaction was to want to slap Adam's grinning face and those of his teammates in the training room. Crate had struck again and she'd been pranked. The whole thing had been pretty funny, in a way.

But there wasn't anything funny about her lusty feelings for the man. Even if she wasn't treating him, even if by some stretch of the imagination, her feelings were returned, his being a sports icon stood in her way. He was a jock, and athlete, and she'd promised herself she would steer clear of guys like him. It didn't take much to remember that agonizing night twenty-five years ago. The horrifying and sickening crunch of the metal...the agonizing pain of her leg...the surprised cry from her father, the last thing she heard from him...

Normally, those memories were enough to warn her off serious relationships with guys in sports. But this time, her hormones were subduing her memories.

"There's no way he'd be interested in me," she mumbled. "He's got his groupies and they're a lot younger and more attractive than I am."

She shook her head, thinking about the young women who flung themselves at the goalie. A couple of them had snuck into the training room the other day and stood gawking until security came and escorted them out. "Typical day," was all Adam had said, with a shrug, before returning to their discussion on politics. That was another thing. He was an intelligent guy who had some wonderful insights and a clever way of looking at things.

He was also pretty clever with his seduction attempts, at least in her fantasies.

Sighing, Susannah slipped her fingers between her legs, unsurprised to find herself soaking wet. Almost unconsciously, she stroked herself, massaging her slick folds, then rubbing her juices along her lower lips, Adam's face and voice in her mind.

I wish he was here. I want him to be watching me. I want him to get hard, to watch me come.

She allowed her imagination to conjure Adam standing at the foot of the bed, watching her hungrily as she played with herself. Slowly, almost hypnotically, she moved her hands up her belly and across her rib cage to her breasts, feeling a warm glow move between her legs as her fingers brushed the slowly hardening peaks.

"Adam," she whispered. "Watch me."

She caressed herself, running her fingers over her flesh, feeling her breath grow raw in her throat as electric lust sang along her nerves.

Open your legs.

The fantasy was so real, she could almost hear him whispering.

"I'm hot for you, Adam," she said softly. "I need to be fucked. I'll go crazy, otherwise…"

I'll take care of you, Anna. I promise. Just open your legs for me, okay?

She followed his instructions, and her hand drifted between her nether lips, her clit hard and swollen against her fingertips.

Oh, my God. You're beautiful down here. All creamy…

A sane, contemptuous part of her was convinced she was losing her mind, her fantasies weaving into a strange reality about a man she barely knew. But she couldn't let it go. In her mind, Adam was on the bed with her, a master of seduction and eroticism.

I want to taste you. I want to see if you taste as good as you look.

"Yes. Please." Her moans sounded unearthly to her ears as she allowed her imagination to roam free. His touch and voice stirred her passions, heated her blood and she gave herself over to the incredible fantasy as his mouth moved from her ear, across her body and between her legs. His tongue flicked in and out of her crease and she gasped, feeling the heat spread from between her legs to the rest of her body.

I wouldn't have thought it possible. You taste better than you look.

His breath was hot on her soaking pussy and she spread her legs wider to give him better access.

"Make me come." Her words came out in a whimper and she felt the breath of his laugh on her lower lips.

I want to savor you, sweetheart. Don't rush me.

His tongue slid inside her, his mouth sucking at her juices. She arched her back at the incredible electricity he was building in her nether regions, wanting to feel him move deeply inside her. But as he withdrew and touched her clit with his tongue, painting it with broad, slow strokes, the wanting became something different.

"There," she told him, shakily. "Oh, God…"

The tip of his tongue continued caressing her clit, which became engorged under his touch. His teeth grazed her folds and she whimpered, thrashing on the bed, wanting to speed the process toward her climax, while enjoying every single lick of erotic fire racing through her veins with this fantasy that was more like reality than anything she'd ever experienced.

He opened her wide with her thumbs and took her swollen clit between his lips. She screamed as he continued moving the tip of his tongue across the swollen, slick scrap of skin, his lips holding it firmly in place. Then, as he sucked greedily, her orgasm exploded through her body.

After a long while, she stirred, then opened her eyes. She was alone. Of course. But that—vision—or whatever it had been had been so real…

If that was just fantasy, what in God's name would the reality be like?

She shoved that thought out of her head, fast. Using brisk movements to overcome her sensual languor, Susannah got out of bed, put on her robe and tied the sash tightly. Maybe the pain of her actions would dull the small, still worm of sexual craving that fluttered in her gut.

Susannah glanced at her bedside clock and sighed. One in the morning. Figured. The man wasn't only playing with her hormones, he was robbing her of beauty sleep. Not that more sleep would help in the looks department. Nothing would help there.

With a shrug, she moved into the living room and saw the glow of her laptop. Maybe checking e-mail would put her to sleep. But there wasn't much help there, either. Just a note from Steve Barton, the Blaze's team doctor, wondering when Cryder would be ready to get back onto the ice.

Susannah grimaced at the man's e-mail. Barton had been after her, three or four times a day, with that same question, wanting answers. But Susannah wouldn't give him anything specific. She couldn't. Yes, the tendons were healing. No, she didn't know how extensive the nerve damage was. She was also reluctant to give a specific timetable—if Cryder went back too soon, he could re-injure everything. But if he was kept out too long, he could lose his starting spot on the team.

Another main concern was that Cryder was petrified about moving his fingers and hand. She'd tried everything from gentle prodding to outright contempt. Sometimes the latter worked with guys who were petrified of being thought of as "girlie-men" and would push themselves simply to spite her. It hadn't had any effect on Cryder though.

Susannah didn't blame him for his fear. His reaction was common to those who'd had serious injuries—they were afraid that they'd re-injure something if they so much as moved a muscle. And if Adam Cryder was Joe Schmoe, normal citizen, she'd let him move at his own pace.

Problem was, Adam Cryder wasn't Joe Schmoe. He was a high-profile goalie for a team demanding his immediate return. Didn't matter if she didn't think Cryder was ready or not mentally. If she couldn't speed that return, her own reputation could be in tatters.

"I just need a week," she mumbled. "That's all. He can do this." She didn't think she'd get that week, though.

Sighing, Susannah sent a non-committal response to the doctor, hoping she could keep him at bay for another day or two. Then, resigning herself to a long night, she plugged into the Internet, trying to find information on how to get a stubborn goalie to move his locked hand. She could draw on her years of experience, sure. But sometimes other physical therapists posted cures and methods on line that were helpful. Maybe that would be the case tonight.

As she logged on and began typing in various search terms, Susannah reflected she'd need as much help as she could get in this situation.

CHAPTER 4

The look of surprise on Susannah's face as she strode into the training room several days later was its own reward. Adam treated her to an almost malicious grin as she scowled at him, listening to the opera straining through the speakers of his boom box.

"What's wrong, Robers? Stunned that a jock likes opera?"

"No. Stunned that you like *La Boheme*. I thought better of you."

Not waiting for his response, she moved to one of the desks and put down her files. Her response stunned Adam to an irritated silence. He'd thought to shock her with his love for opera, demonstrating to her that athletes could also be arts patrons. But she managed to confound him once again. She knew her opera.

Another of the Blaze players, Eric Sodderheim, was in the training room today, working out on some of the light weights, and he nodded at Susannah as she shuffled papers. She smiled back at him, chatting with him easily, and Adam fought a spurt of jealousy.

He'd probably been one of her clients. Like you are, idiot.

Problem was, the rationalization didn't wash. Adam had a helpless crush on Susannah, one that obviously wasn't being returned, despite the odd intimacy that had sprung up between them. In his two weeks of therapy, they'd discussed everything from politics to literature. But nothing beyond that. Nothing personal. Adam itched to know what drove her.

And yeah, okay. Being totally honest, he itched to get her into his bed.

But she treated him with the same informality she treated everyone else who wandered in and out of the training room during the therapy sessions.

He'd gotten a reaction out of her from *La Boheme*, all right. Problem was, it wasn't the reaction he wanted.

She returned to his therapy table with his grips and cones.

"Here, take the cones and stack them. Squeeze 'em, if you can. *La Boheme*," she muttered, under her breath.

Adam suppressed a smile at her sub-vocal rant. "Have a problem with it?"

"Other than the fact you're the last person I'd imagine liking it? Everything. God, Rudolpho was pussy-whipped and we won't even talk about Mimi. 'Oh, God! I'm so frail! I expire! I die!'" Susannah put her hand to her forehead in an exaggerated faction and coughed consumptively. She snorted in contempt. "These hothouse heroines drive me nuts."

"Yeah, tell him to turn that shit off." Sodderhiem had apparently been listening in and decided to add his two cents' worth to the discussion. "Sounds like cats fucking."

"Sodderheim, of course, is speaking from experience," Adam told Susannah confidentially.

"Wrong, Crate," the other man said, leering at Susannah. "I like my pussy between a woman's legs. How 'bout it, angel?"

Adam wondered what Susannah was making of this sudden locker room talk. But instead of being morally offended, she just shook her head and grinned. "In your dreams, Sodderheim. Nowhere else."

Sodderheim sighed theatrically. "It could be magic with us, Susannah."

"Black magic, Eric," she said solemnly. "Save it for one of your groupies who'll buy that load of crap."

Sodderheim laughed again and returned to his weights. Adam relaxed a fraction, then chided himself for his jealousy. Susannah began working on his hand and he tensed for a moment, then relaxed. She looked at him narrowly.

"Is it hurting?"

"No. I took the pain pills."

"Okay. Good."

She continued flexing the joints in silence for a few moments, and Adam allowed the opera to flow over him and through him. Though Susannah expressed her contempt of Mimi, he found the opera lovely to listen to, and not too much of a strain in the interpretation department.

As he listened, he marveled at Susannah's touch. Though she stretched his hand and wrist to capacity, she managed to do it without a lot of pain. Some, yes. But not as bad as that first day here. Maybe he *was* getting better.

"If you don't like Mimi, then who would you choose as an ideal opera heroine?" he asked.

Susannah paused for a moment, then a wicked gleam came into her eyes. "Lucia di Lammermoor."

Big surprise. "Isn't she the one who killed her groom within minutes of marrying him, then went mad?"

"Yep." Susanna had a smile on her face.

"And you think the plot of *La Boheme* is s travesty?"

"Okay, you're right. The plot stinks, but some of the vocal gymnastics are marvelous."

"We should go to an opera some night, you and me," Adam decided.

Susannah looked at him, her turquoise eyes wide. "Seriously?" She looked at him suspiciously. "Okay, what are you trying to pull?"

Adam shrugged. "No one else'll go with me."

"No shit," Sodderheim called out. The forward was clearly following the conversation with way too much interest, and Adam bristled.

"Fuck off," Adam responded, wearily. Just as he was trying to ask Susannah out on a date, a know-it-all was elbowing in and trying to ruin it for him.

Sodderheim looked at him in some surprise, but didn't respond. Susannah frowned at Adam and stared down at his hand again. "I'd be glad to go to the opera with you, Cryder," she said quietly. "I don't get out much these days."

"No girlfriends? Boyfriends?" he inquired, gently. She shook her head, still focusing on his hand.

"Most of the single ones my age are on the prowl and the married ones are tied up with family and the PTA. And men?" She looked up at him and shrugged, but a flash of pain darkened her eyes for a moment. "I'm not exactly some guy's wet dream. In all honesty, I want to be more than some guy's wet dream, anyway."

Her sudden vulnerability wrapped around his heart and squeezed painfully. Something about the loneliness of her tone struck him, made him want to take her in his arms and comfort her. But he sat on the impulse. She'd likely misconstrue it.

She'd have every right to misconstrue it. You've got more than comforting in your mind, and you know it.

"Yeah, I'm an oddball, too," he said. "A single hockey player who would love to be married and raise a passel of brats. But I think most of the women I run across are those friends of yours, who are on the make. They're interested in rubbing elbows, and other things, with famous guys who have a little money. That was great in my twenties. But now that I'm in my mid-thirties, it sucks."

She let out a shaky laugh and put his hand on the therapy table.

"Well, I'm sure somewhere out there is a Mimi who will cater to your every whim."

But I don't want a Mimi. I want a Brünnhilde. Like you.

Susannah rose to her feet, went to the counter where various odds and ends were cluttered, and returned with a rubber ball. She squeezed it a couple of times and placed it in his useless left hand.

"This is soft. Try squeezing it," she said.

Adam sighed and grimly tried to follow her lead. His fingers moved a little. But not enough. Not nearly enough.

"I thought you said you could get it moving," he said, crossly. "It's been two fucking weeks, Susannah. When the Christ is this going to happen for me?"

"Adam, I'm doing my best." She spoke with compassion, but he was too pissed off to really care. "You can move this. You're ready. Beyond ready."

Though her voice was soft, he flushed angrily. Damn it, couldn't she see he was trying his best? The hand was simply not budging, no matter how hard he tried to move it.

"You don't know anything about it," he mumbled.

"Did you say something?"

There was something suddenly dangerous about her tone of voice, and Adam backed off.

"No."

She studied him, two spots of bright color staining her cheeks. "Because it sounded suspiciously like I don't know what you're going through, which is a crock, Adam." As though to emphasize her point, she picked up her cane. "You'll be able to skate again. I never was. This cane is because of an accident close to twenty-five years ago. Drunk driver, an *athlete*, no less, wasn't looking where he was going. A jock, Cryder. Minor league baseball player. He got off with a warning and an order to detox, thanks to an involuntary manslaughter charge and the best attorneys money could buy. I got off with my father being killed and me being lame for the rest of my life. So don't sit there and spout off that I don't know what you're going through."

She got up abruptly and went back to her desk. Just as well—Adam didn't want her to see him kicking himself.

"I'm sorry, Anna," he finally said softly. She shook her head, her back still to him.

"Forget it, Cryder."

The cold words told him to leave it alone, but a perverse part of him refused to do so.

"Did you want to play hockey?"

She nodded and his heart sank lower.

"It's why I went into PT," she said, after awhile. Her voice was a monotone as though she'd compartmentalized her pain and locked it up. "I didn't have the patience for med school, but I wanted to help people." She laughed a little. "Ironic that I'm helping athletes, isn't it?"

"I think that's pretty noble of you," he said, and he meant it. What she'd admitted to him moved his respect and admiration for the woman up a few notches.

"Well." Susannah stood and smiled at him, the cool professional PT back. Adam was sorry she'd closed herself off to him again, but went along with it. She came to him and curled his fingers around the ball. He closed his eyes, enjoying her soothing touch on his hand. The joints weren't sore anymore, thanks to her tending, but the fingers were still stiff. She shook her head and looked at his hand, frustration etched on her face.

"I still can't figure this out," she said. "Just keep doing your best on that. I'll be back in a couple of minutes and we'll try something else."

She left the room and Adam closed his eyes, thinking about the confession she'd just made. He could now see why she had no patience with others' complaining and whining. He especially realized why her distaste of jocks went so deeply.

How to convince her that I'm not another jock?

Adam wished there was a way to let her know that while he loved hockey and felt damned lucky to be making a living at it, it didn't rule his life. It was why he discussed everything *but* sports with her. It was also why he'd brought in the *La Boheme* recording. But instead of looking at him in a whole new light, her reaction had been to beat up on poor Mimi.

Eyes still closed, Adam sensed Susannah's presence as she returned and sat next to him. His eyes flew open as he felt her hand between his legs. Her flushed face was inches from his, her turquoise eyes filled with purpose behind the gold-rimmed specs. As she caressed him, she smiled and winked.

Stunned, Adam felt himself grow hard under her seeking hand. Frantically, he looked around—Sodderheim was still working the weights on the other side of the room, apparently oblivious to what was going on.

"Susannah—" he began, but she shook her head.

"Keep trying to squeeze the ball," she said softly.

She suited actions to her words, gently squeezing his groin and, as he grew harder, running her fingers over the tip of his cock. Even through his layer of clothing, her touch burned, and he restrained himself from groaning.

This whole thing was wrong, wrong, wrong. But the fact she was doing it, almost right under the eyes of his teammate, was unbearably exciting. Adam closed his eyes again, acutely aware of her scent and her desire, which rose in tandem with his own lust.

Susannah's fingers moved to the snap and zipper of his jeans, and in a moment, she had his fly open. Reaching in through his briefs, she drew his erection out and began rubbing the tip. Adam gasped and jerked back, opening his eyes. Through his rising sexual haze, he saw Sodderheim finish with his weights, pick up his towel, and leave the training room. They were alone now, but Adam knew anyone could walk in at any time. The thought only served to arouse him more.

He looked at Susannah again, and she gave him a knowing, provocative smile. "Next time, leave the underwear at home," she said. "It'll speed up the process. Keep trying to squeeze the ball, Cryder."

The ball? She had to be kidding. He was too hard to concentrate on the stupid piece of rubber in his hand, but almost unconsciously, his hand on the ball flexed in tandem with what she was doing to his cock.

"I wish I could take you in my mouth, Adam," she whispered. "I want to lick you, to make you scream. God, just thinking about doing you is getting me hot. And wet."

As she cupped his balls, a sudden image of her lying naked, open and ready for him danced across Adam's vision. He pictured himself plunging into her moist heat, feeling her slick walls contract around him. The vision and her hands were his undoing, and Adam climaxed, pumping into her palm, frantically squeezing the ball in his left hand...

"Adam."

He opened his eyes at the sound of her voice. Susannah stood before him, looking mystified. For a moment, he was confused. Hadn't she just jerked him off?

Then, to his shame, he realized what had happened. He'd fantasized the whole thing. The only reality was that he was squeezing the ball. He looked at his hand, feeling it detached from his body.

"Okay, stop." Susannah touched his hand gently, and he stopped. "How does it feel?"

For a moment he wondered frantically if she was referring to his erection.

"Fine. A little sore," he managed to croak.

She nodded and sat next to him, studying the hand and ball, then turned to him, relief in her eyes. "I'm glad it's moving, Cryder. I'd tried everything to get you moving and I was about ready to tear out my hair because of it. Now we need to start strengthening it."

Without a word, Adam leaned over and kissed her. He felt her surprised "umph" at the contact. But she didn't pull away. Instead, her lips moved beneath his and he felt lust warm his body. He wondered, for a moment, if this was a continuation of the fantasy he'd just experienced. But no. She was warm against him and as she returned his kisses with an almost wild passion, he caught a whiff of her scent— Jean Nate, combined with the musk of desire.

Keeping her face still with his hands, he deepened his kisses, feeling her heated response. Reading the invitation of her open mouth, Adam slid his tongue past her lips and teeth, stroking the underside of her tongue, feeling the shudders of excitement move through her body. His hand moved to cup her breast, his fingers brushing against the taut nipple, and he tasted her moan.

Suddenly, she wasn't there.

Susannah had pulled away from him abruptly and stood, facing him, her hands clenched, clearly fighting for control. Her face was flushed, her eyes wide with a mixture of dismay and desire.

"No," she said. "This can't happen."

"It already has." Adam fought to get his heart rate back to normal and his hard-on under control. He'd known he'd wanted her—what had stunned him was the fire of her response. He glanced down and saw her nipples clearly outlined against the silk of her blouse, hard with her arousal. He had the desire to slip one of those hardened peaks into his mouth and suck and nibble at it.

"It's out of the bag, Anna," he said gently. "We both want it. We can't tiptoe around this any more."

But she looked at him, troubled. "No," she said. "You're my patient. If anyone else had been here—"

"I wouldn't have tried this," he said, trying for a joke.

"Damn right. This is my license on the line. The Texas Physical Therapists Association has a few things to say about therapists becoming involved with their patients. And besides—"

"I'm a jock," Adam said. He leaned forward to trace a delicate blue vein on the back of her hand, noting in some triumph the trembling that seized her at his touch. "But I'm not a jock, Anna. I have a life outside of hockey and isn't booze and women."

"Adam—" her voice was helpless, but he pushed on.

"Besides. You don't strike me as someone who adheres to rules. Angel of Pain. Pushing it to the limits with your patients. You just pushed it to the limit with me. Do you know how I began moving my hand? A wet fantasy about you, Anna. A daydream. While you were squeezing me down there, I was squeezing the ball—"

Susannah drew her hand away suddenly and turned her back on him.

"*No*, Adam."

"Susannah—"

"We're done for today," she said, stubbornly. "Please leave."

Casting a final glance at her back, Adam picked up his brace and left.

CHAPTER 5

Susannah worked the leg press grimly in her North Dallas clinic. It had been a full day, with an overload of patients and a ton of paperwork to be dealt with. But the patients were long gone, the paperwork filed and the clinic closed. Rather than going home and facing another sleepless night, Susannah had decided on her own physical therapy. Her leg had been seizing up all day. It always happened in colder weather, and exercising it helped.

But the exercise wasn't doing anything for her state of mind. That had been thrown into grand confusion two days ago when Adam Cryder had kissed her in the training room at Carlysle Arena, almost melting her into a puddle of lust-riddled goo.

She hadn't been back to see him since then. She gave herself all kinds of excuses. Told herself the patient case load at the clinic needed to be dealt with. With Adam's hand moving now, he was more than halfway there, on the road to recovery. Another physical therapist could take over for her. Besides, despite the healthy fee Brian was paying for her services, the downtown commute was wreaking hell on her gas mileage.

But none of the excuses washed. The simple truth was, Susannah had a crush on Adam Cryder, but she hadn't dreamed, in a million years, it would be returned. When he'd kissed her, she'd panicked.

Gratitude. Nothing more.

She clung to that thought. If Cryder were healthy and whole, he wouldn't be looking twice at her, not with all the cute, short and slender groupies surrounding him. Compared to them, Susannah felt like a cow. Klutz supreme. No way could Cryder want that. Transference was all it was, she rationalized. Wouldn't be the first time.

Problem was, she was attracted to the man. She liked the way he looked. Adored the way he kissed. Even better, she liked his sense of humor, the wicked glint in his green eyes when he was up to something. That, and his grasp of everything non-sports, from politics to opera.

But he was a jock, she reminded herself. A jock had killed her father. A jock had left her permanently lamed.

Even if Adam wasn't her patient, even if a physical involvement with him wasn't something that could get her fired from her job, that small wall was enough to kill any thought of romance.

So why wasn't her body agreeing?

Angrily, Susannah pushed the press out again, then let it fall back. Out. Then in. Out again. In. Focusing on the physical stress on her legs took her mind off the other agony she was experiencing about Adam. At least, for the moment.

She was so into the soothing and repetitive rhythm of her weight-lifting, Susannah almost didn't hear the rattling at the front door. It was after hours, so the door was locked, but someone seemed desperate to get in. She hesitated for a moment, hoping it wasn't some evil person wanting to break in. Then she shrugged and smiled at her thoughts. Probably a patient who'd forgotten a purse or wallet or something. Breathing heavily and sweating from her exertions, Susannah wiped her face on a towel, draped it around her neck. She'd see who it was and send that person on his or her way.

Susannah stood, wincing a little as her leg muscles tightened. She moved into the reception area, then stopped short as she saw Adam through the glass door. He grinned at her, and she stood for a long moment, her feet rooted to the spot. She never dreamed he'd try to find her in person. Since that fateful afternoon, he hadn't contacted her, which had been fine by her.

Now here is was, in the flesh.

"Let me in. I want to talk to you," he called through the door.

Susannah swallowed, cursing the butterflies banging against her belly. "Adam, there's nothing to say."

"I'm not leaving until you let me in."

He crossed his arms and planted his feet. Goalie stance. Susannah sighed, irritated with his stubbornness. For a moment, she thought about sneaking out the back way, then decided against it. She'd have to face him at some point. No time like the present.

Not liking the glad desire crawling in her belly, Susannah moved forward and unlocked the door, then backed away as he came in, closed the door, and leaned against it. His eyes moved warmly over her body, intimate as a caress, and she felt heat pool between her legs. Belatedly, Susannah realized she wore only a sports bra and tights. Why not? She'd been by herself, working out. But now she felt exposed in the tights that clung to her hips and outlined her pubis, not to mention a bra that left nothing to the imagination. Looking down, Susanna saw her nipples press against the bra's stretchy fabric. She looked away, her face flaming.

"I was about ready to leave," she said, not liking the husky sound of her voice.

"You're avoiding me," Adam said softly. "Why?"

"You're not my only patient."

"I've needed you." He moved closer and she could smell the cold radiating off his coat. That, and the menthol of the aftershave he wore. Unconsciously, she flared her nostrils at his scent which, combined with his nearness, made her weak in the knees.

"Angel of Pain," he continued in that same, soft tone. "You wrap me up with your intelligence and personality and healing powers. I kiss you. Then you go away. I don't hear from you. I don't like that."

Susannah took a deep breath, trying to ignore the sensuality crawling through her body. "I know you're grateful—"

"It isn't gratitude, Susannah. That kiss the other day wasn't a pity kiss. Not from my end."

She looked at him, troubled. "I don't want to become part of the Adam Cryder harem."

"That harem isn't around right now."

"So time to get your rocks off on Susannah Robers, is that it?" She spoke more sharply than she'd intended.

"If I wanted to get my rocks off, I'd use my hand," he told her, and despite herself, she trembled at the image in her mind his words conjured. "I don't want a hand, I don't want anyone in my nonexistent harem. I want you. I want your mind, I want your intelligence, your conversation. Your compassion. Your body. Period."

"I can't believe that." She took another step back, and he followed. Almost as though he were stalking prey—guess who the prey was? Susannah repressed a shiver of excitement.

"Why do you think so many guys come on to you? Why do you think Sodderheim made that verbal pass at you the other day?"

His words made her uneasy. "He was kidding. Flirting a little. Happens all the time."

Adam shook his head. "Nope. And if you say 'gratitude' one more time, I'm going to smack you."

They stared at each other and he moved closer to her. But this time she didn't step back.

"I'm overweight, I limp, and I wear glasses," she said.

"You're beautiful and I don't give two craps about your limp or your glasses. If you haven't noticed, I'm not one hundred percent whole myself."

She felt her face stretch into a bitter grin. "The lame leading the lame, huh?"

"Don't. Don't do that."

She gestured helplessly. "Adam, I'm glad to be your friend—"

"I don't want your goddam friendship." His voice was hard and clipped. "What will it take to get that through your head? And please don't tell me I'm a jock. Don't lump me with the asswipe who killed your father and left you lame."

Susannah flinched at his words, and Adam's face softened. "I'm sorry," he said. "But let me show you I'm not like him, Anna. Give me the chance."

Adam's words reached into her, turning her inside out, and Susannah swallowed uneasily. She was sweaty, disheveled, but he was looking at her as though he was starving man and she a five-course meal. Worse still, her body was responding to that look and his words.

"I'm sweaty," she blurted out, and he gave her a crooked smile.

"I'm used to sweat. You smell better than a lot of my teammates do. You look better. And I bet anything you feel better." He reached out, snagged a drop of perspiration on his finger, and she shivered at the feel of it on her flesh. "I don't think I've ever been so turned on by sweat before," he whispered.

He stepped forward, pulled her into his arms, and pressed his lips against hers. She felt his hands tangle in her hair, keeping her head steady as his mouth moved with tortured sensuality on hers, branding her with a torrid desire. Any thought of breaking away from him was gone, not with his body pressed against hers, his need for her evident against her belly. His kisses were like an addictive drug; the more he gave, the more she craved.

"This is insane," she whispered against his lips as the kiss broke.

"So commit me." His voice was harsh, urgent, and, taking a deep breath, he brought his lips to hers again, his tongue making its way into her mouth. Helpless against the onslaught of desire raging through her body, Susannah wound her arms around his neck, pulling herself closer to him.

"Susannah." His breath was hot against her ear as he broke free from the kiss and she trembled at the need, the longing in his voice. "God help me, I've wanted you for awhile. I never thought it would be returned."

"Are you kidding?" Susannah leaned back in his arms, studied his flushed face. "I've had a crush on you. For years. It was one reason I almost turned Brian down when he ordered me to take you on."

"Do you think this is what he had in mind?" Adam leaned forward and began pressing feather-light kisses on her eyelids and cheeks.

"No." Her heart was thumping in her throat, her legs trembling. She caught her breath as he moved against her. "I'm so hot for you, Adam. Damn you."

"Why damn me?" He whispered the words in her hair and she closed her eyes.

"I could get my license revoked—"

"Not if we don't tell anyone."

Susannah took a deep breath and forced herself out of his arms. She turned her back on him and looked out the front door at the almost empty parking lot, rubbing her hands on her arms. Adam moved behind her, close to her, but not touching. Still, she was conscious of the warmth of his body. It was that warmth she was responding to, the need to have him touch her, to kiss her, to bury himself deeply in her.

"I'm not trying to give you the rush or anything." His voice was husky, languid. "We'd be damn good together, and you know it, Anna."

She clenched her fists and lowered her head, practicality warring with her need to be in his arms and in his bed. Or wherever else he could take her.

"There's too much going against this," she whispered.

Adam turned her gently and, putting a finger under her chin, tilted her face to his. His eyes were filled with affection, sympathy and desire.

"There's everything going for this," he responded. "All it needs is a chance."

A chance.

Your father never had a chance once that damned driver hit him.

Susannah wearily pushed the thought from her mind. None of that had been Adam's fault.

"You're persuasive," she told him, her voice unsteady.

Susannah saw relief and triumph flash across his face.

"You learn those skills as a hockey goalie," he said softly. "They come in handy from time to time."

He cupped her face in his hands and kissed her again. Susannah caught her breath at the heat tumbling through her body. She was hot for him, her wanting spiraling out of control.

But they were too exposed here.

She broke the kiss and, locking the door, then taking his hand, led him from the front office, through the weights room, into one of the therapy rooms. They'd be secluded enough in here. At least, they wouldn't be on display in a plate-glass window.

But all practicality fled as he pulled her against him roughly and kissed her with an almost savage passion. She responded urgently. Now that she'd made the decision to be with him, she wanted him fiercely.

As he savaged her mouth, he yanked down the straps of her bra and cupped her full breasts with his hands. Breaking the kiss, Adam dipped his head, running his tongue across one hardened nipple, then slipping it into his mouth and sucking on it, his tongue dragging across it, stoking the heat that roared through her veins.

As he continued working on her nipple, Adam moved his hand between her legs and pressed hard. Almost frantically, Susannah ground herself against his hand, craving the pressure on her swollen clit. Sensing her need, Adam worked his fingers with controlled violence between her legs and Susannah gasped as he bit her nipple gently.

"Take off the tights. Then lie down on the table and spread your legs for me. Christ, I'm so hungry for you."

In a daze, her hands trembling, Susannah did as she asked, stripping off her soaked tights and bra, then lying on the therapy table and spreading herself in a wanton, erotic offering. A moment later, she arched her back in an almost mindless ecstasy as his lips and tongue began their work between her legs. He lapped at her eagerly, then slid his tongue deeply into her before returning to tease her clitoris, roughly stroking the sensitive bud until it was swollen and hard. She bucked against his face, her hands gripping the edges of the table as carnal fire licked through her veins. His mouth continued its sensual torment of her, nibbling and licking a fiery path across her moist, swollen folds. Finally, when it became almost too much to bear, her climax slammed through her, shaking her, until she thought she might faint from a pleasure overload.

But he refused to release her, his hot tongue continuing to caress her engorged clit and driving her over the edge again into a mindless ecstasy.

Finally, he stopped his ministrations and stood. Susannah gasped for air, shudders holding her captive as she tried to come down from the amazing sexual high. She felt the heat in her belly quicken again as she saw him staring at her, his face flushed, his red hair mussed, his mouth smeared with her juices, a wild look of passion in his eyes. Eager anticipation sliced through her body.

"Fuck me," she whispered to him. "I need you in me."

As though her words released something in him, Adam quickly slid out of his clothes, then joined her on the therapy table. He entered her swiftly, almost brutally and she accepted him at once, loving the feel of him stretching her. Her moan was cut off as his mouth claimed hers, and Susannah trembled as she tasted her juices on his lips.

As he drove deeply into her, she matched her hips to his rhythm, feeling herself contract around his hardness. The pressure on her clit was intense, and she felt herself rising toward another orgasm.

"Harder," she cried out. "Oh, my God."

Following her request, he pumped in her almost violently, his thrusts creating a wanton, mindless pleasure that shook her body.

"Come for me," he hissed. "I want to hear you come. Loudly."

His words trigged something deep and primal within her, and she climaxed, screaming his name, digging her nails in his back. As she came down, she felt him shudder violently, felt his release inside her.

They lay together for a long moment, against the hard surface of the therapy table. Susannah struggled to calm her breathing, and she sensed Adam was doing the same. "Wild woman," he finally whispered, kissing her neck. She closed her eyes, marveling at her still-trembling body. She was right about one thing. The reality of Adam's lovemaking far outweighed the fantasies.

"How long had you been planning this?" she asked.

He propped himself on an elbow, and traced her profile with a finger.

"You're talking like I held a gun to your head," Adam said.

Susannah laughed, shakily. "Yeah, it sounds a little like that, doesn't it?"

"I guess the question could be, how long were you waiting for it?"

Susannah turned away from his probing gaze, unable to answer his question. "Several years" smacked of desperation. "I still can't believe I'm a topic of locker room conversation," she said instead.

"Believe it." He stroked her hair, and she relaxed into the soothing rhythm.

"Just don't add to it, Adam. I don't want to end up as one of your locker room stories. One of your conquests. How I fucked the Angel of Pain."

"No, Susannah. I think too much of you to do that. If I'm no jock, you're sure no Angel of Pain."

"Then I'm not doing my job." Sighing, she sat up, stood, and moved away from him. "You're supposed to be in pain when I'm done with you."

"You're afraid to move this along, aren't you?"

She jumped a little, wondering if he could read minds, and he shook his head and grinned.

"Your feelings are all over your face, Anna."

Susannah considered him for a long moment. "We're from two different worlds. You're the guy who loves to prank everyone and who doesn't mind getting hit with a lot of pucks for fun. I think pranks are rude and the closest I get to sports is treating sore joints of athletes."

"But our values are the same," he said, quietly. "I've gotten that from our conversations during the past several weeks. Plus you have strong family ties; you cared deeply about your father. I love family, too. Eventually I want to get married and have a whole bunch of kids."

A slight pain tugged at her. "Not with me, you won't, then. I can't get pregnant." At his startled look, she continued. "I had my tubes tied several years ago. I was told the stress of a pregnancy could be a problem with my leg so…" She let her words trail away, her voice suddenly thick with tears. She thought she'd worked that particular emotional glitch out, but apparently she hadn't. "I figured if it was ever an issue, I could adopt."

She turned her back on him, not wanting him to see her like this. He was silent for a moment, and her heart broke.

Great. Way to drive the guy away from me.

"I'm sorry, Susannah," he said slowly. "I can't give you back your leg or your father. I wish I could. But I'm going to ask you again. Give me the chance to prove myself. The minute I start acting like an egotistical asshole, kick me out. All I want is a chance."

She hitched a breath and turned back to face him. "There's still the matter that you're my patient."

He shook his head, his green eyes glinting. "I won't tell if you won't," he said softly.

"You're impossible. This whole situation is impossible." Still, she returned to him, feeling the welcoming embrace of his arms around her. She simply couldn't resist Adam Cryder. If she had to be discreet, she'd do it.

"I like being impossible. Keeps you on your toes."

"Keeps me on something," she whispered, and tilted her head up for his kiss.

It started off sweet and soft. Susannah had never before experienced a kisser like Adam, who could rouse her so thoroughly with his lips, without the pressure of his tongue. As they kissed, she moved her hand between his legs. He was rock-hard, and she shivered.

"I want to taste you," she said quietly. "Just lie still, okay?"

He smiled at her. "You're the boss, lovely."

Susannah smiled back. "I've said it before, Cryder. You learn very quickly."

Moving her lips over his shoulder and chest, she laved his nipples with her tongue, feeling them grow hard. She felt the harsh rise and fall of his chest beneath her hands and mouth, as she traced the muscles of his broad chest. She picked up his left arm, and lay kisses against the scar that was there, wishing she could heal him in such a simple manner.

But she had another destination in mind. Licking and tasting him, Susannah moved lower, brushing her lips and tongue over his still-taut belly and between his legs. Well muscled legs, the legs of a man who spent hours on the ice.

His large cock rose from its nest of light-colored curls, and for a moment, Susannah pressed her nose into those curls, inhaling deeply of his musky scent. She trembled in excitement as she ran her tongue on the underside, hearing him groan. As she continued licking him, she cupped his balls with her hand, feeling them contract as she fondled them gently. She moved her head back and caressed the tip of his penis with her other hand, feeling him catch his breath. It was slick with his pre-cum and her saliva and she spread the moisture around, feeling him twitch in her hand. She continued slowly palming him in her eager hands, while running slow kisses up and down his shaft.

Finally, she slid his length into her mouth and she felt, more than heard, his strangled cry of desire. As she moved her lips and tongue slowly on him, she heard him babbling, pleading with her for his release.

Then he was climaxing, his hips moving almost violently. For the first time, Susannah found herself liking the taste of a man's cum, and she swallowed eagerly. Her only regret was that he was spent. She would have liked to taste him again. Well, time enough for that.

She moved up to his side and held him as he caught his breath. His orgasm had been wild; she could still feel the aftermath rocking his body. After a while, after the trembling subsided, he moved his hand between her legs, but Susannah gently removed it.

"No," she said. "I'm fine."

"You're sure?"

"Trust me, Cryder. I'm fine."

"Mmm. Good." He buried his face in her shoulder and brushed his lips against the skin there. Susannah shifted and grimaced. While she was enjoying every single hot minute of this erotic encounter, making love on a hard therapy table wasn't exactly one of life's greatest pleasures and she was stiffening up. But other, more important things were on her mind.

"How are we going to keep this quiet?" she wanted to know. "Adam, if you come into the training room tomorrow looking at me like you did tonight, it's going to cause some huge problems."

"It'll cause more problems if I act on it."

She heard the smile in his voice and sat up, scowling. "This isn't funny, Cryder. One of my colleagues had a heap of problems because one of his clients accused him of sexual harassment. It never happened, but it sure caused him some difficulties until his good name was cleared."

"Relax, Anna." His eyes reflected her concern. "I still think we can be discreet about this whole thing. I can be the soul of propriety."

Susannah snorted and managed a laugh. "I doubt that. But the problem is, I don't think I can stop myself from wanting you. Not now. It's like chocolate. I take one bite and I have to have the whole bag." She looked at her wide hips and full breasts and shook her head. "Then it ends up showing."

Adam smiled and reached for her, pressing her closely against him. "Don't worry so much," he said into her hair. "Chocolate can be enjoyed, one bite at a time, lovely. Let me teach you how."

Susannah closed her eyes and nodded against his chest. She didn't have much choice, not any more. She was well and truly addicted to him and there was no going back.

CHAPTER 6

The next day, Adam made his way to the Blaze's training room, feeling very pleased with himself.

He'd stayed with Susannah at the clinic the night before until ten o'clock or so, talking, listening and making love. Discovering a whole new side of this woman he was really beginning to admire. But what he hadn't realized was what a wild lover she'd become when he'd finally gotten past her defenses.

A little too wild he thought, with an amused grimace. Therapy tables and floors were not exactly the right place for frenzied lovemaking, and his back and neck were stiff. Well, maybe some of the weights could help out with that. As long as he kept the arm immobile, he'd be okay.

But his arm was feeling better these days, too. Score another one for Susannah.

Adam was doubly pleased when he saw the object of his affections working away on Adrian Donelson, one of the Blaze's defensemen. Correction. One of the Blaze's thugs. Donelson did okay on-ice, keeping the opposition away from the forward when they were trying to score goals. Off-ice, though, Donelson was a pain in the ass. Come to think of it, he was a pain in the ass on the ice, too.

Still, Adam nodded pleasantly at the man, who growled invectives at him. Nothing new about that. Adam was used to it. After a moment, Donelson turned his expletives to Susannah who, in a supreme mode of indifference, kept stretching his leg. She looked up at Adam and he felt

41

his heart catch at the laughter in her blue eyes, though her face was solemn.

"Seems Donelson here had a run-in with a goalie," she said. "His own."

Adam cocked an eyebrow at her in surprise, while Donelson sat up and glared at her.

"Why'd you have to open your goddamn mouth——*owwwww!*" Donelson's tirade was cut off as Susannah stretched his leg farther and Adam barely restrained a laugh.

"How'd you piss off Thoreau?" Adam asked, getting himself under control.

"It wasn't Thoreau," Adrian snarled. "KC Arden. Female goalie, believe it or not. Some dumb-fuck stunt thought up by Corrigan to boost ticket sales. Stupid cunt didn't know her job, then whacked me on the leg when I tried to tell her."

Adam was mildly intrigued by the thought of a female goalie taking his place, then shrugged. He'd heard of KC; she was a close friend of Kristen's. She was okay. No competition for his starting spot or anything like that though, so nothing to worry about. Donelson had said it—putting KC in goal had publicity stunt written all over it.

"So did it work?"

Adrian glared at him, his face sullen. "What?"

"Did she fill the house?"

"How the fuck do I know?"

"Well, shit, Donelson. You were there, weren't you?" He spoke with a grin on his face, but Donelson looked ready to kill.

"All right." Susannah's calm voice cut into their conversation, and she met Adrian's glare with a calm one of her own. Didn't take much to know what she was thinking—*mess with me and you'll get more pain.*

"I think we're through here today." she said, evenly. "Go see the trainer, get that leg iced. It's a nasty contusion, so just take it easy for the next day or two."

"Fucking goalie practically lamed me," he grumbled. "I'll never walk again."

Susannah's eyes were suddenly blue chips of ice. "Stop griping," she told him in clipped tones. "I'm tired of your God damned bitching. You'll walk and you'll skate. Get the hell out of here and get some ice on that."

She turned her back on him and stalked off to the desk. A red-faced Donelson opened his mouth, and Adam was interested to see what might come out. Then the defenseman clamped his lips shut, glared at Susannah's back and left without another word.

Adam hesitated for a moment, wanting to give her a chance to cool down.

"You okay?" he finally asked.

"Yeah." Susannah turned and gave him a chagrined smile. "I probably should have kept my temper, but he'd been grousing at me for the past thirty minutes. It was getting old. I wouldn't have even worked on him, except Brian asked me." She rolled her eyes. "Brian Corrigan's going to owe me a lot of favors by the time I'm through here."

Adam approached her and slid an arm around her, drawing her close. "Maybe I should be thankful you don't treat me like that."

She shook with laughter. "No, there are other ways to deal with you, Cryder. All of them a lot more fun."

"Hmm." He pulled back slightly and ran his finger around her mouth. Her lips parted slightly and he slid his finger between them. She sucked gently at the finger and Adam shuddered, feeling sexual heat head south between his legs, feeling himself grow hard.

"It's addictive, like chocolate," she whispered, closing her eyes. "Oh, my God. Adam..."

He replaced the finger with his mouth, starting off with gentle kisses, then deepening them at her passionate response. Kissing her was an incredible high, unlike anything he'd experienced with any other woman. Her lips were sensual, moving on his with an unrestrained passion combined with tenderness. The thought of her total abandonment and openness when it came to lovemaking had made him weak in the knees the night before, and the same thing was happening now.

Her arms snaked around his neck and she deliberately ground her hips against him. In rough excitement, Adam cupped her rear end and pulled her against him hard, wanting her to feel his need. Susannah caught her breath, trembling against him.

A moment later, she broke away and stepped back, her face flushed and wild. "Better stop that before I beg you to take me right here," she said huskily.

"The door has a lock—" Adam moved toward her and she laughed and backed away.

"Yeah, but the idea of making love on a therapy table doesn't have too much appeal right now. My back is aching. I think *I* need a physical therapist."

Adam let forth a mock groan. "You're a mind-reader, Anna. I woke up with a backache this morning, too. Very happy. But with a backache. Still, I'm not here to seduce you, as tempting as the idea is." Adam reached into his back pocket, pulled out an envelope and handed it to her. Smiling a little, Susannah took it from him, opened it and drew out two tickets. She burst out laughing.

"*La Boheme?* You're kidding."

"Nope. Dallas Opera Company has it, tomorrow night."

Susannah shook her head slightly, still grinning. "You're really up to hearing me gripe about Mimi?"

Adam put his hand on his heart and bowed. "I can't think of anyone I'd rather hear griping about her. But let's make a deal. You dress up, and I'll put on a suit. Let's make this an occasion."

"An occasion," Susannah repeated, her eyes sparkling. "Okay, Cryder, you're on. An occasion for tomorrow night it is. We'd probably better get started with your session."

*   *   *

The next night, Adam drove to Susannah's house in far North Dallas, trying to tell himself he wasn't nervous. But it wasn't washing. Sure, they'd been lovers. And, yes, the physical therapy on his hand had brought its own non-sexual and platonic intimacy between them.

But this was their first date, and Adam swore under his breath at the butterflies in his stomach. He'd had countless women during his lifetime and had been mildly serious about one or two of them. But he'd never before experienced the palm-sweating, gut-wrenching nerves he was experiencing now. He'd rather be on the ice, defending his goal and crease against an onslaught of five thugs rather than be in that first date position.

He took a deep breath and told himself to relax, wondering in wry amusement why he was getting so worked up about a woman, especially one he'd already slept with. But he knew the answer. To him, desire didn't start between the legs, but between the ears. Given that, it didn't take a genius to figure out his almost insane attraction to this woman. Susannah wasn't just any woman. She was intelligent, with great wit and courage combined.

As Adam neared her apartment, he wondered if the attraction was reciprocated. Sure, she liked what he did for her sexually—two nights ago had been proof of that. But he wanted her to be as attracted to his mind as he was to hers. He desperately wanted her to think of him as anything other than a jock. That was the whole reason for this date.

Pulling in front of her house, Adam took a couple of deep breaths.

Steady, Freddie. You've helped your team win the Tannen Trophy. You can take a woman out on a date.

Bolstering himself with the pep talk, Adam stepped out of his car, but before he could move two steps, the door opened, and Susannah almost flew out to meet him, despite her awkward gait and cane.

Adam wasn't one for clichés, but all of those sappy romance stories had it right as the hero beheld his heroine in a lovely silk dress that matched the color of her eyes and clung enticingly to her full breasts and hips. Her short blonde hair curled softly around her flushed, smiling face. That face didn't have glasses either, he'd noticed with an inward grin. Contacts? He didn't know, nor did he care. There was no doubt in his mind—Susannah was breathtaking.

She smiled at him, and took his arm. Absently, he realized she was only a few inches shorter than his six-foot-three height.

The better to kiss her with your lips, my dear.

"I've never seen you speechless, Cryder," Susannah said. "I guess I'm making an impression. A good one, I hope."

"A very good one." Adam was relieved his voice didn't tremble. He flared his nostrils slightly, taking in her scent.

I think I'll write a letter to Jean Nate. Tell them I get off sexually on their body wash.

"You make a good impression, too, Cryder," Susannah was saying as they walked to his car. "I love guys in three-piece suits. You look great."

"Good enough to eat?" He roused from his sensual bemusement to needle her a little, and she rewarded him with a brilliant smile.

"Well, if you insist—"

Adam couldn't help laughing as he opened the car door for her. "You're insatiable, Anna. I'm not sure what to do with you."

He settled her into the car, went around to the driver's side, and climbed in.

"For starters, you can feed me," she announced. "A fancy place, I assume. I don't dress this way for just anyone. Then try to convince me why I'd waste my time watching *La Boehme*—"

"Other than the company."

"Yes, other than the company," she amended. "Then—well, who knows?"

Who knew indeed? Adam wasn't about to speculate, but he did begin to relax as he listened to her chatter on about opera and politics. She carefully avoided any mention of hockey, and he was grateful to her. Though his hand was doing well, he still had his doubts about his ability to return to the ice.

Throughout the excellent dinner at The Old Warsaw restaurant near downtown, Adam derived great pleasure observing a side of Susannah he'd never seen before. She was outgoing and sparkling, charming to the waiters at the restaurant, and entertaining him with her observations about everything. She was miles away from the cool, professional physical therapist who'd been hired to get his hand moving and getting him back on the ice. Also miles away from the wild lover she'd been a couple of nights before. He'd never seen so many different sides of one woman before. Correction, he told himself, he'd never *allowed* himself to become so involved with a woman to determine her different sides. Until now, his focus had been hockey, reading and opera, with a few women taken for physical relief. Never before had he wanted to make a woman part of his life as he wanted Susannah to be part of his.

While the thought exhilarated him, it petrified him, too. He knew her feelings about athletes, and he realized he was taking a chance trying to encourage her. She could shy away, shut him down. Or worse, decide she was tired of him and move on to someone like Sodderheim.

Adam shuddered at the thought and drank down half his wine. She cocked her head at him and treated him to a smile.

"You okay to drive?" she wanted to know.

"Yeah. Fine." He glanced at his watch, then motioned at the hovering waiter to bring the check. "But we'd better get going. Otherwise we'll miss the opening and I'd miss your diatribe on Mimi."

She pouted and he grinned back at her. Her face softened into a smile and Adam turned his attention to the check, his heart hammering in his chest. He felt like an adolescent in the throes of puppy love. The hard-on between his legs reminded him that his feelings for Susannah were well beyond an innocent flirtation, though.

He considered it all as he signed the check and escorted her out of the restaurant. He put his arm around her as they waited for the valet to bring his car around, and she leaned against him, almost trustingly. Adam closed his eyes for a moment, aware of the cool fall breeze against his face and the scent of this woman. He realized a sense of contentment he'd never felt before, the feeling that everything was going to be just fine. When his car arrived, he reluctantly released

Susannah, and helped her into her car seat, before walking briskly to the driver's side and climbing in.

"Okay," she said, as he began driving. "Are you a Puccini fan, or did you get these tickets to *La Boheme* just to tease me?"

Adam grinned. "Partly both. I like Puccini and I like the way he makes his singers work for their notes. But Puccini isn't my favorite. It's Wagner."

He felt her surprise as she shifted in her seat to look at him.

"Somehow I didn't expect you to be the Wagnerian type," she said. "*Die Meistersinger* or *Lohengrin*?"

"I like both of those, but I'm partial to the Ring Cycle. Now I suppose you're going to go all cynical on me and complain about Brünnhilde's sacrifice to protect Siegfried."

She was silent for a moment, and Adam kept his eyes on the road, not daring to look at her. He realized he was falling for Susannah—but given her cynicism and her buried anger, he didn't know if the feeling was being returned, or if she was simply a willing bed partner and nothing more.

"No," she finally said. "I think what Brünnhilde did was incredibly brave, sacrificing immortality for the sake of her lover. I don't know of any other woman who would have sacrificed that much. I'm not sure I could."

Astonished, Adam glanced at her. Susannah's face was turned from him as she looked out the window. He wanted, desperately, to see her expression. Instead, he turned his attention back to the road.

"Maybe that's what you're doing now," he said quietly. "Sacrificing your need to…be mad at jocks because of what you've been through. You're healing people, Susannah, instead of taking your anger out on them."

"Maybe I push them because I want them to hurt as much as I did." She paused for a long moment, then turned her stricken face to his. "When does it stop hurting, Adam?"

The pain in her voice wrapped around him, and, unaccountably, he found his eyes blurring with tears. He pulled over to the side of the road and took her in his arms. He felt her trembling and, after a moment, felt the wetness of her tears on his shoulder. He continued holding her, feeling her agony as his own as she continued sobbing her grief and fear.

"I'm sorry." Susannah's tears trailed off, leaving her voice hoarse and muffled against his shoulder. Adam took her face in his hands and studied it for a long moment, taking in the red-rimmed eyes, the tear streaks on her skin.

"Don't apologize," he said, gently. Adam was humbled, humbled that this proud woman had the courage to open her emotions to him.

"Brünnhilde," he whispered, then kissed her gently, feeling her soft lips respond under his. He didn't want to go to the opera any more. He wanted to take this woman home and make love to her in every way possible—violently, tenderly, quickly and slowly. Drive the pain out of her heart with his lovemaking. Then maybe they could go on from there.

"Take me home, Adam. Please," Susannah said, as though reading his mind. "I'll owe you for the tickets but—I just want you alone tonight. Just the two of us. Brünnhilde and Siegfried, if you want to think of it that way."

Adam slid back and put the car into gear. "Don't worry about the tickets," he said quietly. "All I want tonight is to be alone with you, too."

CHAPTER 7

Susannah closed her eyes and leaned her head against the backrest of the car seat. She felt exposed and vulnerable, entirely too open to the man next to her, who drove the car with an almost insolent ease.

The evening had started out well enough. Adam looked great and the banter that was the hallmark of their relationship saw them through an excellent meal at an elegant restaurant.

But something had flipped inside her when he'd brought up Brünnhilde and Siegfried. She knew it was only a silly libretto, but she realized that Brünnhilde had given up her own immortality without complaint for the man she loved. She, Susannah, couldn't get past her jock-block, her anger against all men athletic, to open herself further to Adam.

That dichotomy had hit her with a sudden, fierce pang, driving her to tears. Adam holding her in his arms as she cried made the pain go away, at least for a little while. Replacing the pain was her desire to be alone with him, to be taken with the wild passion she knew him capable of.

Swallowing, eyes still closed, Susannah felt the car shift and sway beneath her, feeling her body adjust to the car's rhythm and turns. Never before had she been so aware of physical sensations—the feel of her soft, silk dress against her flesh, the stickiness of drying tears on her face, and even the pain of her leg, which was, thank God, not too bad right now.

Then there was the growing throb in her lower belly and between her legs as her physical awareness focused on the man sitting next to her. She tasted his scent—the menthol aftershave he liked, mixed with his own, unique essence. She reveled in the sensual vision of his hard body pressed against hers—demanding, taking and giving.

Susannah caught her breath and opened her eyes as Adam picked up her hand and placed a kiss on her palm. His warm lips on her sensitive flesh sent a gnawing lust through her veins, bringing the focus to her almost insatiable physical hunger for this man.

"Stop the car. Please." The plea came from her lips in a whimper, and the sane part of her regarded it contemptuously. She'd never had to beg for anything in her life, but now she was pleading with this man to pull over so they could screw.

Adam shook his head, a smile touching his full mouth. "We're not animals," he said softly. "I'd love nothing more than to pull over and take you. Now. I'm so hard I'm about ready to explode." He took her hand and put it between his legs. Susannah shivered at the feeling of his hard flesh in her palm, steel wrapped in hot silk. "But I want to take you in a bed this time," Adam continued, releasing her hand. "Softly, slowly, touching you everywhere. Kissing you everywhere, from your pretty head down between your legs. Slowly this time, okay?"

His words caressed her brain, stimulating her excitement, and she almost groaned. But she saw the good sense of his words. She was also touched. Adam wanted to make this a romantic interlude, rather than two people getting their rocks off on one another.

They arrived at Susannah's house, climbed out of the car, and she opened the door for them. Once inside the dimly lit living room, Adam took her in his arms and kissed her deeply, sensuously, slanting his lips across hers. He made no move to tongue her, but rather, used his lips to rouse her.

He pressed her against him, and Susannah wound her arms around his neck and moved her hips against him, dry-fucking him, almost moaning as his cock found her hot, sexual core, even through their layers of clothes. Adam gasped, placing his hands on her rear and thrusting almost violently against her, whispering hot, dirty words in her ear that only fueled her passion. He'd talked about taking her slowly, but Susannah wasn't in the mood for slow, not right now, not with hot urgency pounding through her veins.

She was close to losing control, when sudden awareness hit her.

Adam wasn't using his left hand.

Damning her instincts as a physical therapist, she broke away from him, trying to reign in her lust. Adam breathed heavily, his face flushed, eyes looking questions at her.

"Is your hand okay?" she asked quietly. He smiled at her, moving his right hand across her breast and down her hip.

"What do you think?"

"I think you need to use your other hand," Susannah said.

Adam dropped his hand, a flash of frustration skittering across his face.

"Can you leave the physical therapy act at the office?"

"Just tell me, Adam."

He glared at her for a moment, and Susannah stared at him back, neutrally. God knows she wanted him. But he was her patient first.

"I'm sorry," she said, gently. "I'm sorry about the PT act. But that was my first charge with you. To get that hand moving. To get a muscle strong, you need to use it."

Adam grinned at her. "Susannah, there's only one muscle I'm thinking of right now."

Well, she couldn't blame him for that. This was why they were here, wasn't it? She took a deep breath, an idea popping into her head.

"Maybe there's a way we can do both. Follow me."

She went into her bedroom, Adam close on her heels. Before she could react, he had her in his arms, and was kissing her again, his lips burning a trail on her lips, cheeks and throat. For a moment, she moved against him, desire cramping her belly and moisture pooling between her legs.

"I like this idea," he murmured against her ear. Gathering all her wits about her, Susannah pushed him away.

"Patience, Cryder," she said, slightly out of breath. "I want to try something."

Susannah went to the closet and took out a silk scarf, feeling the cool silkiness against her palms. Then she returned to him and handed him the scarf, excitement hot in her throat. She'd never asked any man to do this to her. Never.

"You're going to tie me up and make love to me. Just with your left hand."

Adam stared at the scarf, then looked at her.

"You're kidding," he said, in disbelief.

"Part of your therapy," she said, trying to still her pounding heart. Had she erred, thinking Cryder might agree to this?

"Therapy?" He parroted her words.

51

"Fine motor skills. Nothing develops those better than tying knots."

Adam burst out laughing, and she relaxed. "This isn't a side I've seen of you, Susannah," he finally said. "Good God. I never had you for bondage."

"Therapy," she corrected, with a smile.

"Okay. Therapy."

He moved the scarf through his fingers, considering it for a long moment, then looked at her seriously.

"How far do you trust me?" he asked, quietly.

"Trust— What do you mean?"

"I mean, in bed. How far do you trust me?"

"Well..." Susannah was a little bewildered by the question. "I'm suggesting you tie me up and have your way with me. Is that trust enough?"

"I want to blindfold you, too."

Gee, and here she'd thought Adam was a reluctant participant in bondage games. Far from it.

"Sure." She could barely get the word out, as excitement held her captive.

He smiled at her crookedly and caressed her cheek with his left hand. "I think you'll like it."

Before she could respond, Adam went back to her closet, returning with another scarf. He gently wrapped it around her eyes and she could feel him fumbling with the ends as he tied it behind her head.

"Too tight?" he wanted to know.

"No. Fine."

Her heart was beating in a mixture of apprehension and excitement, and she felt him fumble with the zipper on her dress. He slowly lowered it and she shivered as the cool air in the bedroom touched her flesh. Robbed of her sense of sight, the sense of touch, of being touched, was bolstered.

"Left hand." Her voice came out in a whisper.

"Yes, ma'am. Garter belt and stockings? Nice touch, Anna."

"You're the only one I'd wear frilly underwear for, Cryder."

"You won't be wearing it for long." She heard him chuckle and she jumped as he dropped kisses on the tops of her breasts, his hands cupping them, thumbs rubbing across her nipples, which were pulled into hard, aching peaks at his actions. He took her in his arms again, trailing his fingers down her back, and she arched against him as his touch burned. After a moment, Susannah felt him awkwardly unhook her bra and slide it off her shoulders. Her breasts sprang free, and though she couldn't see his face, she fancied she could feel his hot eyes caressing her.

"Your nipples are hard," he said huskily. "I like them that way."

"Touch them, Adam." Her voice didn't sound like her own. "Please."

He laughed softly and took her in his arms again. "You're very impatient, Anna. I said I wanted to take this slowly. Besides, my therapy isn't quite done yet."

She felt him hook his thumbs in her underwear and slide it down her legs, leaving her only with the garter belt and stockings.

"We'll leave the stockings on," he whispered, his warm breath caressing her ear and neck. "You look hot in those. Step out of your underwear."

Trembling, she awkwardly stepped out of the underwear that had fallen around her ankles. A moment later, she heard him inhale deeply.

"Your panties are soaking," he said softly. "God, your juices smell so good. Hold up your arms."

She did as he asked, feeling the soft silk of the scarf against her wrists as he bound them above her head. His fingers moved slowly, awkwardly, as if they were still stiff. They probably were, but for Susannah, the slowness simply whetted her arousal.

She heard his heavy breathing as he touched her, caressing her breasts and belly, his callused hands on her flesh causing goose bumps to break out on her body. After a moment, the warm wetness of his tongue on one of her hardened nipples added to the hot ache between her legs. She was dripping wet, fully aroused, and hungry for more. Keeping his lips around one nipple, Adam toyed with her other aching peak, rolling it across his thumb and finger. Her legs were trembling so hard she thought she would fall.

Then Adam stopped his caresses and, taking her hands, moved her gently forward. She stopped as her thighs touched the bed.

"Kneel down on the bed. Lean over but keep your rear end up in the air." Susannah followed his orders, lying her upper body on the bed, her ass high up in the air, arms outstretched. Trembling, she felt him move her legs until they were far apart. The cool air of the bedroom touched her swollen and soaked nether regions, and she shuddered, wondering what he had in store for her.

"You're beautiful down there, Susannah."

His voice was husky, ticking nerve endings already seared raw by lust, and his fingers trailed down the cheeks of her rear end, sliding in and out of her anal crack. He repeated the caress, smoothing the thick cream from her arousal around her anal hole.

"Adam, please," she whimpered.

"Be quiet. Else I'll gag you, too."

His voice sounded strange to her, strange and brutal. But she realized with sudden astonishment that she wanted it this way. She craved his roughness. She wanted to be taken savagely, almost painfully.

"Payback," he said in that strange voice. "Every day, for these past weeks, I've been hard for you. So hard, I've ached with it. Now you'll know how it feels to wait. To be so hot for someone, you can't stand it. How it feels to literally ache with wanting."

Adam caressed her rear end again, then slid his fingers between her nether lips, stretching them wide. With a moan, Susannah pressed against his hands, wanting him to fill her, but he smacked her lightly on the bottom, and she subsided, trembling. The slap was sudden, unexpected, but the slight sting accompanying it boosted her arousal.

"You're to stay still." His voice was low, commanding, and Susannah shivered with the raw power of it. "I want to play. But don't move or make a sound."

While one part of her wanted to speak, to argue, the other part, the one held captive by this almost savage sensuality, remained quiet, willingly ceding control to this man. She was ready and open for whatever he wanted to do to her and the thought excited her almost beyond endurance.

Adams thumb tenderly brushed her anal opening, moving over it with soft, sure strokes, as he continued to spread her cream around the orifice. She tensed for a moment, but as he continued touching her gently between her cheeks, the tension dissolved into something else—the desire for penetration. As though reading her mind, Adam slipped his thumb into her anal opening. Susannah gasped, not anticipating such intense titillation from his actions.

"Okay?" She could hear his breath coming fast. The vision of him flushed and wild-eyed as he seduced her slowly with his fingers caused her to groan.

"I'll take that as a yes," he said, laughing softly. Keeping his thumb in place, he brushed her nether lips with his fingers, barely touching her swollen clitoris. Susannah wriggled, needing him to touch her there, harder. But Adam slapped her rear again, harder this time. The slight pain sent silver lust floating through her body and she bit her lip to prevent herself from crying out.

"Keep still." His husky demand played on her sensitized nerves and she barely prevented herself from collapsing in a heap on the bed. With a will, she held herself still, feeling Adam's fingers crawl around her lips and into her moist folds with a tortured, carnal slowness. She fought the desire to writhe, to beg, as he continued his soft caresses, his thumb still planted well in her anal hole.

Without warning, his fingers slid deeply into her pussy, and she cried out, moving involuntarily against his hand, feeling his thumb slide past her sphincter muscles to embed itself more deeply. Adam stroked her clit again with solid, sure strokes, pressing more deeply, pushing against the engorged flesh until she was squirming and gasping. Her climax came on with a sudden fierceness, threatening to swamp her senses, her being, and she screamed as she came, unable to control the ecstatic spasms as they controlled her body.

Suddenly his fingers were gone, and Susannah felt the hard tip of his penis brush around her anal hole. She tensed for a moment, knowing she wasn't ready for that kind of penetration, not yet. But with the sixth sense he seemed to have about their lovemaking, Adam moved his cock into her slick, waiting pussy. Sliding hard, taking her roughly, brutally thrusting deeply into her with a primal, almost bestial need that had her begging him to do her, harder...harder. He cried out her name as she came and a moment later, Susannah climaxed again, shudders of excitement ripping through her. Her trembling knees finally gave way and she collapsed on the bed, taking him with her as she rolled over on her side. He was still hard inside her, and Susannah squeezed him, feeling him groan as he came again with a shaking violence.

They lay still for a long moment. Adam was still deeply buried in her, her back to his front, but she felt him soften, then he withdrew and rolled her over, keeping her tied arms above her head. She was still blindfolded and she wondered what the look in his eyes might be.

"Care to untie me?" she asked.

She felt his hands on her body again, on her shoulders, breasts, hips and belly, caressing her with a gentle thoroughness.

"Nope," he said, sounding slightly out of breath. "I'm keeping you trussed up for the moment. I promised I'd take it slow, and I haven't kept to that yet. I'm sorry I was so—rough."

"I liked it."

She heard his soft laughter. "Yes, I could tell. Unless you're a hell of an actress and can fake it."

"No. I'm rotten at faking," her voice came out in a whisper. His hands moved over her body; his touch scalded her senses.

"I like to play," he murmured. "You make the perfect playground, you know. God, Susannah. I could drown in you."

She caught her breath at his almost reverent tone combined with the sensual tune his fingers were playing on her flesh. Then the fingers were replaced with his warm, wet mouth, his lips moving down her shoulder and grazing the tops of her breasts before moving to the valley between her mounds. He layered soft kisses on the sensitive flesh there and the touch of his lips seared fire into her lower belly. As Adam licked her nipples slowly, Susannah felt the accompanying throb between her legs.

Lips trailing down her body, moving over her belly, Susannah opened her legs to him, wanting to feel his lips on her nether lips, his hot breath on her soaking folds. But he ignored the tender, aroused area, instead focusing on the insides of her thighs, treating the flesh to small nips, licks and kisses. She could feel his eager lapping of the cream coating the insides of her legs, and realized he was taking his time, leisurely drinking her in.

But she was near the edge of her own endurance, and needed a release. Almost desperately, Susannah arched her back, hoping he'd take the hint. The breath of his laughter was warm against the tops of her legs and she shivered in longing.

"You're so impatient, darling," he chided. "I told you I wanted to take this slowly."

"Oh, God." Her groan was torn from her guts. "Payback? Again?"

"Payback is sweet, lovely. But not quite so sweet as tasting you."

Adam planted soft kisses on her nether lips, running his tongue lightly along the sensitive flesh before sliding his tongue deeply inside her, and touching her swollen clit. As he continued lapping at her juices, his fingers toyed with the engorged scrap of skin. Captive to the wanton heat flooding her, Susannah bucked against him, grinding herself into his face, demanding him to delve deeper. Adam obliged, thrusting his tongue deeply into her slick hole, and pressing harder on her clit. Then he withdrew his tongue and, capturing the swollen clitoris with his lips, dragged his tongue against it.

Susannah cried out as the heat from his ministrations rose from her belly to swamp her entire body, engulfing her senses, drowning her in almost unbearable excitement. The climax was violent, almost as violent as the first time, but not quite so prolonged. When he released her, she lay still, shuddering. He ripped off the blindfold and she blinked for a moment in the dim light. He was between her legs, leaning over her, smiling slightly, his green eyes intense, and she shivered, wondering at the enchantment this man had over her.

"Fuck me," she whispered. "Adam, please. Do it."

"I thought you'd never ask."

"Don't tell me you were waiting for an invitation?"

"Sweetheart, the way you're looking right now is invitation enough."

Before she could respond, he thrust deeply into her, then lay still. Prompted by his response, she lay still, too, feeling him grow larger inside her, feeling little tremors move through the walls of her pussy. She gasped as small orgasms moved over her body, rippling her flesh, quickening her breathing. She felt as if she were experiencing a constant, low-grade climax, and she could tell from the way Adam's body was twitching that he was experiencing the same thing.

He began moving against her, driving deeply into her, and Susannah felt shudders rip through him. He leaned down, taking one of her hardened nipples in his mouth, and she felt her body moving toward its pinnacle.

The sudden orgasm was explosive, leaving her almost gasping for air. Almost on cue, she felt his release, heard him cry out. He quieted, breathing heavily and she chuckled.

"Adam, if you could untie me, I'd really appreciate it."

"I don't know." He propped himself up on an elbow, and lightly traced her profile with his finger. "I kind of like you trussed up for my pleasure."

"Yeah? Well, that's great. Problem is, I'm losing circulation, and I'd like to be able to move my arms again at some point."

He sighed in mock exasperation. "If you insist." His fingers unlaced the scarf and Susannah noticed he was using his left hand almost without thinking. She smiled to herself. Focusing his attention on something else had gotten him over his fear of moving his hand. Not that this had been her original intent when he'd come in for therapy, of course. Nor would she try this with just any patient. But she was glad her spur-of-the-moment idea had worked.

Still, her arms ached from holding their unnatural position for so long. She groaned as blood flowed back into the extremities, and flexed her own hands.

"That doesn't sound good," Adam said, concern in his voice. He reached out to rub the tops of her arms, and she relaxed into his touch.

"It's fine," she told him. "Pins and needles, but I'll live."

"That's a relief." Adam drew her against him and she lay close to his warmth, feeling at peace. "I'd hate to think of the alternative."

"There is none. I'm with you for the time being," she murmured, realizing, to her amusement, that she was falling asleep.

What a cliché.

His reply followed her down into the deep, velvet comfort of sleep.

"Hopefully for longer than that, Anna. Hopefully for a long time to come."

CHAPTER 8

The next day, Adam and Susannah stood by the ice. Her face was calm and composed as she wrapped his left hand. Adam envied her serenity and wished he could imitate it.

He supposed he had a right to be nervous. Dressed in hockey sweats and his pads, this was his first practice since the accident, and he was petrified. A small part of him laughed, reminding himself he was a guy who faced upward of forty to fifty shots in any given game with small, black rubber disks hit hard enough to break the speed limit in most states. But it didn't matter. He still felt the skate move over his wrist, saw the blood seeping onto the ice, felt his own agony as the feeling in his hand drained away with the blood on the ice…

"Flex your hand for me, Cryder." Her cool words broke into his thoughts, and he brought himself back to the present. Slowly, he tightened his hand into a fist, and let out a sigh. Just a little twinge. Nothing to write home about.

"You okay?" Her mind was intent on the wrapping, he could see, but he knew, from the trembling of her hands, that she was nervous, too. Somehow, the fact she cared steadied his own rising fears.

"Yeah. Fine." He took a deep breath and tried a smile. "No pain. Just a little twinge."

She nodded. "Good."

Her face was remote as she concentrated on his hand. She was miles away from the fiery lover he'd held in his arms the night before. The image overlying the cool professional in front of him was a hot-blooded woman, wantonly offering herself to him for his pleasure. He'd buried himself in that offering, taking her in primal heat, wanting more. He'd dominated so thoroughly and to his pleased surprise, she'd submitted, willingly, giving everything he'd demanded, and more. Afterward, they'd slept together, curled around each other like kittens. He'd awakened early, kissed her gently, then left to prepare himself for the all-important practice.

Payback.

Adam hadn't been aware, until he'd had her tied up and at his mercy, how badly he'd wanted to torture her through sensuality. And she'd loved it, wanting more, craving more.

"Shit," he said now.

"Now what?"

He felt himself flush. "I've got a hard-on the size of Texas," he mumbled. "Try becoming aroused in a cup sometime and see how it feels. Hurts like hell."

She shook her head, a smile playing about her full lips. "You'd better learn to control your animal urges, Cryder."

"Stop grinning at me like that and I might have a chance," he retorted.

She shrugged, and the blouse she wore tightened over her generous breasts. He felt his groin tighten in response. *Animal urges.* Yeah, that just about described it.

Snorting with laughter, he reflected he wasn't any better than some dumb sixteen-year-old kid, beating off to the image of a naked woman in Playboy.

"Share the joke?"

"You make me feel like a teen-ager."

"Uh—yeah. I can see where that would really be a knee-slapper." She looked at him, clearly confused, and he laughed again and shook his head. His hard-on was subsiding, thank God, and he thought he could probably focus on this practice.

"Thanks, sweetheart."

"Uh—you're welcome. But for what?"

"For making me forget how to be afraid."

He leaned over and kissed her gently on the cheek, then skated out onto the ice. His teammates greeted him like a long-lost brother coming home to roost. Even Dirk Reneau, the arrogant French-Canadian coach of the team, unbent enough to twitch his lips at him. Adam thought suspiciously that it looked like a smile.

The trainer came to him and nodded. Like Susannah, he poked and prodded at Adam's hand and wrist. Unlike Susannah, he wasn't very gentle about it. Adam finally pulled away and grimaced.

"Are you trying to re-injure the hand, Bob?" he asked, and the trainer shrugged.

"Sorry, Crate. You okay for some shots?"

Adam felt a cold tightness in his belly. What if he re-injured his hand? What if he couldn't flex? What if he couldn't *play*?

He glanced over at Susannah. She nodded at him calmly, smiled encouragingly at him, and he settled down.

She'd be great to have around, to watch my back.

He shoved that thought out on wheels. During their torrid meetings, none of the talk had gone much beyond the here-and-now. Trying to take it any further at this point would be a problem.

"Yeah. I'm fine for shots, Bob. Thanks."

Adam took a couple of deep breaths. Pulled on his mask. Assumed his goalie's crouch. After so long off the ice, the once-familiar movement felt rusty and his back protested slightly. But as he began moving side-to-side on the ice to get the feel of the crease and the net behind him, his muscles warmed up, loosening on his bones, and his body moved with the flow.

One of the players, Kevin Johnson, skated to a puck on the ice, gave him a questioning look. Adam nodded to him, and Johnson slapped the puck in his direction. For a moment, Adam's muscles tensed and his breathing stopped. He felt the puck hit him in the mid-section and swallowed. No problem there. Then came Chris Onter. Same thing. Body block. Welcome feel of a fast-traveling rubber disk hitting him. Pucks hitting him meant they weren't in the goal.

Another puck. Then another. Easy blocks, easy shots. Suddenly, Adam's sixth sense picked up something outside his range of vision. Almost on instinct, his left hand, in its catching glove, flew out. Snagged something in mid-air. He felt a twinge. Nothing more.

Not daring to breathe, Adam opened his gloved hand, saw the puck nestled in its depths. He looked at Craig Jablonski, the forward who'd fired the puck toward him. The other man nodded, grinned, tipped his finger at Adam.

He turned his attention to Susannah. She was standing behind the boards, her body tense, expectant. He nodded at her and waved, flashing his smile, a smile that broadened as her body sagged in relief.

He was back. And the feeling was glorious.

*   *   *

An hour later, the coach pulled him out of goal, warning him not to strain his arm any more. But Adam could tell the man was pleased. He could see it in the normally dour man's eyes. Of course, the fact the man had mentioned he'd be playing in his first game next week was a pretty good indication, too, that all seemed to be well. Good reasons for him to be on a high when he entered the locker room. He stripped off and showered, his relief and joy enormous.

His joy increased when he entered the therapy room and saw Susannah, a broad grin on her face. Smiling back, Adam went to her and hugged her. She hugged back fiercely and in that gesture, he felt her concern and affection for him..

"Feeling better?" she said, against his shoulder.

"Oh, God. Yes." His eyes closed, and he held her tightly.

"You're hand's okay?"

"Yes. More than okay. It's great."

They held one another in silence, and he could feel her relief; relief that matched his own.

Finally, he held her out at arm's length and gently kissed her.

"Not to sound cliché, Anna, but I owe it all to you. All of it. Even your unorthodox therapy."

"Mmm. There's more of it where that came from." Her voice was low, sensual, and it curved around his thoughts, sparking a sudden wave of desire. He captured her lips with his, feeling her arms move around his neck. The triumphant return to practice, combined with her soft body pressed eagerly against his, released the floodgates of his lust, and he savaged her mouth, showing his insane want for her. His hands slid beneath her sweater to cup her breasts, feeling the outline of her hardened nipples through her bra, and she shuddered.

"Adam, not here," she said, her voice low in his ear.

"They're still at practice." He wasn't in the mood to be stopped, not now.

"But if we're caught—"

He stilled her doubts with his lips, taking her captive almost brutally with his kisses. He felt her struggle, and he released her, reluctantly. She stepped back a moment, flushed, breathing heavily, a smile on her face.

"Down, tiger," she said. "Discretion, remember? I'm sorry I started that, but maybe we can finish it elsewhere—"

"What's the problem?" He sounded a little snarky to his own ears, then he smiled at his impatience. "I want to tell everyone we're together."

"I know. We just can't right now." She shrugged. "There's still my license to think about."

"Well, seeing as you're not treating me any more, I don't see where that's a problem."

Susannah looked confused and her lips pursed. "No longer treating you? What do you mean?"

"What do you mean, what do I mean? The practice. The skate-around. My hand's moving again. Everything looked fine."

"Yes. In *practice*. But no way would I authorize you to participate in a game."

Adam stared at her, feeling as though he'd been sucker-punched. "I looked good out there—they all said it—"

"You did great. *In practice*. But Adam, a game is a different situation."

Anger slowly ate away at desire as he stared at this haughty woman who apparently didn't understand.

"Don't talk to me about the difference between a game and practice, Anna," he said, his voice low with the effort to restrain his anger. "I've been around this sport longer than you have. And Steve Barton has okay'd me to play in tomorrow night's game."

"Without telling me?" Susannah's face flushed in her own anger.

"He's the team doctor and he's right, Anna. It's time to stop treating me with kid gloves. You said it yourself."

"Adam, this injury *needs* to be treated with kid gloves because if you go back too soon…"

"This isn't about the injury, is it?" Realty slapped Adam like a cold, wet towel in the face, and he didn't like the implications of what she was suggesting. "You're just trying to keep me off the ice, for some perverted reason of your own. Lots of guys with torn tendons go back within a few weeks."

"It's more than torn tendons."

"You're right. It's that I'm involved with you. That if I go back, I'm suddenly the target of the babes. You're so fucking petrified that once I get back to playing, I'll forget about you and ignore you. You're so insecure, you can't stand the thought of what might happen once I'm back in the limelight. That's what all this is about, isn't it?"

The words flowed out, unfamiliar, hostile, even to his own ears. Susannah looked at him, clearly stunned. "Do you think I'm so insecure that I'd use—something like this to keep you from doing what you love?"

"I do." He faced her, his hands clenched, daring her to contradict him. He tried to forget she was the reason he could actually clench his hands now. Instead, he gave himself over to his powerful rage. How dare she keep him off the ice, once he'd proven himself more than able to be back there?

She was, Adam saw, as angry as he was. He sensed she was ready to hit him with her cane. He would have welcomed that. He would have welcomed an excuse to dissipate this violent confrontation by lowering her to the floor and taking her brutally. To his surprise and shame, the conversation was turning him on, and not in a good way.

But she fought to get herself under control then turned away and spoke quietly. "You said you weren't a jock. But you're behaving like one. A jock who thinks he's the center of the universe. Who thinks that he knows everything. Who can mouth off and say awful things and get away with it."

Her words cut deeply, but he'd slit his wrist—again—before letting her know that. Before he could respond, she turned to him, stared at him. "All right," she said coldly. "If the team doctor says you're fine, then my opinion doesn't matter. Do what you want, Adam Cryder. But count me out."

Her eyes, anger laced with bewilderment, met his, and he met her stare with a bland one of his own. Then she nodded, her mouth grim.

"Good luck," she told him, then left.

CHAPTER 9

"Susannah, it's Kristen."

Susannah stared dumbly into space, barely cognizant of the voice on the other end of the phone. She was on her way to being well and truly drunk, and resented like hell being interrupted in her quest.

Well, no reason not to be polite. Kristen wasn't the author of her misery right now. At least, not directly.

"Hi, Kristen." Susannah hoped her words weren't slurry. Last thing she needed was the rumor getting out that she was a lush. She had enough on her plate right now. At least emotionally.

"Did you see the game tonight?" Kristen said.

No question what game the other woman meant.

"Nope." Susannah suppressed a drunken giggle with an effort. Well, why shouldn't she be giggling? She was drinking to reduce her internal agony. Probably a good thing she could laugh about *something*, given how Adam Cryder had screwed her over. Literally and figuratively.

I'm not a jock, he'd kept telling her.

Yeah. Sure.

When the chips were down, he'd sure acted like one.

She'd seen the pre-game show that evening, and the commentator's interview with Adam. The sexy green eyes and that great smile as he talked about how hard he'd worked to get back to the ice had roiled her stomach. Plus there'd been a rumor she'd heard that day about a certain young lady Cryder had taken out the night before.

That was the point when Susannah switched off the television set and decided to get seriously drunk.

65

But even through the alcohol, the pain of his accusations kept coming back to her.

You're so insecure, you can't stand the thought of what might happen once I'm back in the limelight.

What hurt her wasn't that he'd said it. What hurt her was that he'd been one hundred percent correct. Yes, it was too soon for him to be back on the ice. But if it had been up to her, she would have kept him off as long as it was feasible—and beyond. Because she knew what would happen once he went back. The triumphant return to the ice. The inevitable woman on his arm.

And she'd be tossed aside, like a used rag after a furniture dusting.

It didn't help Susannah to realize she'd been right about him in the first place. What he felt for her had been nothing more than gratitude. That was what she got for agreeing to become involved—seriously involved—with a jock.

Well, never again. No way.

"He re-injured his arm."

Kristen's words penetrated through her alcoholic haze, and Susannah sat up, yanking herself from her self-pity with an effort. She'd been so wrapped up in her own anger and inebriation, she hadn't been aware of Kristen's tone of voice. Worry, sliding into shades of panic.

"What happened?" Susannah spoke calmly, grabbing for her professional PT persona with an effort. Why had she drunk so much anyway? It was an effort to think straight.

I told him so, I told him this would happen, what the hell was wrong with that fucking team doctor to give him the go-ahead on the ice, why the hell didn't he LISTEN TO ME...

"His arm was wrapped up pretty tight and he told Brian he wouldn't take any stupid chances." Kristen's voice shook. "But he left the goal to try to retrieve a puck in back of his net and—and a goon from the Express checked him into the boards. He—he fell, Susannah, but he didn't get up. He was bent over, holding his wrist..."

The other woman stopped, but Susannah could visualize the scene. Adam, his face white with pain and despair, being helped to his feet and skated off the ice. The removal of his catching glove and the swollen wrist beneath.

"They had to cut off his glove," Kristen said, her throat clogged. Susannah swore under her breath. The thing must have ballooned up.

"He's in surgery?" Susannah asked.

"Yes. That's why I'm calling you."

"For a re-injured tendon? How about the nerve?"

"They don't know. All they know is that he's had an allergic reaction to the anesthesia," the other woman said quietly. "His blood pressure skyrocketed and they had to sock him with some morphine. They're monitoring his heart, but he seems okay now. He's in recovery."

Susannah felt something inside her break and bleed, and she gripped the phone for support. *High blood pressure. Elevated heart rate. Allergic reaction.*

"Why are you calling me now?" Susannah wanted to know. "Couldn't this have waited?"

"I had reason to believe you two had become—close."

Susannah couldn't stop the warmth from spilling through her veins as she remembered how *close* they'd been. She also wondered how Kristen had known about her relationship with Adam. So much for trying to be discreet.

She cleared her throat.

"He made it clear he didn't want to talk to me again," Susannah said.

"Okay." Kristen spoke amiably, but Susannah heard the no-nonsense steel beneath. "Let me tell you something about hockey guys and career-ending injuries. I'm married to one of those. These guys are going to have their black moments in their lives. They're going to lash out and fight against everything we advise. And as tempting as it is, acting like a selfish bitch isn't going to get anywhere."

Susannah became angry. "How dare you—"

"Because I've been there," Kristen said quietly. "It's hell, Susannah. But Adam needs you. And he needs you not to be judgmental, or to tell him you were right, or to play the wounded martyr. And if you care anything at all about him, you'll help."

A moment later, the smooth silence of a disconnected phone brushed against Susannah's ear. She slammed down the headset, her hands trembling.

Adam. Adam in surgery, having a potentially fatal allergic reaction to the anesthesia. Adam, who re-injured his arm and was facing a near-term future of no hockey. Again. From a career perspective, it could kill his chances of being starting goalie for the year. And what would that do to him psychologically?

Had Kristen been right? Had she been so much of a martyr about her own feelings, so self-righteous about her path, she'd failed to realize that a career-ending injury could be a serious emotional blow for Adam?

She closed her eyes, remembering the agonizing car accident that had ended her father's life and left her disabled. That's why she became a physical therapist, she'd told Adam. To help people, to make them healthy.

But she hadn't helped Adam much, she realized, to her shame. She'd called him as a jock, just like the same arrogant asshole who had destroyed her life at age ten. But Adam wasn't the typical jock. He'd gone out of his way to prove it to her, and when he'd made one slip, she'd written him off.

And now he was in recovery from a dangerous surgery that had had his blood pressure skyrocketing. They were trying to control it with drugs. *High blood pressure. Elevated heart rate.* Susannah swallowed, bowed her head.

The thought of a life without Adam in it clutched at her suddenly, causing her to catch her breath. She loved him, she realized helplessly, even after such a short time of being with him. If he couldn't return the feeling, that was fine. But the least she owed him was honesty.

Brünnhilde and Siegfried. Except this time, instead of Siegfried awakening the sleeping Valkyrie, Brünnhilde would need to step in and take on the task of bringing Siegfried back to a semblance of life, likely without hockey.

"Adam," she whispered. "God in heaven, I hope you're okay."

CHAPTER 10

He swam up through the thick darkness with an effort, trying to reach the light at the end. Not the infamous tunnel that people talked about before death. Rather the bright light of a hospital room.

He'd been here before. The fuzziness in his head and hand. The fear of injury brushing lightly across his body.

The Angel of Pain by his bed.

Déjà vu?

If he'd been able, Adam would have sat up. But his body was heavy with the drugs, and all he could do was gaze at her. They'd fought. She'd left. He'd skated. He was injured. That was all he could remember.

But this wasn't like before. She was crying this time, glasses off her face as the tears flowed. That moved him to wakefulness more than anything else. Susannah Robers made her clients cry. She wasn't much of a crier herself.

"Hey." His voice was a croak, and she started crying harder.

"Oh, my God. Adam. How are you feeling? Thank God you're awake."

Her babbling reverberated in his brain and he closed his eyes in an effort to sort it all out.

"Why? What happened?"

His voice wasn't croaking any more, but he sounded exhausted to his own ears.

Susannah clenched her fists, making a clear effort to get herself under control. She wiped her arm across her face, much like a child would, and he felt an unexpected moment of tenderness for her, even through the drug-induced confusion.

"You re-tore your tendons," she said softly, her voice trembling slightly. "They don't know yet about the nerve."

Adam closed his eyes, taking in her comment. He wasn't surprised, actually. When that goon had checked him into the boards and he'd fallen, he had felt, more than heard, the tearing in his wrist, and assumed the worse-case scenario.

"You were complaining that your wrist was hurting. A lot. They pulled you off the ice and when they cut the glove off and tried to move your hand…"

He'd screamed. He remembered that now. The trainer hadn't hesitated after that, but hustled him into the locker room and shot him full of pain-killer. Things had blurred out, until now.

"How bad is it?"

"I—" She shook her head, looking as though she would cry again.

Weakly, he reached out with his good hand and she took it, gripping it tightly..

"The truth, Anna," he said gently. "I won't go ballistic again. I promise."

"You had to go through another surgery and they had to stitch you up again. But you were allergic to the anesthesia. At one point, your blood pressure skyrocketed. They had to whack you with a dose of morphine, but—but they were afraid…"

Afraid he might end up in that hockey rink in the sky.

"Were you afraid?" he asked.

"Damn straight." She snuffled and looked at him, her red-rimmed eyes serious. "When Kristen called me and told me you were having a weird reaction to the anesthesia, well, I—I was afraid that would be it."

"Gee, Susannah. I didn't know you cared."

She managed a smile at his weak sarcasm. "You must be feeling better, Cryder, if you're snapping at me."

He studied her for a long moment, bemused to see a light shining from behind her, painting a halo around her.

Like an angel. Angel of Pain.

Angel, sure. Of a lot of things. And he'd stupidly driven her off because of his macho behavior. Accusing her of keeping him off the ice. Then the next night, taking out some stupid groupie for a drink. He'd done it for revenge, but the date had been empty. He'd missed

Susannah, pure and simple. After an hour of inane chatter with the groupie, he'd taken her home and, much to the woman's irritation, left.

Now Adam closed his eyes again, his gut clenching. For someone who claimed to disdain jock-type behavior, for someone who'd been hell-bent on proving to Susannah he was different from the typical athlete, he hadn't done such a great job.

He opened his eyes and tightened his grip on her hand. "I'm sorry."

"Oh, God." She began crying again and he felt her pain, felt it become his own.

"Anna, don't."

"I can't help it. Damn you, Adam Cryder. Why'd you have to make me care so much?"

Adam managed a hollow laugh. "I could ask the same of you, sweetheart. You're way outside of my realm of experience."

"Mine, too."

They sat silently for a moment, their hands clinging together. Adam fought off the drugs, not wanting to drift off right now.

"I behaved like a dumb jerk," he finally said. "You were right, Susannah. I needed to stay off the ice a little longer, to heal. Now I really wracked myself up." He hesitated for a moment, tasting the words. "This could be career-ending." He felt a slight jolt of internal pain, then a strange sort of peace.

Susannah's hand tightened on his. "I'm sorry, Cryder. You didn't deserve this."

He looked at her for a long moment. She'd been disabled from childhood, yet had managed to turn it all around and help others. There was a lesson to be learned there, he thought.

"It'll be okay, Anna. I can always coach. The league is always screaming for decent goalie coaches." He treated her to a grin. "Besides, it'll keep me off the ice and out of the hands of those grasping groupies."

She managed a smile for him. "I guess that's one good thing, right? I never thought I was the jealous type, Adam, but when I heard that rumor about you on the town the other night—"

"I know. She meant nothing to me."

Susannah burst out laughing. "Stop with the old lines."

"But it's true." Adam struggled to keep his exhaustion at bay. He could sleep, after he said what he needed to. "I mentioned before that I want to settle down. Have a few kids. Stop being Crate, the jock. I want to do it with you, Susannah."

71

"Isn't this a little sudden after just a few weeks?" She was obviously trying to make a joke of it, but Adam wasn't buying it.

"We're good together, Susannah," he said. "I don't think we need to be dating for the next year or five to realize that."

Her face fell as she released his hand and turned away.

"I can't have children. You know that Adam." His heart lurched at the pain in her voice.

"So we'll adopt."

"I thought most guys liked the idea of their own genes in their kids."

Adam sighed in exasperation, then a grin split his face. "I keep trying to tell you, Anna. I'm not like most guys. I'm especially not a jock. And I sure as hell don't care if my kids have my genes or yours. I just want them to be mine. Ours."

Susannah put her face in her hands and started crying again. "What the hell is it about this hospital that drives me into tears?" she choked out.

"Blame the patient," Adam said. "I'd drive the devil into tears. Not to mention the Angel of Pain. It's not quite the romantic location or circumstances I'd envisioned, and maybe this question is coming a little sooner than I'd like, but would you marry me?"

She looked at him, grabbed a tissue from the box on his bedside table, and blew her nose. "Just don't call me Brünnhilde."

Then she dropped the tissue and flung her arms around his neck. Adam winced, and she pulled back suddenly. "Crap. I'm sorry. Some physical therapist I am."

He reached out with his good arm and hugged her close, loving her size, her strength, her compassion. "You're a wonderful therapist," he whispered into her hair. "I'll take that as a yes?"

"Yes! Yes, you can take this as a yes."

"But sometime, we'll have to discuss payback."

"Only when you're ready."

She hugged him, fiercely, then relaxed against him. Adam cradled her with his good arm and shut his eyes. Despite the pain in his arm and his uncertain future, he felt an overwhelming contentment with this woman in his arms.

Only when you're ready.

He'd been ready for someone like her all of his life. Someone with her fortitude, guts, passion and empathy. Someone willing to see him not as Crate the buff jock, but as Adam Cryder, human being. She'd

72

seen his worst side, and hadn't gone screaming into the night. Instead, here she was by his side, ready to pick up his pieces.

"I think we're both ready," he said gently.

She looked up at him, gazed at his face with those heartbreakingly beautiful eyes, and nodded, clearly catching his meaning.

"I think you're right. We definitely are."

HUNKS OF HOCKEY

TWO ON ONE

HUNKS OF HOCKEY

CHAPTER 1

Jeanne awoke in her sun-washed room to the sound of her husband singing in the shower. Nothing atypical about that. Since their marriage three years before, Gary's awful singing had been a way of life, a sort of off-key alarm clock that exasperated her because it woke her up, and touched her because he sang when he was happy.

At least one of them was happy today.

Jeanne closed her eyes for a long moment, analyzing the deep ache in her chest and throat as though the pain was a kind of physical specimen that could be objectively studied, categorized and then put away. But she couldn't be objective about this—it was just too much. The night before, she'd been awake for hours, lying on her empty bed, crying bitter, angry tears until her nose clogged, her throat turned raspy and her eyes stung. Then when the tears had run out, she'd stared into the darkness, her body one huge ache of exhausting numbness, until the ache spilled over again into tears. At some point, the vicious, weepy cycle had shut down, and she'd fallen unconscious until awakening to this sunny, smiley day.

She desperately wanted to turn the clock back to yesterday morning. Just twenty-four hours ago, everything had been All Right. She'd been a working woman, secure in her career. The happy wife of a well-regarded major league hockey player. Still passionately in love with her husband and he with her, or so it seemed.

What a difference a day makes.

The chest-ache threatened to turn into tears again, and Jeanne

77

fought both ache and tears with an iron will. The solution was simple, of course. She'd have to end the marriage. God knows he wouldn't. Why should he? Gary was having his cake and eating cookies on the side. He had had it both ways—literally.

But did she have the guts to do it? Jeanne wasn't sure; she knew how charming her husband could be. He could say a tender word to her, or touch her in that special way he had, and she'd be like putty in his hands. He'd always been so skilled in bed, and she damned her sexual attraction to him. It was making it difficult to consider kicking him out of her life.

The water shut off and Jeanne braced herself for Gary's appearance. As he came from the bathroom, a towel wrapped around his middle, Jeanne reflected that Gary was a very attractive specimen. Though topping out at a relatively short five-ten, he was in excellent shape, with a lean, yet well-sculpted body and strong legs resulting from his hours on the ice as a forward with the Dallas Blaze hockey club. Despite everything, Jeanne found her mind lingering on the other muscle that was hidden by his towel. The one between his legs; the one that brought her so much pleasure…

Gary smiled at her, a smile that reached his light gray eyes. Jeanne had always loved that smile; it told her how glad he was that she was in his life. But now she didn't trust it.

Is he really that good an actor? Or am I just imagining what happened?

No, it was no imagination. The cold hard reality of what had confronted her on the computer screen the night before flowed into her memory like sewage into a drain. That horrible ache clawed its way back into her throat and chest, and Jeanne forced herself to swallow and take a deep breath to calm herself.

Gary ran a hand through his short-cropped, light-blond hair, and bent to kiss her cheek. It was all she could do not to turn away from him.

"Sleep well?" he wanted to know.

Tell him! her brain screamed. *Tell him what you saw, what you uncovered!*

But she couldn't make herself do it.

Instead, Jeanne gave him what felt like an artificial smile. "I did have some trouble sleeping. Allergies are kicking in again, it being spring and all."

That would at least explain her swollen, red eyes.

Sitting on the bed, Gary studied her and gently stroked her hair back from her forehead in a comforting gesture.

That's the hand he used to get another man off. That man being my best friend.

Jeanne fought the censuring inner voice as she lay quietly under his caress.

"You were zonked out when I got home," Gary said. "I'm sorry I got in so late yesterday. The plane was delayed due to rain, and I didn't get in until around four or so. I hope I didn't wake you."

Jeanne let loose another fake-feeling smile. "I didn't hear you come in. Thanks for being so quiet."

"You're welcome, sweeting. I'm sorry your allergies are kicking up. Did you take anything for them? No? I'm guessing you have to work tonight—we have a game—so you might want to think about taking something and sleeping during the day."

Jeanne nodded and shrugged. "I can't, Gary. I have a meeting with the North Texas Panthers marketing staff in a couple of hours. Brian will be there. Rob and Kristen are coming over from Fort Worth to meet with us." She managed to get Rob's name out with only a small catch in her voice, but Gary didn't seem to notice the hesitation.

"On a Saturday? That sucks. Well, at least you'll be at the arena this afternoon. That's great. I'll be able to meet you during practice."

Jeanne was startled for a moment out of her self-pity. "You have practice today? You just got in from a road trip, you have a game tonight and the coach is still calling practice? Unbelievable."

Gary grimaced and shifted. His towel draped open invitingly, but Jeanne kept her eyes away from the gap. Time was she might have taken advantage of what lay beneath the thin terry cloth. But knowing that another man's mouth might have been on it sort of took away the urge to play.

"Though we won last night, it wasn't good enough," Gary said glumly. "I swear to God Dirk the Dick is into torturing the players, and nothing more."

Jeanne felt real sympathy for Gary. As the Blaze's marketing director she had all too often of late been soft-pedaling grumpy players who complained to the media about the asshole coach that team owner Brian Corrigan brought down from French Canada. Like the rest of the hockey world, she'd wondered why Brian had hired Dirk Reneau in the first place, since the man was known for inspiring hatred among players. When she asked Brian about it at one point, her boss had simply grunted.

"Reneau has a talent for building teams," he'd said. "He knows the right players to pick, and to bring up from the Panthers. This sorry excuse for a team needs all the help it can get."

Jeanne had to admit Brian was right. Since winning the Tannen Trophy a couple of years ago, the Blaze was on a downhill course as free agencies and lucrative trades decimated the team. At least the team was improving this year. Players were probably sticking together in their mutual hatred for the coach.

"I'm sorry, Gary," Jeanne said slowly. "I'm sorry this is so difficult for you."

Her husband shrugged, and the towel fell open again. Jeanne swallowed and forced herself to look away from the enticing view.

"Can't you cancel that meeting today?" he asked. "You don't look too well."

He had that right. Problem was, canceling the meeting wasn't the solution. For a moment, Jeanne felt herself wanting to blurt out everything she'd discovered. The words gathered on the tip of her tongue, demanding a release. As tempting as it was to be brutally honest with Gary, now wasn't the time. She needed to be calm and rational when she confronted him. She also wanted to look at the e-mail again. Provided Gary hadn't deleted it. She cursed herself for not making a copy so she could go over it again, when she wasn't so blindsided by it.

"I'm okay," she forced herself to say.

She heard Gary sigh. "I disagree, but suit yourself, sweetheart." The bed rocked as Gary stood, and she turned just in time to see him go into his huge, walk-in closet. She should probably get up, too. She'd have to shower, force herself to eat something. Today's meeting promised to be a long one, and there'd probably be no time to break for any kind of lunch.

As Jeanne sat up, Gary came out of his closet, wearing black sweats with "Property of the Dallas Blaze" stenciled across his chest.

Out of the closet, she thought sourly. How symbolic.

He came to her, smiling, leaned over, and kissed her on the forehead. She closed her eyes at the gentle caress of his lips on her skin, and tightened her hand on his arm. If only she didn't care about him so much. If only she hadn't believed him close to four years ago when he told her he loved her, loved being with her, wanted her as his life mate. She'd said no for close to a year before she gave in, faced her feelings and agreed to marry him.

Jeanne pasted yet another artificial smile on her face. "Good luck, sweetheart. I'll pray for you."

He made a face at her, but his eyes twinkled. "I'll need all the help I can get, so your prayers are definitely welcomed and encouraged. See you later, love."

He walked out and Jeanne heard his light footsteps as he moved through their spacious, one-floor house. Despite his grousing about the coach, Gary seemed happy. Like a man who loved his job and loved his life.

When she heard the front door close, Jeanne felt the agony to wash over her once again and she buried her head in the pillow, wondering if the heartache and horrible feeling of betrayal would ever end.

It was like some stupid romance novel. Best friend sleeps with husband. When the best friend was a man, and unabashedly gay, that only added to the whole messy setup.

"Life with a major league hockey player," that same best friend, Rob, quipped when she'd griped to him long ago about the perils of romance with a hockey player. While she and Gary were dating, willing, nubile women came up to him, putting their arms around him, kissing him in public, and clearly ignoring her. One particularly aggressive groupie even offered to give Gary head while they were dining in a fancy restaurant.

Gary politely, yet emphatically, declined all invitations, even from the ballsy broad with the blowjob offer. But Jeanne had continued worrying about what might be happening behind her back; a worry she shared with Rob.

"Are you kidding?" her friend asked when she'd told him about the blow-job incident. "Gary is thoroughly monogamous. Trust me, darling. If he's with you, he's with no one else."

Rob Gartner. Her marketing counterpart with the North Texas Panthers, the Blaze's minor league hockey affiliate. Her best buddy. The guy to whom she could confide almost anything. The man who'd been her "bridal attendant" when she finally broke down against Gary's relentless pursuit. The man who had been so happy for her when she confessed, almost shyly, that she and Gary were going to make their relationship legal and forever.

The asshole who'd slept with her husband.

Jeanne swallowed and flopped back on the quilt, her mind playing with the idea of the two of them getting it on. Where had they done it?

Would Gary have had the bad taste to bring him here? To make love to the other man in the bed he shared with his wife? No, betrayer or not, her husband wasn't *that* crass. Rob's apartment, then. That's where it would have happened.

In her mind's eye, Jeanne could see Rob's elegantly appointed, two-bedroom apartment near Sundance Square in Fort Worth. She was a regular visitor to Rob's home, frequently spending the night when business or pleasure took her to the Panthers' side of town.

Now she could visualize Rob's bedroom, painted in eggshell white, the walls sporting two colorful Chagall prints. She saw the large, four-poster bed, covered with its quilts and blankets of dark brown and beige, reflecting Rob's masculine tastes.

Then, unwillingly, Jeanne saw her husband and Rob together, undressing one another on the dark brown quilt.

Jeanne was helpless before the image of the two men touching one another with growing passion. She saw it all; her well-muscled husband with the light sprinkling of blond hair on his chest, stomach, and groin. And Rob, at six feet tall, with a sexy, strong build, the dark hair on his chest a match for the long, dark hair on his head. Two different physical specimens, fused together in love play, penises erect as they strained toward one another, lips and tongues meeting, tangling, as they kissed. The kisses started out softly, gently, then grew heated. Their legs twined with one another as hard flesh pressed against hard flesh in an incredibly erotic dance.

Gary broke the kiss, and trailed kisses down Rob's chest, flicking at his nipples with his nails, them following the caress with his hot tongue. Jeanne caught her breath at Rob's groan as Gary moved down the other man's body, sliding his lips across Rob's taut stomach, then between his legs. She felt the sensual shock in her own groin as Gary teased Rob's cock with his fingers and tongue, lapping at the swollen purple crown that dripped with pre-cum. Skillfully stroking Rob's balls with his fingers, Gary layered soft kisses on the swollen shaft, his tongue sneaking out to explore and tease the hard flesh. Rob arched his back, demanding from his actions that Gary take him all the way in the mouth. But Gary chuckled almost tauntingly, keeping his caresses light and teasing. Jeanne knew from experience that Gary was a master with his tongue. He used oral sex on her frequently and would tease her to the brink of insanity before allowing her a release. Now, in her vision, he was doing the same thing to Rob.

And she wouldn't have believed it, but her body was responding to this incredible fantasy encounter between her husband and best friend. Her nipples grew tight and hard, and warmth tingled between her legs. The images were so vivid in her mind, Jeanne felt as though the two men were in the same room. Her breath caught as Gary slid Rob's penis into his mouth, and Jeanne shuddered as lust-filled moans assaulted her ears.

Rob's green eyes glazed with an almost demented desire while Gary sucked in erotic rhythm, sliding the hardened shaft in and out of his mouth as he hefted and fondled the tightening balls.

"Oh, God. Yes." Rob's voice was hoarse with his impending climax, hips gyrating in a frenzy. A small moan escaped Jeanne's lips as Rob shuddered, fingers clinging to the brown quilt, a prisoner of an almost violent orgasm. Gary's mouth and throat worked, swallowing the other man's cum and Jeanne's teeth came down hard on her lip as she lay on her own bed, horny, but unsated.

Her powerful imagination continued its grip on her as Rob leaned to his bedside table, picked up a tube of K-Y jelly, squirted the thick lotion onto his hands, then rubbed the lube on Gary's swollen penis. Gary lay still for a moment, clearly enjoying the sensation of the other man's caressing hands on his hard flesh. Jeanne had to admit Rob was thorough, at least in her fantasies, slowly and sensuously massaging her husband's erection and balls with the clear lotion. Gary threw his head back at the other man's erotic fondling, his lower lip caught between his teeth in extreme pleasure.

Jeanne's breath came hot in her throat at the scene in her mind's eye. As Rob continued pleasuring Gary with his hands, Jeanne's fingers crept between her legs, unsurprised to find herself wet and swollen.

At a look from Gary, Rob ceased his intimate touching and knelt on the bed, legs slightly spread, eyes closed, face alight with anticipation. Gary positioned himself behind the other man and, licking his lips in anticipation, slowly slid his cock into Rob's ass.

Jeanne, who'd been taken from behind several times by Gary, felt the shock of his swollen penis entering her own anal area as he sank deeply into Rob. As she touched her engorged clit, she moaned at the vision of the ass-fucking playing itself out before her.

"Give it to him," she whispered to the imaginary Gary. "Oh, Jesus, lover. Give it to him hard. Make him come loudly."

Gary moved in and out of Rob's tight hole slowly, almost tauntingly. Jeanne jerked at the sight, feeling hot lust sear her body, enslaving her to the vision playing itself before her closed eyelids.

Jeanne roughly caressed her swollen sex, driving herself toward a desperately needed climax. As both men cried out, Jeanne felt herself go over the edge and she screamed.

Awash in passion, Jeanne came off her climax, shuddering deeply, eyes still closed. A moment later, her eyes jerked open as she felt a grip on her wrist. Her heart pounded as she saw Gary above her, naked and smiling. As he captured both of her hands, pinning them above her head, Jeanne was confused for a moment. Wasn't he somewhere off screwing Rob? Then she remembered. It had been a fantasy. A bizarre wet dream.

"Is that why you were in such a snarky mood this morning?" he asked softly. Keeping her hands imprisoned, Gary moved against her, and Jeanne eagerly shuddered as his swollen shaft pressed against her thigh. "You were in the mood? And I didn't pick up on it?"

"Yes," she croaked. Better to play along than admit she'd been fantasizing herself into a climax. Besides, after the experience she'd just gone through with her overactive imagination, she *was* in the mood.

"What were you thinking about while you were doing yourself?" Keeping her captive with one hand, Gary moved his other down her body and slid it under her nightgown. His fingers played with the curls between her legs and Jeanne's breath caught as a spear of lust sliced through her.

"What were you thinking?" he repeated.

"You," she said, her voice husky. "You pleasuring me."

Gary continued toying with her nether regions and Jeanne's legs fell open. She desperately wanted him to touch her, but Gary apparently had other ideas.

"You were a bad girl for not telling me," he said softly, removing his hand. "For playing with yourself without me here to watch. You'll have to be punished."

Jeanne's body tightened in anticipation at his words and at his flushed face, knowing full well what would happen now. They'd played this scene out many times, and Jeanne craved what was to come.

"Yes," Jeanne said, almost in a whisper. "I was a bad girl. And I need to be punished."

"Take your nightgown off and lie on your stomach."

Not trusting herself to speak, Jeanne sat up and slid the garment off, then rolled over, pressing her face against the silk of the quilt. Her body clenched in anticipation, but the first smack of Gary's hand on the right cheek of her ass was still a shock and she yelped. Holding her down with one hand as she began to writhe from the pain, Gary spanked steadily on her right side. Heat bloomed on her rear end, which throbbed in counterpoint to the warmth growing in her nether regions. The pain became almost unbearable, yet Gary's continued the sensual assault, the sound of his hand striking her flesh boosting her arousal. Just when she thought she had enough, Gary moved his ministrations to her left cheek. Jeanne was beyond coherent thought, the pain and pleasure almost overwhelming. She was no longer human, but a throbbing mass of desire as Gary meted out his punishment with slow, sure strokes.

Then he stopped abruptly and tenderly stroked her bottom, his fingers moving sensuously against the bruised flesh of her cheeks. Her legs had fallen open during the spanking, and Gary took advantage of her vulnerable position, lightly playing his fingers over her nether regions, adding to the heat blossoming in her loins. Forgotten was the fact her husband might have cheated on her. As usual, his forceful dominance turned her on beyond coherence and she wanted him with a raw need that had her gasping. She tried to turn over, but Gary pressed his hand to her back, keeping her face down.

"Problems?" he queried. Listening to him, Jeanne could almost believe he was unaffected by the punishment he'd just doled out to her. Only his quickened breathing gave away that he was as turned on as she was.

"Gary, please."

He chuckled, continuing to fondle her, his fingers playing up and down the crack of her ass, and wandering over her nether regions, sending tendrils of lust through her body.

"Please what?" he wanted to know.

"Do me," she whispered. "Oh, dear God."

"Hmm." His fingers moved tauntingly, teasing her lips, brushing over and over without penetration. Jeanne groaned in frustration, needing him to touch the hot core of her sex, to penetrate her. "I really respond a lot better to politeness, J.B. Ask me nicely and we'll see."

Gary could draw them both out for hours doing this, but she didn't think she could wait that long.

"Please," she whimpered. "Please do me."

Gary slid his fingers deeply inside her, and she spasmed momentarily, almost breathlessly. Then he withdrew his fingers, massaging her cream around her anal hole. Teasingly, he slid a finger into the tight hole, then out again. In and out again, over and over, until she was writhing against the bed, her body hot with the need to climax. She was on the very edge when Gary withdrew his hand and gently played with her crack. Jeanne groaned in frustration as he chuckled.

"I'm still not convinced," he said softly. "You have to convince me you really want it."

Inflamed with need, Jeanne wanted to kill him. She had to have her release or she'd go nuts. His laughter washed over her and she moaned in sensual agony.

"I'm still waiting, J.B."

"Oh, God, Gary. I'm so fucking wet for you. So hot...please...do me...finger-fuck me..."

"Beg me for it, baby." She couldn't see his face, but she heard his husky voice, heavy with desire and need. "I want you to scream, to beg."

Restraint gone, wanting him so badly, Jeanne begged him to be fucked. Screamed it, as he'd demanded. And was rewarded by the feel of his fingers sliding deeply into her soaked pussy. Moaning, she thrust against his fingers, wanting him to go deep and hard. He obliged her, pushing deeper, his fingers swirling against her slick and swollen walls.

"You know what it does to me to see you play with yourself like that," he said harshly, as he moved his fingers. "I'm not sure what turns me on more. Watching you do it. Or disciplining you when I catch you at it."

"Gary..." In the grip of a pending orgasm, Jeanne could barely say much more. Gary thrust deeply, almost painfully with his fingers and Jeanne screamed again, feeling her climax wash over her, holding her body captive, writhing on the bed as he continued pleasuring her.

He released her as she came down, and she felt the mattress dip as he joined her on the bed.

"Get on your knees and get your ass up in the air. Damn it, you get me so hard..."

Legs trembling, Jeanne did as he commanded, knowing what he wanted, ready for it. Craving it. She felt Gary's cock at her backside, slowly moving along the crease of her ass, then feeling the swollen tip caress the anal hole.

"Yes," she said hoarsely. "There, lover. Give it to me there."

But he moved lower. "No, my love. Today you get fucked in the pussy," he said softly. "I want you to milk me good." He slid into her hard and Jeanne let out a gasp of pleasure. Then he withdrew and slammed into her again. Thrusting deeply, Gary moved quickly inside her, and Jeanne clenched around him, relishing his groans. As he drove deeper, Jeanne reached between her legs and stroked the engorged, sensitive flesh in tandem with his thrusts. Roused beyond belief, it didn't take much for her to climax again. As she hit, Jeanne felt the liquid heat of his release throughout her body. Trembling in the aftermath, she collapsed face down on the quilt, Gary sliding out of her as she did so.

After a moment she heard him chuckle and she rolled over on her back. Her husband was propped upon his arm, grinning down at her, and he smoothed her hair back from her face.

"I'd forgotten my spare set of pads," he told her. "Now I'm glad I did."

Despite everything, Jeanne found herself smiling back at him. She loved this man. And even if he was a betraying cheater, he was a phenomenal lover.

"I hope I wasn't too rough," he continued and Jeanne shook her head and stretched.

Her butt still hurt from the beating and she smiled. "You got it right this time," she told him. "It was perfect."

"Good. I always assume you'll speak up if there's a problem. Then again, shyness has never been an issue with you in bed." Sighing, he climbed off the bed and pulled on underwear and sweatpants he'd apparently dropped on the floor.

"I gotta rush," he said, as he hunted around for his sweatshirt. "If I'm late again, Reneau will have my butt for supper. And I'm sorry, J.B., but telling him I was watching my wife play with herself wouldn't be a good excuse for him."

Jeanne sat up as Gary found his sweatshirt and pulled it on.

"I could always offer to blow him to get you off the hook," she said, facetiously.

"Naw," he said, with a broad grin, his face appearing in the sweatshirt's neck hole. His spiky blond hair was tousled, and Jeanne found herself wanting to smooth it down. She wanted him to come back to bed. Maybe they could both stay in bed all day. Make savage love, sweet love, and she could forget about that dreadful e-mail that lurked at the back of her mind.

"The days of your sleeping with men to get me ahead are over," he said, continuing their private joke. He moved quickly to the closet, reappearing almost at once with the extra pads in hand. "Now. If you want to consider sleeping with a woman or two, I wouldn't object. I'd even bring a couple of the guys over to watch."

Jeanne managed a laugh, though her heart was suddenly heavy at his words. Not at the post-coital banter, which was typical of their relationship. But the idea he wouldn't have a problem with her screwing around on him hit her hard.

Was he saying it to justify his own actions?

"Maybe we'll consider it some night when we've got nothing else going on," she said, forcing a lightness she was far from feeling. "You could get some tips. Learn something new about how to please a woman."

"Thanks, J.B." Gary spoke wryly, and leaned forward to kiss her lightly. "I'm not sure whether to be insulted or pleased at that remark." He stood up and looked down at her, his light gray eyes filled with laughter. "Anyway, as tempting and delicious as you look right now, I gotta go. Reneau awaits."

"Don't let me keep you, then."

He tipped a wink at her and left.

Jeanne dropped her cheerful façade as she heard the door shut again. This time she waited a few moments until she heard his car start, then pull away. Getting to her feet, she went to her closet, pulled open the door, and looked critically at her reflection for a long moment in the full-length mirror. She shook her head and stuck her tongue out at the tall, slender body that confronted her. No boobs or hips to speak of, but at least her skin was flawless. She was in her mid thirties, and supposed she was aging well. Her shoulder-length, chocolate-brown hair framed her face, which was flushed from recent lovemaking. Her full mouth drooped slightly and she sighed at her dark brown eyes. Doe eyes, they were, and still slightly red and swollen from last night's bout of weeping. No wonder Gary had wondered about allergies.

Turning her back on the mirror, Jeanne grabbed a robe from the hook, slid it on, then went to the third bedroom, which served as hers and Gary's home office.

Jeanne sat in the chair in front of the computer, wincing. She was still feeling the effects of her husband's enthusiastic punishment. To her irritation, she found herself becoming aroused again at the slight sting on her bottom.

Maybe I should do myself again. See if Gary comes back a second time and we can have an encore.

Jeanne logged into her husband's account. They'd long ago traded passwords, and why not? They had no secrets from one another, after all. Jeanne trusted Gary enough not to snoop around on him. Unlike some of the other hockey wives, who regularly monitored their husbands' e-mails with almost zealous attention.

Scrolling through her husband's inbox, Jeanne thought, at first, that Gary might have deleted the e-mail. But there it was, in all its glory. To Gary. Love Rob. With the same sick feeling in her gut that she'd experienced the night before, Jeanne's eyes roamed over the words.

> *It was a night to remember for me, too, Gary. Your touch and your smell are still with me. I remember your moans. How hard your dick was in my ass. How good you tasted. Most of all, I'm touched you trusted me enough with this and I'm glad, more than glad, that I could be there for you. Rest assured that I'd never let Jeanne know what happened. All my love, Rob*

The thread was dated three weeks ago. While she and Kristen DuChein, owner of the North Texas Panthers, had been out of town at the Women in Sports Management conference. She couldn't find the original e-mail Gary must have sent. Maybe it was just as well. Given this graphic response, she could well imagine what Gary had sent. She, herself, had been on the receiving end of several of his erotic e-mails while they were dating, and even into their marriage. Now, it seemed that Rob was the recipient.

Trembling, Jeanne ran her hands over her face. Lucky her—Jeanne would be facing her husband's lover in just a few hours, across a conference table at the Dallas Blaze corporate headquarters. She didn't know how she'd be able to sit calmly, trading business strategies and marketing insights with Rob when her instinct would be to fly at him, kicking, screaming and damning him.

"Okay, Jeanne Bradley-Jacobsen," she told herself. "No going off the deep end like some dumb female in a soap opera. Not until you get the facts straight about this whole sordid mess. You're going to march up there, take a shower, get on your business suit, and stay in control."

She took a deep breath, got to her feet, and turned off the computer.

"When you have the facts straight," she said to the computer, "then you're allowed to go into hysterics."

CHAPTER 2

"The graphs show that if we can continue on this course, and encourage sponsors to come on board with us, revenue should probably increase for the next season."

Blaine Etherington, Jeanne's assistant director of marketing, rambled on and on. Jeanne studied her notes, trying to find a good point to intervene without pissing the man off. She'd asked Blaine to keep the numbers presentation under fifteen minutes, but his discussion was already flirting with the half-hour mark.

It wouldn't be so bad if Blaine's presentation had some interest. But Blaine was a numbers man, nuts-and-bolts, bottom line. He loved stats, lived for them and now was rolling them off his tongue almost lasciviously. Normally, Jeanne found her subordinate's passion for his spreadsheets more than helpful. Jeanne hated numbers; her particular skill lay in organization and personnel.

But Blaine's droning irritated her. So did Rob Gartner's serene attitude as he sat across the table from her, scribbling notes. Jeanne tried to keep her attention away from Rob. Despite everything, though, she couldn't stop visualizing the damned e-mail that seemed to take up permanent residence in her brain. The one written by the man who sat across her.

I remember your moans. How hard your dick was in my ass. How good you tasted.

Keeping her head down and scribbling meaningless notes on her pad, Jeanne glanced at Rob through her eyelashes. He was dressed casually today, in khaki pants and a tan button-down shirt. Still, he managed to look sexy. Six feet two of well-muscled chest, strong legs, and the mop of brown, longish hair over those bright green eyes. Eyes that often enough sparked with good humor, intelligence, and vitality. The entire package attracted a lot of women, despite the fact that Rob was openly gay.

Still, his preferences had never daunted many of the hockey wives, who had wondered from time to time what it would take to get him to the other side. In her position as Faggot's Best Friend, Jeanne came in for her own share of questioning about whether she'd ever slept with him, or ever had the chance. Her answer was that the thought had never crossed her mind.

It was a lie, of course. But she'd slit her throat before acknowledging to the chattering group of wives that there was one time when she and Rob had come close to crossing the line between friendship and the bedroom.

As she sat listening to Blaine drone on, Jeanne hurriedly pushed the memory from her. Bad enough her husband had apparently enjoyed Rob in the Biblical sense. The last thing she needed was to fantasize about the gay man.

It's not like you haven't fantasized about him in the past, a little voice inside her said. *Maybe your anger isn't because Rob slept with Gary, but because he didn't sleep with you first. Especially given the relationship you both have. You knew Rob a lot of years before Gary came into your life.*

Bullshit.

Not at all, the voice went on serenely. *Remember how Rob kissed you all those years ago.*

Jeanne stiffened at the well-worn theme running around her brain. *We were both drunk at the time,* she told that voice patiently. *We were drunk, it was late, we were tired and I'm still not sure I didn't imagine the whole thing. It never could have happened, nor will it. Kiss or not. You know his beliefs about homosexuality and genetics. That people are born to be gay.*

The voice sniggered. *Not necessarily. All men can get hard, given the right provocation. And given your track record, you're pretty good at getting them hard, Jeannie-boo.*

"Okay." Jeanne smiled at Blaine, praying she hadn't interrupted him in the middle of some important factoid. While her intent had been to cut off the flow of numbers from the man, she also wanted to shut up that smug little voice inside her; the one that kept insisting Rob would be a hot bed partner and given the close relationship she shared with him, she'd be the logical one to seduce him.

"Blaine, thanks for pulling together those figures." She felt Rob's amusement from across the room—the two of them were so often on the same wavelength, they were almost telepathic and she knew he was about as bored with the numbers as she'd been.

"I think the point Blaine's trying to make, that we're all trying to make, is that economically, it makes sense to offer the teams as a double sponsorship deal," Jeanne went on smoothly, fighting the temptation to exchange a smirk with Rob.

Brian Corrigan, who had also been taking notes during Blaine's presentation, put down his pencil, and leaned across the table, a scowl marring his face. Jeanne rolled her eyes mentally, getting ready for the onslaught of whatever criticism he had. This time she did look at Rob, who was doing his best to keep a straight face.

"Yeah, but the problem is divvying up the funds," Brian said. "The Blaze is a major league franchise. We require more resources than the minor league affiliate. Is it fair to ask a sponsor for the Blaze to turn over part of his or her money to the North Texas Panthers?"

"The Panthers aren't bleeding money anymore, Brian," Kristen DuChein chimed in. Kristen, who was Brian's wife, was also owner of the North Texas Panthers, was also an extraordinarily savvy businesswoman. Not to mention the only person who could control Brian when he went off on a rant.

"I know, my love." Brian tossed a rare smile to his wife. "But I want to make sure that the Panthers don't end up bankrupting the Blaze again. Once was too much."

"That's where the marketing comes in," Jeanne said, stepping in. She'd anticipated Brian's concerns and was ready. "The problem we've had in the past is that the Panthers have been marketed as a minor league team, separate from the major league franchise."

"They *are* a minor-league team," Brian said, glancing at Kristen. The light-haired woman said nothing, just waving at Jeanne to continue.

"True," Jeanne said. "But maybe we need to position the Panthers differently. Instead of dubbing the team a minor league affiliate, why not position it as the Blaze's future? A partnership, in which one club is developing potential for the other's future success." She turned to Kristen. "You've had some outstanding talent coming from the Panthers. Onter, Donelson, Cryder to name just a few."

"And Jacobsen?" Kristen said, with a grin. Jeanne chuckled.

"I'm trying to leave nepotism out of this," she responded.

Kristen tapped her upper lip thoughtfully, then nodded. "What you're suggesting, Jeanne, could fit into the other proposal that Rob thought up."

Brian scowled. "Which is?"

"Sponsors buy a part of Panthers players," Rob said promptly. "Not the real players, of course, but maybe a player's time. In return, the players go to grand openings and other events the sponsors have. They're photographed by the local press at these things, stuff like that. That way the sponsors feel as though they have ownership in the Panthers. Gets them into the arena, and as their players are brought up to the Blaze, the sponsors continue to have that feeling of pride and ownership."

Brian sat back, staring into space. "Do we do that just on the minor league level?"

"It couldn't work on the major league level," Jeanne said. "I checked it out. The player's union won't stand for it. But they don't care what goes on among affiliates, as long as it isn't illegal or immoral."

Brian frowned for a moment, thoughtful. Jeanne could almost see the wheels turning in his head. Mentally, she braced herself for the man's merciless questions. Brian normally didn't let an idea go through without poking about a zillion holes into it.

But Brian surprised her this time. "You know, that's not a bad idea," he finally said. "We'd have to make damn sure, though, that there'd be a line in the sand. That players aren't required to go to birthday parties or bar mitzvahs or whatnot."

"That would be outlined in any contract we write," Rob said, with a grin. "I can't see Craig LaFaucet being willing to attend some five-year-old girl's princess fairy party just because daddy bought a share in LaFaucet's career."

Brian smiled back. "Maybe that wouldn't be such a bad idea at that, keeping the guys in line with that type of threat. Now I'm sorry we can't do this on the major league level. Keep some of those idiots in line. Your husband excluded, of course, Jeanne."

Jeanne stomped on her look of surprise with an effort. Brian

Corrigan wasn't one to make jokes, but here he was, doing so. Rob raised an eyebrow in her direction and it was all Jeanne could do not to dissolve into giggles.

"Okay, let's think about it and if it works out, get it into action for the next season. I think we've done good work here." Brian dusted his hands and stood. "We're about ready to go into the playoffs, then summer break. Both teams, thank goodness, have a playoff berth, not that I think any of them will get too deep into the playoff series. By the way, that comment stays in this room, hmm?"

He looked at Jeanne, who nodded, trying to keep her face expressionless. Did he honestly think she'd pass something like that to Gary?

Brian shrugged in the face of her silence, then went on. "Maybe a meeting in June to get everything firmed up for next year, but then I think that's it. Thanks, everyone, for coming in on a Saturday. I appreciate it."

Brian sat down next to Kristen, and the two began comparing the spreadsheets on the table. Thankful for the implicit dismissal, Jeanne gathered her papers and pens and left the glass-enclosed conference room, Blaine following her. Rob tipped her a salute and headed in the direction of the restrooms.

"Marketing revenues," Blaine said, giving her the spreadsheets. Jeanne looked at them, then shook her head with a sigh.

"We're a little over budget on advertising," she told her assistant. He nodded, his eyes bright under his sandy hair.

"First time in a while, Jeanne," he responded. "We've usually been under budget. But it's offset by the increase on add revenue from the flashers. And the Zamboni advertising."

Jeanne blew out her lips and perused the figures once again. "Do me a favor and pull together a graph or something to give me a better idea of the cost-benefits here," she finally said. "You know I'm a lousy numbers person. Also, I want to see if that extra spending has led to extra ticket sales. Let's spare us all a tongue-lashing from Brian."

Blaine rolled his eyes. "Nothing will lead to extra ticket sales, not right now. Not so long as the Blaze is in the tank with its win-loss record."

She suppressed a smile at his didactic tone. "They're in a rebuilding mode," she said, mimicking Brian's deep voice. She cast a quick glance at her boss, who was in deep conversation with Kristen, then looked at Blaine, whose lips were twitching. Then she couldn't hold it in any longer and she burst out laughing, Blaine joining in.

"Something funny?" Rob came behind her, and lay his hands on her shoulders. Jeanne jumped slightly, stunned at the small but sudden worm of desire moving through her belly at his touch. Maybe the remnants of her fantasy were still hanging around in her brain.

Or maybe your desire for Rob has always been there. Maybe you're finally leaving the land of denial and being honest with yourself about this.

Jeanne forced an easy grin on her face as she turned to Rob, wishing she could stuff an imaginary sock in the mouth of her chatty inner voice.

"Just making fun of Brian," Jeanne told Rob.

Rob glanced into the conference room, where Kristen and Brian were still engrossed in the paper litter that covered the huge table

"Yeah, that's a favorite past-time with us in Fort Worth, too," He said. "But we don't do it out loud. Kristen gets pretty bitchy if we start slapping her husband around verbally. Not that it stops *her* from doing it." Rob shrugged. "I could never understand why people think it's okay to knock their significant others down in public."

"I've never done that with Gary." Jeanne didn't like the tension underlying her voice as she defended her actions. Rob raised an eyebrow at her.

"Darling, I wasn't talking about you. You've been good for Gary."

Yep. Warming him up for you, right?

The words were ready to spill from Jeanne's mouth when Blaine pointedly cleared his throat. "Jeanne, I'd like to have part of the day off," he said, plaintively.

"I'm sorry." Jeanne was irritated with herself. She'd been so lost in her own shit, she'd forgotten that her assistant was standing by patiently. "These can wait until Monday. Thanks for coming in today, Blaine."

"It's okay, Jeanne." The other man seemed mollified. "I'll catch you Monday. Have a good weekend. What's left of it, anyway."

"You, too, Blaine."

Jeanne watched the man hurry away, spreadsheets clutched to his chest like a sacred offering.

"There goes Dactose, slave to the god Numeros. Off to put in his daily offering for the results which are...numbers." Rob spoke softly and Jeanne snorted in amusement. Part of the amusement was relief though—relief that Blaine prevented her from blurting out what was on her mind.

You're a coward, Jeannie-boo, the voice inside told her.

So call me chicken.

"I'm glad Blaine's the numbers guy," she said to Rob. "Someone has to do it and I'm allergic to Excel. By the way, next time you make faces at me, please don't do it with Brian around, okay? Last thing I need is to start losing it in front of him."

"I don't know," Rob said reflectively. "Maybe you're losing it in front of him might loosen him up a little."

"Fine. Then you try it. I like my job too much to try to test the limits of Brian Corrigan's sense of humor."

Rob smiled, then fingered the material of her tweed jacket.

"Nice outfit," he said admiringly. "New?"

"K&G," Jeanne told him and grinned at his shocked look.

"Discount," he sneered.

"We can't all be pulling down huge salaries like you do." She gazed at him pointedly. "Besides, you aren't exactly dressed for success today, so you're not one to talk. Did you bike in?"

He nodded. Well, that explained his casual look. It also explained the beat-up leather jacket. Jeanne knew that jacket well—he'd had it for years. It was part of his persona. It also made him look dangerously sexy.

"You didn't come with Kristen?" Jeanne asked, pushing the thought out of her brain.

He shook his head. "I wanted to stick around for the game tonight. I thought we could sit together."

"How long have you had that jacket?" Jeanne suddenly asked.

Rob raised his eyebrow in surprise, then she could see him calculating the answer. "Four years ago, just before you came on with the Blaze...and right before I was promoted to marketing director. I wore it at that first joint meeting, when you and I went for drinks afterward and confessed our latest romantic scandals."

That was right. Two months into her tenure as marketing director with the Blaze, she and Rob had met at the business meeting at Carlyle Arena, then gone for drinks at Antares at the Hyatt nearby to discuss marketing strategies. As the drinks flowed, discussions turned from business to personal and it came out that both had been recently dumped by long-term lovers. By the end of the evening, the two realized they shared more in common than broken hearts, though. Like a love of hockey, theater and stupid movies. And a great friendship had been born. Until three weeks ago.

"It was a lot better looking then," she said and winced. Her voice was more cutting than she'd intended. She suddenly realized how badly she wanted to hurt this man. Her best friend. Yeah, right.

Rob raised an eyebrow at her. "No need to get bitchy about it, J.B. We're none of us as young as we used to be. Given what the jacket's been through, it's held up well. Listen, I have some work I can get done here today. Can I crash at your place tonight?"

That was the usual M.O. Nights that Rob wanted to see the Blaze, he had carte blanche to stay with her and Gary. Nothing new about that. Problem was, she couldn't get the image of Rob and Gary on the brown bedspread out of her mind.

"Sure you can stay over. No problem." She hoped her voice sounded more sincere than she felt. But if Rob noticed any problem, he didn't let on.

From inside the conference room, Kristen looked up suddenly. "Rob, good. I'm glad you're around. I need you," she called out.

"Be right there, boss," Rob said cheerfully.

Kristen nodded, and returned to her discussion with Brian.

Rob sighed, shaking his head. "I need you," he said, mimicking Kristen. "Words I love to hear. But preferably from a hunk with a deep, masculine voice."

"Ah, well." Jeanne smiled. Despite everything, Rob could always make her laugh. "You'll have to deal with hearing it from a woman, I guess. At least until Mr. Perfect comes along."

Rob shrugged and winked. "Too late. You're married to him, darling. I'll just have to hope the gay version turns up in my life." Before she could respond, Rob hugged her briefly. "I have to scoot. I'll set up shop here today, so let's hook up sometime later today, okay?"

Without another word, Rob went into the conference room. Brian and Kristen looked up at him and nodded. Rob sat at the table and took out a note pad and pen. Jeanne slowly turned her back on them and went to her office. It was quiet, and she relished the solitude. Most days, the Blaze offices were a jumping hive of activity.

After entering her office, Jeanne moved to the window and studied the view of downtown Dallas, picking out the Reunion Arena Tower with its distinctive ball. What had Rob meant about Gary being Mr. Perfect? How long had he felt that way about the other man?

Jeanne's computer dinged softly, signifying e-mail, and she sighed. She couldn't help it. The sound made her think of another e-mail, ensconced in her computer at home.

Staring at the skyline, Jeanne realized she would have to stop dodging the situation and accept that Gary might be a homosexual in the process of outing himself. The ardent way in which he'd pursued her, the enthusiasm to which he'd taken to their lovemaking; none of it mattered, not now. It was likely all a sham.

She would also have to face the painful fact that she was a beard, a female Gary used to cover his sexual preferences. She supposed she could see the situation from his point of view. He could be in real trouble as a hockey player if he was revealed as queer. Sexual orientation wasn't supposed to be an issue in sports, but Jeanne didn't buy it. Men were uneasy in the locker room with openly gay teammates.

The whole thing was especially tense among the North Texas Panthers and Dallas Blaze. Kristen's first husband, Marty Pellin, general manager of the North Texas Panthers, had rocked the sports world several years before when he couldn't keep his hands off several of his players. Pellin had died in a fiery auto wreck weeks after the whole story had come out. But Kristen had lived with the stigma long after he was buried.

Given everything, Jeanne supposed Gary's marriage to a willing bedmate like herself would be logical, if he indeed were a closet fag. And why not? Her mouth curled in contempt at her past behavior. She'd all but thrown herself at him in a very public fashion on their fourth or fifth date. The kinky sex had continued unabated throughout their courtship and well into their marriage. Taking risks; pushing the envelope; trying everything, at any time and anywhere. She was an easy mark, hot for the studly hockey player, and he'd taken her up on it. Given her predilection for taking risks, she was probably considered every man's wet dream.

Jeanne swallowed her self-contempt, tried to push it out of her mind as she sat at her desk and stared, unseeingly, at the load of e-mails that required her attention.

Despite her connection with Gary in the bedroom—and on many occasions outside of it, Jeanne knew the bond she shared with her husband went beyond just physical. They'd always shared an innate honesty, an ability to talk about whatever was on their minds. When Gary had been concerned about her close relationship with Rob and what it might portend, he hadn't hesitated to mention it to her. And when she'd shared her misgivings about the groupies that clustered around the locker room, following hockey games, always looking for a free grope, she'd brought it up to him. These were issues they'd been able to resolve, with honesty, compassion and reassurance.

"There's no reassurance in this situation," Jeanne said softly, staring at her computer screen. What she would need to do, she realized, is determine whether her marriage should be continued, and what her options were if her husband, indeed, was making his way out of the closet.

*   *   *

Later that afternoon, Jeanne slipped into a sweater and reluctantly made her way down to the ice at Carlyle for her usual pre-game meeting and chat with Gary. This was tradition with them; whenever he had a home game, she'd slip away from her duties and meet with her husband for a few minutes. They talked, or sometimes they'd sit in silence. But she always came away from those brief encounters glad she was married to Gary.

Today was different, though. Jeanne dreaded the meeting because she had spent some time on the Internet, researching the lives of gays with hetero spouses. While she had a lot of respect for those who chose to stick out their marriage, she couldn't see herself in the position as one of those understanding spouses. If children were involved, that would be another matter. But given their crazy schedules, she and Gary had decided against kids, a decision for which Jeanne was now thankful. It would make leaving him that much easier. Not that leaving him would be easy, she thought despondently as she entered the arena. She didn't think she could do it.

As Jeanne reached ice level, she saw Gary in their usual spot, the home team penalty box. His face brightened as he saw her, and Jeanne's newfound resolution to leave her marriage took a serious nosedive. The look on Gary's face was a private, special one between them, one that told her how much he cared about her; how glad he was to see her.

It was definitely not a look that a man who had cheated on his wife with another guy would have.

*I remember your moans. How hard your dick was in my ass.
How good you tasted.*

Gary must be a hell of an actor, Jeanne told herself glumly.

"Hey," he said, as she approached.

She sat next to him. "Hey yourself."

Gary took her hand and they stared at the clean sheet of ice for a long moment. Jeanne groped for something to say, something impersonal. The accusations trembled on her tongue. But as pissed as she was, Jeanne didn't have the heart to question her husband before a game.

"Are you ready for the Racers?" she finally asked.

Gary shrugged. "They're a bottom team in the division. Shouldn't be too much of a problem."

"Bottom feeders can sometimes be spoilers," she reminded him.

"Thanks, coach," he said dryly. "I already heard it from The Dick. He's very good at telling us that if we can't beat those scrubs, we're not fit to be on the ice. Dirk the Dick is such a great motivator and purveyor of team chemistry. I just can't figure out why more people don't like him." Gary dropped his sarcastic attitude and sighed. "Is Brian letting anything out about when he plans to fire the asshole?"

Jeanne shook her head. "Brian doesn't discuss team strategy with me. I'm his business head, remember? Talk to Rich Huntington. He's ops and player personnel."

"Hunt doesn't know either. But from what I understand, he's just as frustrated with the coach."

They continued chatting in the same vein for a few minutes, as they always did. Nothing hugely important. Just the act of being with her before a game was enough of a tonic for him. Or so he'd told her. As Jeanne watched other players taking the ice for their pre-game practice, she wondered if that was still the case. She studied the players for a moment, then did a double-take.

"Am I sniffing some funny glue or does Adrian Donelson actually look happy?" she ventured. Gary followed her gaze to where the tall, dark-haired defenseman was warming up and smiled.

"Yeah, quite a change for him, isn't it? Seeing a smile on his face. Rumor has it he's in love."

Jeanne shook her head, amazed. Donelson had struck her as a first-class grump, for all he was a great on-ice enforcer. "Anyone we know?"

Gary shrugged. "Old friend, apparently. He's not kissing and telling, and thank God, I say. His sexual exploits were getting pretty boring, even for locker room conversations."

Gary trailed off, his face troubled, uneasy. He turned to her, about ready to say something, and Jeanne waited expectantly, wondering and also dreading if he was going to come clean with her about his own exploits with Rob.

But then Chris Onter, the Blaze's center, skated by the penalty bench and stopped to discuss an upcoming charity event. Jeanne hid her anger at the interruption, chatting in a friendly fashion with the player. As she chatted with Onter, Jeanne reflected on the dichotomy of hockey players. They were blood and guts on the ice, pounding each other in an almost unholy glee in their attempts to get a piece of frozen, vulcanized rubber into the goal. But off the ice, she had yet to meet a more polite group of men. Most were family men, dedicated to their homes and communities.

Like Gary?

Until the night before, Jeanne had thought so.

As Onter skated off, Jeanne turned to her husband, hoping the interruption hadn't cost him his nerve; hoping he would let loose with whatever he had on his mind. Her heart sank as she saw him lace up his skates in preparation for taking the ice.

"Duty calls," he said. His head was down and she couldn't see his face, but his voice was strained.

"Okay." Jeanne forced herself to swallow the lump lodged in her throat. "I guess it does. For both of us."

Gary looked up at her and smiled. Then he sat next to her on the bench and kissed her on the tip of her nose. "For luck," he said.

She kissed him back gently on the lips. "For luck."

He saluted her, stood and skated onto the ice to begin drills. Jeanne looked at him for a few minutes as he handled the puck with almost contemptuous ease, passing it to teammates, then taking it back on his stick. She tried to recreate the awe she'd experienced in the past; awe that this man had selected her for his mate, especially when women regularly threw themselves at him.

But with her newfound knowledge, she simply couldn't bring up the heartfelt appreciation and love. Her heart was heavy with her secret, and she lacked the guts to bring it into the open. And Gary, perhaps understandably, was keeping mum on the subject.

Shoulders slumped, Jeanne turned her back on the practice and left the arena. With a will, she went back to her quiet office, determined to make a dent in her work. Summer was coming, advertising contracts needed to be reviewed and signed and new potential sponsors needed to be contacted. She should take advantage of the quiet to get the paperwork done.

Within fifteen minutes, she was deeply involved in her work, all personal matters shut out of her brain. What seemed like only a few moments later, she was startled by a gentle clearing of the throat. Jeanne looked up from the contract she was perusing to see Rob, standing in the doorway, leaning nonchalantly against the doorjamb, grinning at her.

"You looked so intent, I was afraid to interrupt you," he said.

Jeanne said nothing. She just gawked at him for a long moment, brought from the safe world of contracts and sponsors and advertising to this reality of the long, lean sexy man standing before her, complete with the leather jacket, a mop of longish dark hair that refused to be tamed by a brush, and the amused glint in his green eyes.

Helplessly, her mind went back to that night four years ago in Ozona's. The night in which she and Rob came close to crossing the line of their friendship into a deeper, more intimate relationship…

Get it out of your thoughts, Jeannie-boo. Going over that won't help a damned thing.

Jeanne put the contract down on her desk and tried a smile for her friend. "What time is it?"

He glanced at his watch. "About six-fifteen. With face-off at seven, I thought we should get down there and get our seats."

"Yeah, okay. Give me a few minutes to freshen up and I'll meet you at the elevator."

"You got it, sweetheart."

He left. Jeanne put the contracts in the folder and shut off her computer, forcing herself to go through the motions of finishing her work while her mind tumbled in chaos, her personal life once again clamoring for attention. Husband sleeping with best friend. She wanting her best friend. And possibly, she leaving her husband. The thoughts went around in her brain, like a vicious circle, until Jeanne was ready to run from the building, screaming.

She wouldn't do that, of course. Instead, she forced herself to breathe evenly and deeply, then went to the bathroom and put lipstick on. She ran a comb through her hair and stared at herself in the mirror. Her brown doe-eyes seemed enormous in her face, brimming with unwelcome knowledge about her own needs and desires. Jeanne clenched her hands and turned away from the image.

I need to leave. I want to go home, bury myself under the covers and shut the world out.

Instead, she sat on her panicked inner voice, picked up her purse, and left the ladies' room. A moment later, she found Rob at the elevator.

"I was getting worried about you, J.B.," he told her. "I thought I'd have to come in after you."

"A gay man in the women's rest room," Jeanne said, musingly. "There's something interesting for the grapevine."

He winked and grinned at her. "It'd be more interesting if I was found in the men's room. And not alone. There's your grapevine topic, and it wouldn't be the first time, as I think about it."

Jeanne felt a sudden and unwelcome desire cramp her belly at the sudden image that came to mind. Rob and Gary...together...on the brown bedspread...

The elevator came and they stepped on.

"Don't tell me you've done that here," she said, relieved that her voice sounded humorous.

He shook his head. "God, no. It happened years ago, at another job. I was young and stupid and came damn near close to losing my job over it."

Yeah, and speaking of young and stupid...

The memory of what happened at Ozona's all those years ago assaulted her. It had been after a Blaze game, before Gary had come into her life. She and Rob ended up at the popular bar and grill on lower Greenville Avenue and proceeded to tear apart that night's game, and drinking a little too much.

When she was ready to leave, she stood, giggling as the room swayed around her.

"Oh, shit," she'd said, and Rob began to snicker. "You try to stand up," she told him.

"I'm not that stupid, J.B.," he said, and they both started laughing. Still giggling, Jeanne leaned over for the customary good-bye peck on the cheek from her friend. But instead of giving him a smooth on the cheek, Jeanne found her lips meeting Rob's. She was startled into inaction for a moment, unable to move. Rather than pulling back as she thought he might, Rob deepened the kiss, sliding his hand behind her neck to hold her head steady. Jeanne found herself opening her lips, inviting his tongue to explore her mouth, which he'd done with a smooth, sensual beat that had her reeling.

Suddenly realizing what she was doing and with whom, Jeanne

frantically broke the kiss and stumbled away. Away from Rob, away from the booze, away from the knowledge this was no kiss a gay man would give to a woman friend. Jeanne almost ran into the dark, humid night, looking for a cab, her mind reeling with the combination of too much booze, the feel of his lips on hers, and the recollection of his tongue sliding sensuously into her mouth. As she leaned against a light post, she damned herself for drinking too much. And in the deep recess of her mind, she damned herself for not sticking around and seeing where that kiss might have led. She was aroused beyond belief, wanting Rob in her bed, his mouth on hers, his flesh pressed against her, his cock buried deeply inside her.

She hadn't seen Rob for several weeks afterward and had wondered, almost fearfully, if the kiss would change the dynamics of their relationship. But the next time they were together, Rob had been his usual friendly self, not mentioning the hot, dark kiss they'd shared in the dim bar. Jeanne, taking her cue from him, never referred to it again. And it had remained in the back of her mind, only coming out during periods of extreme exhaustion, frustration or confusion.

"Jeanne?"

She started, brought abruptly back to the present. The elevator. The upcoming game. And this dangerously sexy gay man, who was stirring all kinds of unwelcome emotions inside her. The elevator doors were open, facing out on the lobby of the arena, where throngs of hockey fans awaited eagerly and loudly to get into their seats.

"We're here," Rob said, staring at her curiously. "Bottom level. You looked gone. Off in the ozone or something."

Yeah. Ozona's.

Jeanne sat on her almost hysterical laughter and shook her head. "I'm fine," she said. "A little tired. Wanting to go home and climb into bed."

With you.

Rob studied her for a moment and Jeanne felt as though he was reaching inside of her and giving her thoughts and emotions an unwelcome stir. She couldn't tear herself away from his intense gaze to save her life.

Maybe I should have confronted him with it after it happened. Maybe I should have really asked him how he felt about me, why he kissed me like that. Maybe I should have forced him to take the next step.

Thinking about that "next step," Jeanne felt a shiver course through her, partly fear, partly anticipation.

"Are you okay?" His voice was soft, concerned, and Jeanne trembled again, angry and aroused in turn. Bad enough he was gay. Worse was that he'd slept with her husband. Now she wanted him. This whole thing was sordid, stupid. But try as she might, she couldn't stomp on her body's yearning for the guy. She remembered that kiss in all of its darkly erotic detail, and Jeanne found herself hungering for it again.

The elevator doors closed, effectively blocking out the fan noise and lobby lights.

"Jeanne, what is it?"

The tenderness of his voice almost made her break down. She longed to confess everything to him, as she was used to doing. Ironic, really. Rob was her best friend, her number-one confidante. They'd weathered a lot of problems and crises together.

But this was the one thing she couldn't confide to him. The one thing that would drive him away. Not that he'd slept with Gary. But that she wanted to sleep with Rob.

Swallowing, she looked away, feeling her eyes fill with tears. Then jumped as he touched her arm.

"Jeanne…"

The welcome vibration of the pager clipped to her belt saved her from hearing what he might have to say. She unclipped the pager and saw, with relief and inevitability, that it was from Brian. Her boss found it hard to believe his staff might actually like to see a Blaze game for fun every once in awhile. His feeling was that if his employees were in the building they were automatically on call. While the attitude irritated Jeanne, right now she was grateful for her boss's type A personality.

"Duty calls." Jeanne forced herself to speak lightly.

Rob shook his head, rolled his eyes and punched the button on the panel. The elevator door slid open and the wall of light and noise almost assaulted Jeanne.

"Jeez, can't the guy let you enjoy a game for once?" Rob said, half in exasperation. "No wonder you look so friggin' tired these days. Tell Brian to leave you alone."

Jeanne gave him a perfunctory smile. "You tell him, okay? See how far you can get. But maybe I can cage something tasty from the owner's box for the both of us. There are some perks to working on the job. I'll meet you at the seats."

Rob waved, good-naturedly. "No you won't. I know Brian and that means I'll be by myself at this one. I'll see you later at the house."

Oh, crap. She'd forgotten he would be spending the night. For a moment, Jeanne thought about not going home, about booking a hotel room near the Carlyle for the night. It wouldn't be the first time; sometimes if she was working late, she would stay the night at a hotel and spare herself the drive home.

But if she did that, Rob and Gary would be in the house together...alone...unseen...able to do almost anything...

The erotic images suddenly assaulting her were as agonizing as they were arousing.

"Okay. Enjoy the rest of the game. Cheer Gary on for me," Jeanne managed to say, then hurried away without waiting for his response. First Ozona's, now this. Just like her, to run off before some Moment of Truth could be explored.

"I'm a fucking coward," she muttered, as she made her way to the owner's box. "I can be a woman in a man's world, I can interact with hockey players like one of the guys, but I can't tell my fucking best friend that I've wanted him, or tell my husband I know he cheated on me."

She managed a calm demeanor until arriving just outside the box, where she was alone, and out of sight from the crowds. Jeanne leaned against the wall and clenched her fists, praying for control.

We're playing this stupid game of guess who'll spill the beans first. We all know a secret, but none of us has the guts to admit it. Or to be honest about it. I hate this.

"Now's not the time," she told herself, softly. "Be brave, little one. Get through whatever the hell Brian wants. Then you can decide what to do."

Taking a deep breath, Jeanne pulled herself together, knocked on the door to the owner's box, heard Brian's voice inviting her inside. She responded to the request and went inside, noticing the typical scene. Brian Corrigan, his long, dark hair neatly tied back, was dressed in his usual shirtsleeves and slightly loosened necktie, while playing host to some business bigwig or another, or simply in deep discussion with his wife. But Kristen was gone, presumably back to Fort Worth. Jeanne wished Rob had gone back with her.

Brian's companion tonight was Eric Jardin from Jardin Jewelers. The two sat at a small conference table, papers spread across the smooth, dark top. Jeanne glanced through the window, and saw the players warming up. Her eyes lingered on number 34. Gary's number. Her cheating, lying husband...

Jeanne forced herself to meet Brian's welcoming and somewhat apologetic smile with one of her own.

God, any more fake smiles like this and my damned cheeks will crack. They hurt already.

Eric stood, grinned at her, and held out his hand. "I'm glad to see you, Jeanne." The man was sincere and polite. In contrast to Brian's business look, Eric was totally casual, a dark blue sweater and slacks setting off his blond hair and blue eyes admirably. Jeanne took his hand politely, meeting the man's blue-eyed gaze with a cool one of her own. Eric Jardin was a bonafide flirt who knew how to charm. He was also single and constantly on the prowl. Or so the grapevine hinted. The rumor mill even implicated Kristen as one of his flings. But Jeanne always dismissed that tidbit—from what she could tell, the North Texas Panthers' boss was loyal to Brian.

Just like I've been to Gary. And look where it's gotten me.

Jeanne shoved the thought out of her mind and took the seat at the conference table, Eric following suit. He smiled at her again and, to her dismay, Jeanne felt her heart thumping in her chest.

This is good, she told herself. First Rob. Now a client. Could you possibly get any lower with your depravity?

"I'm sorry to take you away from the game, Jeanne," Brian was saying. "You've already been here most of the day. But Eric is ready to chat up some potential promotional ideas for next season, and we thought we could use your input. I figured as long as you were here, now would be as good a time as any."

"Sure," Jeanne said, relieved that she could dive once again into the relatively unmessy realm of marketing and business. "No time like the present. Probably a good idea to get a jump on it, before the break begins." She searched on the messy table and extracted a pad of lined paper and a pen. "We're already fielding some sponsorship inquiries for next year," she continued. "I haven't committed anyone to anything yet because I want to see who else is interested in coming on board."

Eric raised an eyebrow. "Count me in, Jeanne. What's your assessment on some of the flasher boards and charities we've run in conjunction with the Blaze this year? Think they've done any good?"

She nodded, relieved that she remembered Blaine's figures. She'd looked at them just an hour before, and was ready to quote them. "They've helped our bottom line," she said. "The question is, have they helped yours."

"What's helped are the coupons," Eric said, thoughtfully. "Now we can actually measure how much response we're getting."

For the next fifteen minutes, Jeanne lost herself in the comforting and somewhat mundane chat about business, marketing, response rates and strategies. With a marginal part of her mind, she registered that Gary was having a great night on the ice, clocking in at two assists and a goal and just during the first period. Normally, this would be a night when they would celebrate.

Maybe Rob and Gary can celebrate together. The thought brought her an unexpected pang, and she suddenly wanted to be away from here. Away from the workaholic Brian, the too-knowing Eric. Away from her best friend and her cheating husband. Away from emotions that threatened to swamp her. As far away as she could manage.

Brian nodded at her, signaling an end to the meeting. "I'm sorry to keep you, Jeanne. I know you wanted to watch Gary. He's having a great night."

"I'll throw my apologies in there, too," Eric added, with a smile. "But it's always good to see you."

His remark was innocent enough; the glance he threw her was anything but. Innuendoes and flirting were part of the man's M.O., and she knew how to brush off his comments without causing offense. He was a valued client, after all, and she'd learned to tiptoe that line between business and familiarity with Eric's type.

Tonight, though, she was thinking of taking his remarks beyond the flirtation stage.

Why not? Hubby cheated on me, why not return the favor?

With a sigh, Jeanne stood and moved to the suite's window to study the game. Gary was in play now, partnered with the speedy Chris Onter. The two raced up the ice, appearing to gang up on an opposing team member. Two-on-one; Jeanne could spot it, and she held her breath as the play developed. Gary passed to Onter, who shot the puck at the goal, where it slithered under the opposing goalie's stick. Bull's-eye.

The crowd went wild as the celebratory stadium horns sounded. The Racers' goalie's face was covered with a mask, but his body language showed dejection and anger. For no good reason, Jeanne remembered a conversation she had with Blaze goalie Adam Cryder before a season-ending injury had taken him out of the line-up. She'd wanted to mike him up at some television network's request, but he turned her down.

"If I get scored on, my language gets pretty ripe," he confessed with a wry smile. "It wouldn't look too good for us or the network if that happens."

"Two-on-one. Possibly one of the most exciting moves in hockey."

Jeanne started. She'd been so involved with her own thoughts, she wasn't aware of Eric's approach. Or his nearness. He was standing close enough for her to feel the heat radiating from his body. Jeanne's nostrils flaired at the mint scent of his body cologne. Eric was good-looking in a smooth, urbane way, with his almost white-blond hair a direct counterpoint to his vivid blue eyes. He was a little too thin for Jeanne's tastes, but what the hell. He dressed nicely, he looked hot, and he smelled delicious.

Good enough to eat, hey, Jeannie-boo?

Behind her, Jeanne could hear Brian talking on the phone. Based on the intimate tone of his voice, she thought he might be talking with Kristen. She damped down the sudden feeling of jealousy. Whatever else Brian was, he was fiercely loyal to his wife. *He* wouldn't sneak around on her.

Swallowing, Jeanne looked in Eric's eyes, and the knowledge and sensuality there sent a thrill along her nerves, straight down to her toes.

"What do you think?" he said in that same, soft tone. "Do you think two-on-ones are exciting?"

Eric's words and tone conjured sexy, erotic visions in her mind of bedroom games. Two men, one women; the woman the recipient of unimaginable pleasure. It didn't take too much to put herself in that spot.

But who were the two men?

"I think…I think you're right," Jeanne found herself responding in a halting voice. "Next to a penalty shot, it's a pretty exciting move. On the ice."

Jeanne slapped herself mentally, forcing herself to look away from Eric's knowing eyes and to move away from him. She turned to Brian, who snapped his cell phone shut.

"You seem a little peaked, Jeanne," he said, concerned. "If I could spare Gary, I'd suggest you two head off to some sunny climate or something. But with playoffs coming up, it's not in the cards right now."

What was this? Was her turmoil actually showing on her face? Now her boss, her type A boss, was telling her to take some time off!

Jeanne opened her mouth to say something sarcastic, but thought better of it.

"We'll get away after the season ends," she said, slowly.

If we're still together, that is.

"Make sure you do," Brian said. "We'll let you go now. Have a good one, Jeanne."

Recognizing her dismissal, Jeanne gathered her things and left quietly, feeling Eric's eyes burn into her back. Outside the suite, Jeanne leaned against the wall, trying to reconcile her body's hunger with her rational mind. Since being fucked by her husband that morning, Jeanne had gone from wanting her best friend to lusting after a client with the reputation of a suave Don Juan.

"It doesn't take much to know what the hell is going on," she muttered, through gritted teeth. Payback, pure and simple. She wanted revenge against her cheating husband. And right now, game or no game, she wanted to confront the bastard. If her knowledge disrupted his game for the rest of the night, tough shit. The whole affair was disrupting her *life*, let alone a stupid hockey game.

Jeanne swiftly made her way to the locker room level. With the game going on, not many people were around, but the first period would end in a few minutes.

As Jeanne waited in nervous anticipation, her eyes wandered past the shut locker room door to a cubby just one hundred yards away. It was there, in the semi-secluded spot, that she'd seduced Gary after they'd been dating for a few weeks. Her body tightened in anticipation as the memory washed over her.

Gary, who was skating with the Panthers, had accepted her invitation to a Blaze game. They'd sat together, enjoying the game, discussing strategy, discussing the time when he might be on that sheet of ice himself someday. Immediately following the game, Jeanne had taken him downstairs for an impromptu tour of the facilities. But there were other sights she'd wanted her new boyfriend to see, sights that had nothing to do with locker rooms or back offices. Pushing Gary into a cubby and pressing against him, Jeanne had whispered what she wanted from him, what she needed for him to do.

To her relief, Gary hadn't shied away in disgust at her suggestions as had another guy she'd brought here. Instead, he considered her for a long moment, gray eyes narrowing. Then he pressed her back against the wall, kissing her with a raw hunger and passion. Jeanne had grown weak in the knees at his touch. The fact he wasn't much taller than her added to the heat of this illicit encounter, and Jeanne moaned as he ground his hips against hers while taking her mouth again and again with his own. Lust flowed through her body like molten honey, and Jeanne became aware that Gary was hard for her, as hungry for it as she was, and willing to fuck her in this public place.

Keeping her lips captive with his, Gary slid his hand beneath her skirt and up her thigh. She sensed his delighted surprise at the bare flesh beneath her skirt; she was naked except for a garter belt and panty hose. His fingers found their way to her mound, toying with the curls for a moment before sliding through her nether lips to fondle her slick folds. She jerked against him as a spasm of white-hot desire slammed through her.

"How long have you been planning to waylay me like this?" he murmured in her ear.

She could hardly think straight with his fingers doing their dance on her swollen clit and the sensitive flesh around it.

"Since our second date," she managed to confess.

"You're dripping wet," he said softly. "Have you been walking around all day like this?"

"Yes." She'd anticipated this scenario in her mind, over and over, since getting dressed that morning. The dichotomy of her nakedness beneath the sensible wool skirt had kept her in a high state of arousal most of the day.

"All day," Gary said musingly, continuing to work his fingers. With his other hand, he slowly unbuttoned her blouse, exposing her small breasts. She felt her nipples pucker as the cold air hit them.

"No bra," he commented.

"I—I don't need one." Gary's bold actions roused her further, almost robbing her of the power to speak.

"That's good." A shiver worked its way down her spine at his husky tone. "It makes it easier for me to do this."

Leaning over, he took a tight nipple in his mouth and sucked hard, running his thumb across the other sensitive peak. Jeanne's teeth sank into her lip and she fought to swallow the moan that threatened to break free.

A small part of her knew she'd be toast if she, the vice president of marketing for the Dallas Blaze, were found half naked, being seduced by a player with the minor league affiliate in public.

But she was past caring by now. She only wished she could rip her clothes off so Gary could run his lips, his hands, his cock over her entire body. She didn't care that a roomful of people was just yards away. The only thing that mattered was Gary, his hard body pressed against hers as his fingers and mouth toyed with her.

Gary raised his head up to look at her, his eyes glazed with desire, with need. "You like to take risks, don't you? I like it, too. Oh, Jesus. I love it that you're so ready for this...that you want me to do this..."

He pressed against her and Jeanne drew in a breath as he touched her clit again, trembling as the sudden heat almost drove her to her knees.

"I should make you wait for this," he said, trembling. "The longer we're at this, the more exciting it becomes. The more likely we are to be discovered. And discovery could mean your job. Not to mention my career."

He slid his fingers deeply inside her soaking cunt and she buckled against him, moaning against his shoulder. She was on fire, wanting him to screw her, wanting him to make her come.

"Jesus, yes, Gary," she whispered. "Right there. Oh, dear Lord..."

Gary continued moving his fingers in and out of her, moving slowly at first, then quickening the pace. As he placed his thumb on her clit and pushed hard, Jeanne's climax moved through her. She muffled her cries against Gary's shoulder as he continued his intense pleasuring of her.

Finally he released her, and she came down from her sexual high, her legs trembling, her breath coming fast. But he wasn't done with her yet.

"The next time, I'll count how many times I can get you to come," he said. "But I'm so hard for you right now, I'm ready to explode. I couldn't wait to save my life."

"Do me. I want you in me." Had that been her raspy voice, heavy with command, with desire? She was insatiable around him, roused with a sexual need she couldn't define.

Smiling at her, Gary backed away and slid down his pants. He returned to her, sliding slowly into her, thrusting deeply, pinning her against the wall as he moved against her.

"Impatient, aren't you?" he said, somewhat breathlessly.

She couldn't reply, as his cock rubbing against her slickness was sensual torture. She moaned his name, then suddenly spasmed as she came again, her orgasm rocking her with a suddenness that had her reeling. Gary let out a soft groan, and she felt his release throughout her body.

Gary slid out of her, his smile lighting his flushed face.

"I think we can save the tour for another time," he said. "There's only one more tour I'm interested in, and that's of your body."

Jeanne, who still craved more from this man, didn't argue, but brought him to her apartment that night. Only later, as she lay exhausted and sated in Gary's arms, had Jeanne brought up the subject of protection. Or rather, lack of it.

Gary had grinned at her. "Fine time to be thinking about it, J.B. But not to worry. I haven't been with anyone for a long, long time. I get into a lot of risks with lovemaking, and not a lot of women appreciate it."

In that way, Gary was her true soul mate. As she got to know Gary better, Jeanne learned he liked to push the envelope when it came to sex. Though they tried many different things, Jeanne's favorite, by far, was public sex, during which Gary would seduce her anywhere and everywhere the fancy took them both. Movie theaters, the library and even, at one point, in the middle of a crowded Carlyle arena during a Blaze hockey game, when Gary finger fucked her under a blanket, making her come again and again, in a silent, ecstatic, and sensual agony.

They hadn't indulged quite so often since Gary had been called up to the majors. But now, as Jeanne stood before the locker room prior to the end of the first period, Jeanne fancied she saw Gary and herself, getting it on with one another for the very first time. She saw Gary fondle her, slowly unbutton her blouse to reveal her nipples, hardened with excitement and the cold air. She saw him slide his hand under her skirt, and slowly into her sticky-slick cunt…

Jeanne cried out, jerked from her reverie by a hand on her arm. She turned and stared into Eric Jardin's blue smiling eyes. One part of her was a little unnerved at the man's stalking of her; while the other wondered how far she could go with him. Or how far he might take her. If his look said anything, he'd go about as far as she wanted him to.

"I'm sorry," he said softly. "You looked lost in thought."

He's good looking. He wants me. It'd be payback.

But that would be turning her back on everything she respected about marriage.

So? It's not as though your loving hubby there exactly respected your wedding vows.

Eric smiled, almost reading her thoughts.

"I thought our meeting had concluded a little abruptly," he said. "I'd love to take you out for a drink to chat a little more."

It didn't take a genius to figure out that Eric had more than drinking on his mind. But as confused and raw and horny as she was feeling, Jeanne had to restrain herself from jumping in his arms right there. Begging him for a quick fuck. Throwing her husband's infidelity right back in his face, in the same place where it had all begun for herself and Gary.

No. She wasn't ready to go that far. She was committed to her marriage, no matter what. But what could one little drink hurt?

Ignoring the condemning voice in her mind, Jeanne gave Eric a crooked smile and lay her hand on his arm. She fancied she could feel it tighten in excitement under hers.

"A drink and talk would be lovely," she said.

CHAPTER 3

Paying off the cab, Jeanne giggled to herself. She was plastered, three sheets to the wind, choose your cliché. She didn't care. The all-encompassing ache she'd been nursing for the past twenty-four hours was successfully smothered under layers of shots and beers. She hadn't drunk so much since college. Even in college, she'd been only a moderate drinker.

"The better to get drunker with, my dear," she said out loud, then snickered. She was drunk, all right. But when it came down to it, she hadn't had the guts to act on her lust for Eric Jardin—and her need to extract vengeance on her husband.

"You're a wuss," she snarled at herself as she stumbled up the sidewalk. It would serve her right if Jardin pulled his account from the Panthers. She'd behaved like a cock tease toward him, then left him hanging. Jeanne supposed she could take comfort in the fact that a couple of pretty girls had sidled up to Jardin as she'd apologized and left him. Turning back to him at the door, Jeanne saw a look of sensual greed infuse the other man's face as he put an arm around both.

She stopped as she saw Rob's motorcycle. Memory came through sluggishly, like molasses on a cold winter morning. That's right. Rob was staying over tonight. He didn't want to hike back to Fort Worth. Bully for them.

Jeanne wondered if she would find the two in bed. For a moment the pain wrestled with the alcohol. But the booze won. Pressing her lips together, Jeanne marched toward the house. She managed to get the key in the lock during the third try. She almost hoped they were together. Get it all out in the open. She'd confront the lovers, and demand an explanation.

But when she marched in the living room, all she saw was Gary, sitting in his recliner, reading a book. When he looked up, he marked the book, stood up, and frowned at her.

"Where the hell have you been?" he demanded. "I was worried sick!"

The concern soaking his tone gave her pause for a moment and she felt a moment of guilt. Then the anger came boiling up again.

"Like you care," she almost snarled. She stalked into the bedroom, hoping to find a naked Rob lolling in the afterglow of some rowdy sex. But all she saw was the bed, neatly made. The empty bed made her stop for a moment. The thought tried to work is way through her brain that the bed was in pristine shape. Not a wrinkle. She peered at it owlishly, in wonder.

"Suppose you tell me where you were until two A.M.?" Gary stood behind her and spoke acidly. "And why you didn't bother to call? Why you didn't answer your cell? Another hour and I was ready to call the police."

She turned to face him. "If you must know, I was out with Eric Jardin." She tried to speak with lofty disdain, but her words came out slurred.

She almost laughed out loud at the shock on Gary's face. "Jardin? That...that letch? What the hell were you doing out with *him*?"

"Business meeting," Jeanne said promptly. "He took me out for drinks, pumped my brains for information, then tried to come on to me. I admit I encouraged it. But then I chickened out and came home. How was the game, by the way?"

If Gary had been shocked that Jeanne was with Letch Supreme, his mouth fell to the floor at her response. He shook his head and glared at her.

"Jesus, J.B. You...you came on to him? What the fuck were you thinking? I knew you had a wild side, but this is going a little too far! I won't stand for it from my wife!"

Jeanne felt her eyes fill with tears. Foolish, drunken tears. "*You* won't stand for it? What the hell do you think I've had to stand for? To put up with? After what you did? Damn you, thanks a lot, Gary. Now I'm sounding like a cliché..."

He grabbed her and glared.

"Don't talk to me like that. This isn't about me. And I just bet that it was Jardin you were fantasizing about this morning, wasn't it?"

The remark was so far from the truth, Jeanne just stared at him in surprise. He shook her a little, angrily. "Answer me, damn you! And you better not lie about it."

Jeanne shook her head, her lips trembling. "No, I didn't lie. I was fantasizing about you. But—"

"But?"

Jeanne straightened her back. She wasn't ready for this confrontation. But sometimes confrontations just foisted themselves on you, whether you were ready or not. Besides, she'd been ready to confront him earlier, at the game, but the timely arrival of Eric the Letch had prevented that.

I hadn't drunk half of Dallas at that point, though.

It didn't matter. The opening was there. It was time to spill the beans, drunk or not. "You weren't alone. And you weren't with me. You were with Rob."

She hoped that he'd look at her incredulously at the confession, wondering how in the world he, a straight man, would be cavorting with a card-carrying homosexual in her sexual visions of him.

But he didn't do it. His hands tightened on her arms for a brief moment, then he released her, his eyes on her face, clearly trying to determine how much she knew, how much he'd have to backpedal. Jeanne decided to put him out of his misery.

"I saw your e-mail," she said, quietly. "The one from Rob. From…from a few weeks ago when I was out of town. I…I know you guys were together. I'm just wondering when you were going to—uh—share that little fact with me."

The effect her words had on him would have almost been laughable if she hadn't felt so scraped raw. Gary's face crumpled, and his gray eyes looked at her, stunned and guilty. She'd hoped, really hoped, that what she'd seen on the computer had been some kind of joke. But his shamed face said it all.

Turning on him, Jeanne felt silent tears sliding down her cheeks. No tears like a drunk's tears. She sank down on the edge of the bed, miserable and exhausted beyond belief.

"Why, Gary?" Her voice was a croak.

He was silent for a long moment. When he spoke at last, his voice was low. "It's complicated."

"Yeah. And it's not because of me, right? It's some deep need in you. Something you can't get from me, your wife. Despite the fact I've done everything you've asked. I've been your sub when you've wanted it. I've let you punish me in the bedroom. I've let you take me in all manner of ways. I thought…I thought we had a great sex life …"

"Jeanne, stop. You've been great. It isn't you."

"Of course not. It's never the wife's fault, is it?"

Jeanne's voice shook and she buried her head in her hands, feeling herself shudder with sobs.

"So you're gay?" Jeanne forced herself to ask through the tears.

She felt his hesitation. "It's not that simple."

"Oh, Christ!" Jeanne dropped her hands and turned to glare at him. "It *is* that simple. It's a simple question. "You're either gay or you're not."

"It's not that simple," he repeated, his face a study in misery.

Gary sounded helpless and for a moment, anger flared through the tears. He had no right to feel helpless, not after what he'd done. She wanted to stand up to him, give him the side of her tongue, to lash into him for the indiscretion. But she was gripped by the mind-numbing alcohol. Problem was, while the booze was muddling her thoughts, it wasn't doing a hell of a lot to stem her pain. Dimly, she felt the weight of the bed sag as he sat next to her and took her in his arms. She wanted so badly to fight him off, but the crying was debilitating her. Never had grief swamped her to this extent. She was helpless before its bitter onslaught. She couldn't seem to stop crying, now that the dam had broken. And the booze was making her tired, so tired…

Gary said nothing, continuing to hold her as her violent weeping held her in its grip.

"Jeanne, I'm sorry," he whispered. "It only happened once and—"

She pushed him away and pulled into herself, rocking back and forth, hoping the soothing motion would calm her down. "Once. Just once? God, Gary, that was one time too much. Was it good for you?" she asked angrily. "He gave you something he'd never give to me. Was it good?"

"I know," Gary said softly. "That was part of the issue. You wanted it from him, didn't you?"

Jeanne stopped her rocking, stared at him in shock, then felt herself move toward denial. "Damn you, this isn't about me!" Her throat hurt from keeping her anger in check. "I may have…have wanted to, but I didn't do anything about it. This is all about you—fucking around on me. With…with a gay man. A man who is—was—my best friend."

"I still am your best friend, Jeanne." A quiet voice from the door prompted Jeanne to look up. She swallowed as Rob's brilliant green eyes pinned hers.

"My best friend seducing my husband." Her voice was raw. "My best friend outing him. Some best fucking friend."

Rob ignored her tirade and came to her. Crouching, he took a foot in his hands and began to massage it as he used to do when she was upset about something. Usually it calmed her down. Right now, it pissed her off. She wanted to yank her foot away in self-righteous anger, but the alcohol slowed her, dulling her reflexes, exhausting her.

"Maybe you need to hear the whole story, J.B., before you start rushing to point fingers." Rob spoke calmly as he continued massaging her foot.

"Rob, no." Jeanne heard the warning in her husband's voice, but Rob ignored him.

"Gary went through a difficult time while he was at the Panthers," Rob was saying quietly as he continued massaging her foot. She felt her husband's intake of breath, but Rob glared at him. "If you're not going to tell her, I will. She deserves to know."

"What, that you two are going to run off together? I hope you're very happy." She tried to yank her foot away, aware she was sounding petulant, but Rob kept a firm hold.

"Don't be a bitch," he said mildly. "The true story is there were problems with Marty Pellin long before you entered the picture, darling. And this is part of it."

This time Jeanne was successful in retrieving her foot from Rob's grasp. She faced her husband, horror moving through her at Rob's words. Marty Pellin, the late, unlamented owner of the North Texas Panthers, who had brought scandal down on the team because he hadn't kept his hands off the players.

"That...pervert put his hands on you?" she said, aghast.

Gary shrugged, his face an unhappy study. "Pellin was threatening to send a bunch of us back to the farm team if we didn't...cooperate. I'd just come on board with the Panthers and wanted to stay for awhile. I didn't want to screw with my future. I didn't figure one...indiscretion would make a difference."

"Why didn't you come forward when everyone else did?"

Gary looked down, his face red.

"Tell her, Gary." Rob's voice was implacable, and Gary's shoulders slumped.

"I enjoyed it." Gary's voice was low, choked. "I liked it with Marty. It's one reason I didn't report it when the others did."

Jeanne felt bile rise in her throat and she took several deep breaths, trying to steady herself and calm her stomach. "How could you have liked it with him?" she whispered. She was afraid she might scream. "You…you just told me you didn't think you're gay."

His gaze met hers somberly. "I thought I might be bi."

Jeanne listened, stunned to speechlessness as she swallowed another spasm of nausea.

"I never screwed around after you and I met," Gary went on. "I never wanted to. I love you too much. I love our sex life together. But I'd always wondered about that other side of me."

"And that gave you license to run to…to my best friend? To ask him to…to fuck you like that?" Jeanne turned to Rob. "And that gave you license to say okay?"

Her voice was raw, and she was trembling. All these years, her worries had been the bimbos. Female groupies accosting her husband for a few quickies. Never, in her wildest dreams, had she expected something like this. Feeling boneless, she put her head in her hands, wanting, more than anything, to shut this whole scenario out of her consciousness.

"It didn't give us license to do this, you're right." Rob's voice was low, filled with pain. "I told you earlier that Gary would have slit his wrists before hurting you. Me, I would have, too. We never meant for you to find out." He reached for her foot again, but she pulled away from him, her stomach heaving. This time she knew she wouldn't be successful keeping it down. She wasn't sure if it was the booze or the conversation, but she stumbled to her feet and stumbled to the bathroom. She barely made it before she threw up her glut of alcohol.

The perfect ending to a hell of a day.

Gasping, she hung over the toilet, wondering if more was going to come up. She felt a hand stroking back her hair. Gently. She recognized Gary's touch, trying to comfort her, and she broke down weeping again. Whatever else he might have done, he was trying to comfort her, trying to soothe her. Distantly she heard the hissing of a shower.

"C'mon." Gary's voice was gentle as he urged her to her feet. "Let's get you cleaned up. You'll feel better after a hot shower."

"No," she said miserably, though her tears. "Leave me alone. Please."

"No, Jeanne," he said softly, but firmly. "Come on."

She didn't have the strength to fight him. She was dimly aware of Rob stepping out of the bathroom as Gary helped her out of her clothes, then led her into the shower. She allowed herself to be guided, like a small child, the tears still running unchecked down her face. She didn't fuss as Gary shampooed her hair, then rinsed it and the soap from the rest of her body.

When finished, he wrapped her in a fluffy towel, dried her off, then slid a nightgown on. He led her to their king bed and Jeanne lay down, exhausted from her tears and from the emotional swirl of the entire day. Gary lay beside her and took her in his arms. She wanted to fight him, fight the betraying asshole. She wanted nothing to do with him ever again. But she was just too damned tired to fight. Her eyelids grew heavy and she fell asleep secure, despite everything, in the embrace of her husband.

*   *   *

She woke what seemed like a few moments later, lying on her right side. The room was dark except for a dim light streaming in from the living room and bedroom. Jeanne swallowed, her head aching, her eyes burning from the tears she'd shed. Given all she'd drunk with Eric, she was thankful a headache was her only problem.

Gary lay next to her, fully dressed, sound asleep, and Jeanne felt an unexpected moment of tenderness for him. Despite the awful emotional turmoil they'd been through, he had still taken care of her. She lay on her back and sighed, realizing she couldn't leave him. She was just too connected with him in too many ways. She'd have to work through the pain and the ramifications of what was going on.

"That was a pretty deep sigh. Want to talk about it?" a soft voice said next to her. Jeanne jumped and rolled over to her left side, somehow unsurprised to see Rob lying there. Unlike her husband, who slumbered peacefully, Rob was wide awake, and also dressed. In the dim light, Jeanne could see concern, care, and love etched on his face.

He touched her hair, gently. "How are you feeling?"

She paused for a moment, wondering how to respond. Then she plunged ahead. "Remember how you felt when you walked in to find Charlie in bed with that stud from the restaurant down the street?" Shortly after her marriage to Gary, Rob had been in agony over his live-in lover's indiscretion for months.

Rob nodded and Jeanne sighed again. "Multiply that by about one

121

hundred and you'll have an idea of how bad I'm feeling now." She felt the pain, a red wave, threatening to come up and swallow her again. But she promised it wouldn't, not until she fully understood what was going on.

"I'm sorry," he whispered. "I'm sorry you got involved with this. But Gary wasn't cheating on you, J.B."

Jeanne closed her eyes with a sense of helpless resignation. She supposed in the homosexual closet world, in which men switched partners with depressing regularity, a one-time fuck with someone else's partner wouldn't count as cheating.

"Rob, I don't agree. Where I come from, monogamy is a part of marriage."

"Gary didn't sleep with me because he was hot for me or anything." Rob spoke carefully, as though trying to ensure she understood what he was getting at. "He was trying to prove a point to himself. That his feelings for Marty were a one-time thing. A fluke. He asked me because…I was safe. He felt I wouldn't try to take him away from you because I care about you too much to hurt you like that."

Jeanne felt the tears gathering. Again. More of this and she could hire herself out as a waterworks. "But you did hurt me, don't you understand? You gave him something you never gave me."

His eyes widened at her admission and she cursed her honesty. She was lying here, hurting over Gary's infidelity, when in the deepest recesses of her mind, she knew she'd always wondered what sleeping with Rob would be like.

If that's the case, I'm no better than Gary.

Rob reached out to cup her cheek. "I never knew you were curious about that," he said softly.

Jeanne hitched a breath. Now that the truth was out, she may as well go all the way. "That kiss at Ozona's four years ago. It brought up the question in my mind. A lot of times. You kept saying you were gay and you weren't interested, but that kiss said something different and… Oh, never mind. You're gay. You like to fuck men, right? It doesn't matter."

"Jeanne—"

"It's a dead issue, Rob. One I don't want to talk about right now. I actually don't want to talk about anything right now because I don't want to wake up Gary."

She jumped as she heard her husband's voice behind her. "Gary's very much awake. And is very much interested in this conversation."

Jeanne closed her eyes and gritted her teeth, not liking the guilty feeling washing through her, feeling as though she'd been doing something far worse with Rob than talking.

Rob propped himself up on an elbow, and glanced at Gary behind her. Then he looked down at her again.

"Okay, as long as we're being honest here, I wondered about it, too, J.B.," he said.

She looked at him in bewilderment. "Wondered about—"

"Wondered about what it would be like to sleep with you. You weren't the only one confused as hell about that kiss at Ozona's. I thought that would go away when you married Gary—it's one reason why I pushed it so hard. But it's still there. That curiosity."

Jeanne sat up in bed suddenly, and leaned against the headboard, staring down at both men, an awful suspicion taking place in her mind.

"That's why you agreed to sleep with Gary when he came to you?" she said. "Because you couldn't—wouldn't—sleep with me? Because you're gay?"

"It's more complicated than that," Rob said slowly.

Jeanne threw up her arms in frustration. "None of this is complicated, goddamn it! You're the ones who are making it such a fucking mess. Gary thinks he's bisexual, but instead of coming to me, he goes to you. You want to sleep with me, you're wondering about it, but instead of coming to me, you go to Gary. And you two end up in the sack, causing me all kinds of shit. Why the hell am I the one out of the loop when this concerns me, too? Why am I the one being caused to suffer over this?"

Angrily, she tried to crawl over Gary to get out of the bed and to get far away from these two stupid idiots. But her husband's arms came around her, holding her tightly, crushing her against his chest. Then he rolled her over, pinning her beneath him, grinning down at her in apparent delight.

"What the fuck is so funny?" she almost growled. She wanted to do something, anything, to get that sudden smile off his face. "Stop laughing at me."

"Sweetheart, I'm not laughing at you," Gary said. "There's nothing to laugh about. But J.B., one thing I have always loved and admired about you is your honesty and your ability to cut through bullshit and confusion. You are absolutely right about everything."

"Jeanne's always had the ability to get to the heart of an issue," Rob agreed. Light suddenly blossomed in the room as Rob turned on the bedside lamp. Jeanne struggled against Gary's hold, glaring up at him, but he kept her captive.

"So what's so funny about this whole mess?" she snarled.

Gary ignored her, directing his comments at the other man. "So here's our situation. I know, based on that one-time experience with you, that I'm likely not bi. No offense. Nothing you did or didn't do."

"None taken," Rob said.

Jeanne lurched against Gary's hold again, but he held her fast and continued speaking.

"Okay. What we have just learned is that Jeanne has wanted you, and you, apparently, have been wanting her."

"Correct." Rob spoke and Jeanne could hear the wariness in his voice.

"Well, then have at her, Rob."

"Huh?" Rob's response echoed Jeanne's feelings completely. She wondered if her husband had gone insane. Or maybe this was his idea of a joke. If so, it was a joke in very bad taste. But she saw that beneath his smile, Gary was serious.

"It could answer a lot of questions if you two make love," Gary said. "It would satisfy curiosity on both sides. And Jeanne's right. She has been left out of the loop on this. By the way, Rob, have you ever slept with a woman before?"

"Well, once. I'm no expert or anything."

"Okay." Gary nodded. "I can help you through this, Rob. I know what Jeanne likes. With the two of us together, this should go smoothly—"

"Are you nuts?" Jeanne found her voice, interrupting her husband's obscenely calm voice, and struggling against his hold. This time Gary released her, and she sat up, studying the two men incredulously. "Gary, I'm not some kind of...of *thing* you can offer to other men for their pleasure...or...or their education. I never knew you were a...a pimp."

Gary winced at her choice of words. "I'm not pimping you. Nor am I offering you to other *men*, love," he said gently. "This is Rob. A close friend of yours. One who, as you just said, you've been wanting for years. Besides, isn't that every woman's wet dream? Having two men pleasure her in bed? Touching, kissing and licking until she's screaming herself hoarse?"

Jeanne shivered, both at the raw tone of his voice and the image he evoked in her mind with his words. Images of the three of them together, making love, being made love to, tantalizing, erotic images of unbearable pleasure, shattering climaxes, flesh pressed on flesh in love, in lust ...

"Gary, I don't believe you're...you're..." Her voice trembled and she couldn't finish.

"The woman I took outside that crowded locker room years ago would be jumping at this chance. The one who had God-knows-how-many orgasms in the middle of that hockey game would have, too. What happened to that woman?"

"I—" Jeanne fell silent, at a sudden loss for words. What had happened to that woman?

Maybe the question you should ask yourself is what kind of a man would suggest this particular threesome.

"Rob's gay," she pointed out, hoping she sounded firm. "He's not attracted to women."

"Why don't you let Rob speak for himself?" Rob said, an undercurrent of humor in his voice. Before she could respond, he took her hand and placed it between his legs. Jeanne's belly spasmed at the feel of his hard-on throbbing against her palm, even while her mind refused to wrap itself around this man's arousal. She yanked back her hand, almost as though burned.

"How—"

"I can get it up for women," Rob said quietly. "It's happened. Granted, not often, but it has. Especially with you." He rolled over on his back, staring at the ceiling. "I never did anything about it, though. I was so afraid of fucking up our friendship because I can't commit to you. I'm attracted to men, J.B. But—there's been a long-time attraction to you, too."

Jeanne swallowed, taking in the incredible admission. Then she closed her eyes, trying to ignore the sudden and eager trembling of her body.

Every woman's wet dream...

"J.B., as you pointed out before, there isn't anything complicated about this." Gary's voice was calm and quiet. "It's just a question of whether you want this."

Jeanne opened her eyes and studied her husband. His face was serious, his eyes gentle and loving as they studied her. She licked her lips and studied Rob, who was lying on the bed, studying her with the same gentleness, the same love.

"Honestly?" she whispered.

"Honestly," Gary said.

Jeanne took a deep breath. "I love you both. I want you both."

There it was, buried under layers and years of denial and avoidance. She'd been brought up to believe that marriage was strictly monogamous. Now she was opening herself to the idea of two men making love to her. Even through the heat, the arousal, and the potential, the whole thing felt right. It would be a perfect fit for the three of them.

"I figured as much," Gary said. "And we're both here."

She stared at her husband, and he nodded.

"What now?" she asked, barely able to speak.

"You might want to kiss him," Gary suggested, a smile tugging his lips.

Swallowing, Jeanne turned to the other man. Her breath caught at the love in his eyes. Restraint gone, she moved into his arms and felt him trembling against her, felt Gary's tacit approval of her actions.

"God, I'm so hungry for you," Rob whispered into her hair, and her breath caught at his words.

"Taste her," Gary suggested softly from behind them. "Lick between her legs. There isn't anything better than the taste of a woman when she's aroused and creaming for you. How about it, Jeanne? Are you ready to let another man taste between your legs? Because the thought of you being eaten by someone else is getting me harder."

The thought was getting her wetter, too. The heat of both men on her body, combined with their varying scents made her a slave to her desire, and she was unable to speak because of the sensations whirling through her body.

"I've never gone down on a woman before," Rob said, a little hesitantly.

"I can help you through that," Gary said, in a soft, matter-of-fact tone. "When you do this, make sure you lick, rather than suck."

"I'm here," Jeanne managed to interject. She pushed away from Rob, rolled over on her back and looked up at Gary. "I can tell him what I like. You don't have to talk around me."

Gary let out a soft laugh. "You're not doing a whole lot of talking right now, lover. It's okay, though. You just lie there and enjoy it, okay? Slowly and gently is the way to go with her, Rob. And it also helps if she's undressed."

Gary reached under her nightgown and in a single movement, slid it over her head and threw it off the bed. Lying behind her, Gary held her hands together above her head and fondled her breasts, tugging on the turgid peaks. Rob leaned over and took a nipple in his mouth, caressing it with his tongue, sucking at it. Pulses of heat rammed through her body at both men's actions and Jeanne cried out, arching her back.

"Caress her with your lips," she heard Gary suggesting. "Move down her body while you do it. She loves that."

A dim part of Jeanne was grateful for Gary's tutelage. Desire swamped her like a wave, robbing her of the power of speech. Rob did as her husband directed, moving his lips and tongue slowly between her breasts and down over her belly and mons, nibbling, licking, caressing her flesh on the way. Jeanne jerked against Gary's restraining hands on her wrists as Rob's wet caresses fired her nerve endings. As Rob placed himself between her legs, Jeanne arched involuntarily at the feel of his hot breath on her soaking nether regions.

"Gary…" she called out. "Oh, my Jesus. Gary…"

"It's okay, babe." His voice was husky with his own need, his own arousal. "I'm here for you. Let him explore. Let him taste. God, you look beautiful right now…"

Jeanne gasped as she felt Rob's tongue touch her crease, almost tentatively, then slowly lick up and down it. Then the man became bolder, moving deeper between her swollen nether lips to taste. As she cried out from the intensity of the physical sensations, she felt Gary tremble beside her.

"French her, Rob," he urged hoarsely. "French kiss down there. As if you were kissing her mouth."

Without hesitation Rob dropped slow, open-mouthed kisses on her slit, his tongue dipping in to touch her engorged clitoris, caressing it slowly, lingeringly, then pulling back before moving in to tantalize her again. Jeanne arched her back, thrusting her lips toward the man who was giving her such intense pleasure while taking in Gary's hot eyes looming above her.

"So damn sexy," her husband whispered.

Gary's mouth claimed hers, his lips moving slowly, erotically on hers, almost in counterpoint with Rob's movements, almost mirroring each other. As Rob continued tonguing her nether regions, Gary slipped his own tongue in her mouth, keeping his eyes open as they searched hers, hot with need, with desire.

Rob opened her with his thumbs, sliding his tongue deeper into her slick core. Jeanne screamed into Gary's mouth, the heat of passion submerging her in a fiery ecstasy.

Gary broke the kiss, breathing harshly. "Keep doing it," he told Rob, his voice hoarse. "Oh, my God. Keep going."

Jeanne was barely aware of the words, panting with a need for fulfillment, out of control, writhing in desperate ecstasy. As Rob's tongue moved faster on her, then slid deeply inside her, Gary kissed her again, savagely, devouring her, releasing her wrists in a frenzy of his own passion. Jeanne clutched his shoulders, desperately needing an anchor, feeling almost out of control on this wildly sensual ride.

"Gary…I can't hold out much longer…" Her breath was coming in gasps as she broke the kiss.

"Let it go, baby. Let him take you there. And let me watch…"

Almost as though her husband's permission to come had unlocked something in her, Jeanne allowed her climax to roll over her, to swamp her in its incredible molten heat, drowning her in an almost unspeakable lust and desire. She couldn't stop screaming, and as she came again, she clung to Gary, who whispered encouragement at her cries. Rob continued his intense pleasuring of her, continuing to lash her clit and the sensitive area around it with his tongue and lips, driving her to new heights.

When she was screamed raw and gasping for air, Gary let out his own breath. "Let her go," he told Rob. "She's had enough."

Rob stopped his ministrations, a little reluctantly Jeanne thought. But she didn't care. She was wrung out, trembling from the intense orgasm and its aftermath. Rob moved up and stared down at her face. He was flushed, aroused, his eyes glittering with a deep and untamed passion.

"You're delicious," he said. Before she could react, he kissed her with a hard sensuality, and the taste of her juices on his lips made her groan. She pushed him away reluctantly, knowing what she wanted.

"Kiss him, Gary," she demanded harshly. "On the lips. Taste me."

Looking at her in surprise, Gary dropped a tentative kiss on Rob's lips. Jeanne caught her breath at the surprising heat caroming through her at their contact.

"No. Like you mean it." Her voice had gone from harsh to husky. Gary didn't hesitate, but lay his lips on Rob's, who responded with a hot passion. Jeanne saw Gary's tongue snaked out to trace Rob's lips, and she knew he tasted her cream on the other man. The thought caused her belly to cramp in a spasm of lust.

As the two men continued kissing, Gary's hand crept down to the other man's crotch. Rob leaned into the caress, thrusting his hips toward Gary, who palmed the bulge behind his jeans and caressed it, almost roughly.

Jeanne was becoming aroused at Gary's fondling, and her hand stole between her legs. She wanted to drive herself to a climax while watching her husband pleasure another man. But Gary broke the kiss, saw what she was doing, and shook his head.

"Not this time," he told her. "This time we all participate. There's a lot to be said for voyeurism, but not right now."

"Get undressed, then. Both of you." She barely recognized the tense, raw tone of her voice. Nor did she recognize the incredible hunger that had her in its control.

Without a word, they climbed from the bed, quickly removed their clothes, then stood before her, almost offering themselves to her. Jeanne lounged on the bed and studied them both. Two incredibly handsome men. Gary shorter, muscle-bound, with little hair crossing his chest. Rob taller, more slender but still well-built, a light mat of dark hair dusting his chest. Though different physically, both cocks stood at attention, Gary's large erection straining from a nest of blond, frizzy curls, while Rob's penis, smaller, but thicker, extended from dark, almost smooth hair. Her belly spasmed at the sight of these two perfect men, and her body craved both of them.

"I want you both in me," she said. "At the same time."

Rob frowned. "Can she take it in the rear?"

Gary nodded. "We've done it. Lube's in the upper left hand drawer."

Rob cocked an eye at her and grinned. "Seems like you've been keeping some details of your sex life from me, J.B."

"I'll try not to do that in the future," she said, sweetly. "You can hear all of the gory details of what my husband does to me in bed after this. Now, give me the K-Y."

Rob rolled his eyes, but handed her the tube. "You're so demanding, sweetheart."

"Just wait. It gets worse," Gary said, with a smile. "What Jeanne says, goes, at least in bed."

Ignoring their teasing, Jeanne put the gel on her hands, and, moving to her husband, began to massage his penis and balls in a way she knew he liked. She took her time with it, moving her palms slowly over his hardened shaft, the combination of his pre-cum and the K-Y making the flesh of his cock slick. Though her attention was focused on Gary, Jeanne burned in Rob's gaze, feeling his hunger, his arousal, as he watched the deeply intimate caresses.

"Jeanne. No more," Gary whispered. "Not unless you want this to be over with before it begins."

"Then watch me do Rob," she said softly.

"Yes, okay."

Jeanne turned to the other man, who eagerly looked at her.

"Is there anything special you want me to do?" she asked him and he shook his head.

"What you just did to Gary—I liked that."

Eager to explore this new, hard flesh, Jeanne took her time, putting more gel on her hands, and slowly moving them around his erection and balls. He trembled under her hands. Glancing up, Jeanne saw his eyes closed, his lower lip caught between his teeth as she continued her fondling.

Handling both men so intimately, touching their hardness, steel-covered-softness, excited her and she felt her nipples pucker in response, and heat pool between her legs.

"Jeanne," Rob said faintly. "If you keep doing that, I'm going to explode."

Gary lay down on his back and beckoned for her. "Let's put the poor man out of his misery," he said, his eyes twinkling with amusement and desire.

"That's you all over, isn't it, Gary?" Jeanne said, with a grin. "Always considering the other guy's point of view."

"Shut up and ride me, J.B. Rob's not the only one who's ready to explode."

Still smiling, Jeanne aligned herself on her husband, impaling herself slowly on his rigid flesh, biting her lip at the throbbing desire threatening to overwhelm her. "Lean over. As far as you can," Gary said, his voice strained and she did, catching her breath at the exquisite sensations of his cock pressing against her swollen walls. She sensed Rob behind her, ready for her, felt the heat of his penis, covered with the smooth lubricant she'd applied. Closing her eyes, Jeanne felt Gary jerk inside her, as the tip of Rob's penis touched her rectum lightly, almost like a caress.

"Please, Rob," she whispered. "Please don't make me wait...do me now..."

Without a word, Rob entered her, going slowly, ensuring she was ready to accept him. Jeanne forced herself to relax, panting instinctively as she felt his hardness move deeper inside her narrow channel. Then he was in all the way and Jeanne gasped. She felt Gary jerk inside her again and she bit her lip, sensation running riot through her body at the hot, hard flesh invading her, rousing her, making her speechless with an incredible, wanton lust.

Rob began sliding in and out of her, and Gary followed the other man's lead, thrusting deeply, sliding out, then entering again. Jeanne moved in harmony with both men, a willing and eager receptacle for their joint arousal.

"Jeanne," Rob whispered in her ear. "Oh, my God...you feel so tight...so good."

She shuddered in excitement at the awe in his voice, and at the sight of Gary beneath her, insane desire glazing his light gray eyes. Jeanne willingly fell into the incredible sensations swimming through her body as both men made love to her, warm, pulsing cocks invading her, teasing her, melting her into a throbbing mass of desire. She dimly heard the moans of the men as they continued their wildly sensual assault of her nether regions, and the sound notched up her feelings of ecstasy.

Then heat engulfed her in a white-hot climax, and Jeanne cried out as her orgasm claimed her, holding her body captive in wave after wave of unimagined pleasure.

As she came down, shuddering from the sexual high, she felt Gary's seed move through her. A moment later, Rob climaxed and she shuddered again, feeling his hot release move deeply into her.

Groaning, Jeanne collapsed on her husband, felt Rob soften and slip from her. As she rolled off Gary, Jeanne heard water running in the bathroom, and surmised that Rob was cleaning himself off. She looked at her husband. His eyes were closed and his face was flushed as his breathing slowed. Then she felt the bed dip slightly as Rob lay down on it and pulled her against him, his front against her back, spoon fashion. Gary opened his eyes, smiled, moved closer, and put his arms around them both. Jeanne closed her eyes, savoring the closeness between the three of them. If anyone had told her this morning that she'd be okay with this whole scenario, she would have thought their minds were in the gutter. Deep, deep in the gutter. But aside from the incredible pleasure she was experiencing, the whole scenario felt right. She felt complete with these two men in her bed, and was stunned at the thought. She lay between Gary and Rob, content. After awhile, she felt Rob growing hard against her and her body felt the sudden and insatiable need to feel him inside her, driving into her deeply, wrenching a climax out of her.

She turned in his arms, regarding his green eyes. "I want you to fuck me again," she told him deliberately. "In the cunt, this time."

Her husband let out a chuckle. "Rob was right about your impatience, love. Let's draw this out a little. I think it's time for a sensual massage. Roll over, face down."

"Now who's demanding?" Jeanne said, but complied. A moment later, she felt soft silk caress her forehead and eyes as Gary settled the blindfold comfortably.

"Too tight?" he wanted to know.

"It's fine." Jeanne's voice trembled. He'd blindfolded her a couple of times before, and the loss of sight boosted the other senses.

She heard the bedside table drawer open and shut. "Put this on your hands and start massaging her feet," Gary said. "Slowly. I'll do her back. Just follow my lead."

A moment later, the scent of vanilla oil assaulted Jeanne's senses and she drew in a breath. She jumped a moment later as Gary's hands touched the flesh of her back, then began a circular, sensual motion, his hands sliding up and down her skin, drawing goose bumps.

"Go on," Gary spoke gently. "Do her feet. She likes it."

Jeanne felt her right foot picked up, then bit her lip as oiled hands stroked up and down the sole, lingering on the toes. He rubbed her big toe, fondling it until Jeanne was squirming, feeling the heat drive into her lower belly.

"How does it feel?" Rob asked her. "Is it too hard?"

I only wish it was, Jeanne wanted to say, but she shook her head.

"It's perfect," she said, her voice unsteady.

"You have beautiful feet," he said. His lips danced across her arch and his tongue sneaked out to taste the flesh.

"I never knew you liked feet." She squirmed as he chuckled against her sensitive flesh.

"I don't get into men's feet much," he confided. "Especially big, ugly men's feet. Like Gary's here. I swear to God, I never thought hockey players had such ugly feet."

"Off my case," Gary growled, but Jeanne heard the smile in his voice. Her husband moved his hands to the middle of her back, continuing to caress her. At the same time, Rob picked up her other foot and caressed it, giving it the same, careful titillating attention as the other. Jeanne felt her arousal continue to ebb and flow as both men touched her slowly and with evident enjoyment.

"Move up her legs," Gary told Rob quietly. "J.B., spread them for us. I love seeing you swollen and creaming for this."

Jeanne swallowed and spread her legs, shivering as the cool air of the bedroom caressed her slick folds. As Rob moved up her legs, his fingers playing a steamy dance on her flesh, Gary's hands moved downward, stroking her lower back, then cupping her rear end, pressing in on the cheeks, as the almost unbearably erotic massage continued.

Then four hands were between her legs, stroking the sensitive flesh, tantalizing her by moving close to her nether regions, but not touching them. Surrounded by darkness, at the mercy of the maddening caresses that taunted even as they roused, Jeanne writhed on the quilt, wanting those fingers to touch her heated core.

"Higher," she pleaded, and she heard Gary chuckle.

"I told you she was impatient," he said to Rob.

"She's beautiful down there," the other man murmured. "Can I touch?"

"She'd probably like nothing better."

Before Jeanne could remind Gary that she was perfectly capable of speech, she felt well-lubed fingers slip between her swollen folds and into her slick pussy, touching her hardened clit, robbing her of speech. Other fingers moved along the crack of her ass, then in and out of her anal hole, causing her to cry out in longing, in need. The fondling continued, slick fingers moving in and out, caressing, teasing, bringing Jeanne to the edge, then down before she could climax. Swimming in the blindfold's darkness, Jeanne was victim to the sweet assault, desperately wanting to climax. But the hands weren't allowing her a much needed release, building her craving for more as they continued their intimate invasion, building her lust.

"Draw it out, Rob," Gary's husky tone raised goose bumps along her flesh. "Make her wait for it. Make her want it. Jesus God, she's hot for it."

"Of course," the other man murmured. "God, she's wet."

"Good sign," Gary responded. "I want her dripping wet before we do anything about it."

"Please," Jeanne couldn't stop herself from begging. Her entire body was on fire, shaking hard, her cunt throbbing with an arousal and hunger that was almost painful.

"No," Gary said, excitement darkening his tone. "You're not ready yet. Nowhere near ready."

One finger, then two slid deeply into her, moving steadily toward her G-spot. Jeanne buckled and cried out at the incredible sensations, a slave to their play, to the movement inside her. She felt a tongue at her crack, slowly licking, imposing more wanton torture on her. Whose hands were in her, whose lips seducing her she didn't know any more, nor did she care. The only thing she cared about was slaking her body's extraordinary hunger.

"Oh, God." She heard herself shrieking. "Please. I can't take this anymore..."

"Rise up on your knees." Was that Rob's voice, thick with desire? Through the sensual haze enveloping her, she couldn't tell, but she obeyed, legs trembling, ass up in the air, eagerly awaiting the assault. Jeanne cried out again as a hardened spear, velvet-covered steel, invaded her, driving deeply into her slickness, coming out, then slamming into her again and again.

"Suck me off." Another voice, hoarse with urgency at her front, and another shaft guided into her open and willing mouth. She took it eagerly, not certain whose it was, not caring. She sucked hard, hearing a moan, then contracted her pussy. She felt a thrust in response, and she moaned around the cock in her mouth, moving her lips and tongue eagerly over the hardened flesh..

As before, Jeanne felt herself moving in harmony between the two men, tasting one, being fucked by the other, penises invading both ends of her body, driving her to incredible, exquisite heights.

She sucked hard on the offering in her mouth, heard a masculine cry, tasted the warm cum on her lips and tongue. She came then, screaming, her body milking the cock buried deeply inside her, feeling it spasm as heat moved deeply into her womb.

Half sobbing from reaction, Jeanne collapsed, her body shaking violently from the release. The arousal had been unbelievable, her climax earth-shattering.

Gentle hands removed her blindfold. A moment later, she felt arms holding her tenderly, soothingly as both men embraced her. Gradually, her shuddering subsided, replaced by a comforting exhaustion. Almost gratefully, Jeanne let the soothing darkness take her into a gentle oblivion.

CHAPTER 4

A slight movement brought Jeanne out of her light doze. Daylight spilled into the room, outlining Rob as he pulled on pants and shirt, then left. Jeanne turned over and saw that Gary was still asleep. She studied his relaxed face for a moment, her feelings a mix of tenderness and incredulity. Tenderness, that he'd allowed her and Rob to explore their physical feelings for one another, and had joined in.

And incredulity that it had all happened.

If she hadn't known any better, she would have thought the whole thing had been a wild, erotic dream. But the soreness between her legs told her otherwise.

Sliding from the bed so as not to disturb Gary, Jeanne slid on her robe and moved into the living room. Rob stood there, his leather jacket on, examining his keys.

"Going somewhere?" she asked softly. He glanced up at her and grinned. His look was intimate, and Jeanne felt herself blush, remembering what had gone on with the three of them just hours before.

"Yeah," he said. "Places to go, people to see."

"That's you, all right. Always in demand."

"Just call me Mr. Popularity."

Jeanne swallowed and dropped the forced banter, suddenly uncertain as to how she should treat Rob. He shook his head.

"Don't. It happened, sweetheart," he whispered. "And it's okay. More than okay." He came to her, ran a finger around her neck and smiled. "You might want to think about wearing a turtleneck for the next few days, though."

Jeanne felt herself flush as she remembered the origins of the hickies now decorating her throat. In their final throes of lovemaking, as dawn pushed through the windows, Gary tied her hands above her head. Then each man took his place between her legs, gently licking and nibbling her swollen folds, drawing out pleasure until she thought she'd go out of her mind. At the end of it all, as Jeanne lay totally spent, Rob put his mark of love, of possession on her neck, and Gary followed. Even after the marks faded, Jeanne knew she'd remember the heat of their lips on her skin; the slight pain-pleasure that occurred as they raised the welts on her sensitive flesh.

"Maybe I should just wear what I always wear and tell the truth if people ask me where I got these hickies from," she said, with a smile. "But as I think about it, no one would have the bad taste to ask me about it."

Rob laughed a little. "No one would believe the truth, either, if you did tell. I'm not sure I do."

"Rob, are we okay?" Jeanne spoke, suddenly anxious. "I don't want this screwing us up as friends. I don't want things to be…awkward between us."

"Like they haven't been since Ozona's?" he asked. "With both of us in denial about what it might be like with each other? Maybe if we'd acted on that kiss, things might have been different."

"Yeah," she said wryly. "I could have been the one to change you. That'd have increased my standing among the female community."

"You wouldn't have changed me. I'm still gay. I'll always prefer men, Jeanne."

"But you've been able to get it up for a woman," she pointed out.

"Once." Rob fiddled with the zipper on his jacket. "The only other woman I slept with looked like you. It wasn't nearly as enjoyable as what we just did and I had to get good and drunk to go through with it. But she wasn't you. She didn't have your personality. Your essence. She was just a substitute." He took a deep breath and managed a laugh. "I'm sounding like some dumb Hallmark Card. I need to go."

He leaned over and hugged her. Jeanne held him, taking in his scent; the mingled remnants of cologne, sex and leather.

"Next time we do this," she said, her voice muffled in his shoulder. "Wear this jacket to bed."

He burst out laughing, then held her out at arm's length, grinning broadly. "I never knew you had such a voracious sexual appetite, Jeanne. I'll have to keep that in mind." He leaned forward and kissed her on the forehead, becoming serious. "Go talk to your husband. Gary's a hell of a guy, and you need to work things out with him. Then we can decide if another time is in the cards or not."

Rob dropped his arms from her shoulders and, taking her hand, walked her to the door. Jeanne opened it and unlatched the screen to let him out. "Call me when you get home," she told him. "I'll worry otherwise."

"Yes, Mother," he said wryly. He walked to the cycle, zipped his jacket, put on his helmet and revved the motor. Before Jeanne could wonder what the neighbors might think about all this noise at such a ridiculous hour on a Sunday morning, Rob waved, steered the cycle down the driveway, and was gone.

As Jeanne heard the roar of the bike fade away, she stared out at the sunlit-drenched lawn. It would be a lovely day and thank goodness, a Sunday. No practice today and she wouldn't have to go into work, so she and Gary could rest. Despite herself, Jeanne shivered a little and drew her robe closed, remembering the night before, all the passion.

Gary had been right about one thing. What had just happened *was* every woman's wet dream, being fucked by two men. But this had been more than simply coupling. She'd bonded with both men in a way she'd never thought possible. Beneath the heat had been a sense of completeness, of rightness.

Jeanne closed the front door and moved through the living room back into the bedroom. Gary was awake and sitting up, a sheet covering him. Jeanne sat on the side of the bed and stared at her hands. She wasn't sure what the proper behavior was toward one's husband following a threesome that he'd initiated.

"Rob gone?" Gary wanted to know.

"Yeah. He just took off."

They were silent for a moment, then Jeanne let out a sigh and looked at him. He looked tired, but at peace.

"What just happened here?" she said.

"If I have to explain it to you, I might get horny again."

"I'm serious, Gary."

He blew out a breath, tucked his hands behind his head and stared at the ceiling.

"I'm not sure," he finally said. "It was more than three people getting their rocks off, wasn't it?"

Jeanne closed her eyes, feeling a profound weight lift from her shoulders.

"And here I thought that was my imagination," she said. "It felt right to me, Gary. Kind of like three puzzle pieces, coming together and fitting together just right." She laughed a little. "Now I'm sounding like a Hallmark card." She shook her head at Gary's questioning look. "Never mind."

They were silent for a moment. "Why didn't you come to me about Marty?" Jeanne finally asked.

Gary made a face. "Sure. Just the thing you want to break to your wife. 'Hey, babe. You know the skank that seduced half the Panthers' squad and caused a huge scandal to come down on his wife and his team? Well, guess what? I was one of them and I actually liked it.'" He dropped the sarcastic attitude and looked at her, troubled. "The thing is, I'm probably not the only one who did. Like it, I mean. Not that any of us who went through it compared notes or anything. You can't do that on a hockey team."

Jeanne nodded in understanding. No way could Gary have asked his teammates about Marty Pellin; he would have been stigmatized for the rest of his career.

And in all honesty, how would *she* have reacted if he'd come to her with the idea he might be bisexual? That he actually might like doing it with men and women?

Before last night? Before last night I would have chucked him out of the house.

The more she thought about it, the more it made a kind of warped sense that he would turn to Rob, the only openly homosexual male he knew, for some kind of advice with his dilemma.

"I felt I could trust Rob with this," Gary was saying, as though reading her mind. "He said it doesn't just hit you like that. That there are other signs pointing to homosexuality or bisexuality and you really couldn't tell on the basis of one encounter."

Gary paused for a moment, then moved ahead, almost reluctantly. "He was honest, and used himself as an example. His feelings for you. That he was gay, but his love for you was a lot deeper than he'd let on. Then our talk got pretty intimate and—and we acted on it. I won't lie. I enjoyed being with him like that. Physically it was okay. But—but it was nothing compared to what I feel when I'm with you. Last night I enjoyed seeing your pleasure more than I liked sleeping with him." Gary held out his hands, his face helpless. "I know what this must sound like, but it's true. I love you. You're my life. But if you feel you need to leave me because of this, I'll understand."

Jeanne felt tears sting her eyes at his admission. She supposed, on the surface, he sounded like a cheating husband who'd been caught red-handed, so to speak, and who was trying to cover his tracks by professing his undying love for her. And, taking it one step further, he supposed that by initiating the threesome, he could take some of the guilt off his own shoulders by offering her the man he'd slept with.

But after what the three of them had gone through the night before, she wasn't in any position to point fingers. Nor did she want to. Not anymore.

"I'm not going to leave you." She took his hand, and stroked his hair from his forehead. "I love you, Gary. Very much. But I was never honest with you about Rob because deep down, I loved him, and wanted him. But because he was gay—"

"You didn't dare try to do anything about it," Gary finished for her.

"Until last night. When you forced me into his arms."

Gary laughed. "I don't think it took a whole lot of coercion, sweetheart." He reached out and pulled her on top of him, so he was staring into her face. "Is it something you're going to want to try again with him? Be honest with me."

Jeanne thought about it, savoring the memory of the heat, the closeness between the three of them.

"Maybe," she said, reluctantly. "Rob hinted he'd be interested. I don't know, though. It might not be fair to him. If he finds someone, no way would I want to turn this into a foursome."

"Thank goodness," Gary spoke wryly. "I'm not in the mood to entertain a whole parade of men in my bed. I love you. I'd do anything to make you happy. But I have my limits."

Jeanne laughed and buried her face in her husband's chest, reflecting on how dearly she appreciated his warmth, his sensitivity, his strength.

"My biggest fear is that last night might screw us up," she murmured against his skin. "Might have screwed us all up."

Gary's arms tightened around her. "If anything, I think it broke down some walls. Whether or not we end up together like that again, it did break down some walls."

Jeanne said nothing, but nodded and lay quietly in his arms, content beyond all belief, watching the sun paint its gold light on the walls.

HUNKS OF HOCKEY

PENALTY KILL

HUNKS OF HOCKEY

CHAPTER 1

"Adriaannnn!!!!"

Even before he glanced up, he knew who was calling his name. Or rather whos. There were two of them. Twins, actually. Tia and Mia. Marla or Carla. Something like that. Names hadn't mattered that night he'd spent with them. All that had matter was what they'd done for him. And to him.

But Adrian Donelson just wasn't in the mood tonight, despite the beckoning four bouncing boobs and erect nipples encased in clinging spring wool. Every part of his body ached and his joints were determined to have a nice, long conversation with him, despite the trainer's best efforts and a whirlpool following this bitch of a game. The left eye where Calder decked him hurt like hell. So did the right cheek where trainer Steve Larson had sunk a couple of stitches after the bench-clearing brawl against the Eugene, Oregon Greyhounds. God, playoff hockey sucked sometimes.

But fans were fans. Adrian pasted the obligatory brilliant smile on his face and looked at the two women. Blondes, both of them. Trying to take after Marilyn Monroe or something like that.

"Adriannn," one of them cooed. Mia? Tia? "We saw that little scuffle on the ice. You poor, poor baby. We're here to help, lover."

Little scuffle? She had to be kidding. The Blaze would be working off penalties from that one well into the next season.

"We can think of some healing to help you out," the other one purred, coming to his side.

Some other night, any other night, he'd be as hard as the ice surface at Carlyle Arena at the thought of getting it on with these two. They were both very inventive.

Maybe...

He checked with his groin. Nope. Not a quiver.

He sighed. The best place for him was a bathtub, nursing a glass of bourbon. Then straight to bed. Alone.

"Hey, ladies. I gotta road call tomorrow. Up at 4 A.M." It was a lie, but no reason why they had to know it.

"Mmmm." The first blonde sashayed to his side and ran her hand across his broad chest, licking her cherry-red lips with almost obscene anticipation. "We can get you up and *keep* you up until 4 A.M. And beyond, if you want."

"Thanks for the offer, but not tonight, ladies. Maybe next home game," he said, allowing true regret to color his voice.

The second one—Mia, he now remembered. Mia liked to use her mouth, whereas her sister was definitely a hand girl. Anyway, Mia was ready to protest. But he was saved by the arrival of another of his teammates, Gary Jacobsen. They immediately turned their attention to the light-hair, light-eyed forward, and Adrian made his escape quietly, snorting to himself.

Good luck with that one, ladies. He's very married. And very devoted to his wife.

Who knew, though? Maybe those two got off on trying. Maybe it was the chase that turned them on. Used to be the case for him. But after enough nights with the Tias and Mias of the world, he was ready to bow out of that scene, thank you very much.

Breathing a silent sigh of relief, Adrian entered the Dallas Blaze's private parking garage. Privacy. At last. He needed it tonight, after that fiasco on the ice masquerading as a game. The Blaze had their asses handed to them on a platter by their arch rivals. This deep into the playoffs, a 7-3 loss just wasn't funny. Especially when that loss put them in the hole two-and-oh, and at home. If they didn't get some magic going in Oregon the day after tomorrow, they may as well kiss any hopes of the Tannen Trophy good-bye and get the golf clubs shined up.

But the loss, as galling as it was, didn't piss him off. The fact he'd been penalized for something he hadn't even done was making Adrian see red. It had been the other player, Greg Calder, who had instigated the slash, but Adrian had drawn the penalty. When he'd protested angrily to the ref, he was kicked off for a game misconduct. It hadn't helped when Calder had taunted the other Blaze players as he skated by them. On his way to his own bench. Suddenly, half the team was on the ice, pummeling one another in a kind of ecstatic anger. It had taken close to fifteen minutes to sort out the penalties. Meanwhile Adrian was in the locker room, receiving a tongue lashing from the trainer as the guy sunk stitches into him.

"Mr. Corrigan will not like this," the man had said.

No, Adrian had no doubt that Blaze owner Brian Corrigan wouldn't like it. Not that Corrigan would mind the fighting; an ex-hockey man himself, he had quite a reputation as a forward before a career-ending injury drove him to the owner and management side. But the spectacular loss would not sit well with a man who lived and breathed hockey like Corrigan did.

Adrian wasn't looking forward to an interview with Corrigan on this one. While he had respect for the owner, he had no desire to cross him. Corrigan was one man who literally gave Adrian the creeps.

Nor would the team coach be much better. No doubt Dirk "The Dick" Reneau would be lambasting the team at the press conference, and his disparaging remarks would be plastered all over tomorrow's newspaper and TV news editions. Why in hell's name coaches always thought it was a great idea to put down players in front of their fans escaped him. Supposedly it spurred motivation. But Adrian hated it.

Willfully shaking his head free from his concerns, Adrian climbed into his Plymouth Solaris. He grinned as the powerful engine came to life and he drove out of the garage. A local dealership had gifted the car to him, and he had no regrets. At first the thought of a Plymouth had made his mouth curl. If he was going to have a gift car, he'd have preferred one with some muscle. But the Solaris's smooth ride and controlled power was like love at first sight.

Traffic was light, thankfully, with all the hockey fans gone home or to bars in the West End or Uptown to drown their sorrows. Adrian himself lived farther east, in Rockwall. Though it was a longish drive from Carlyle Arena, he liked the quiet town, as well as its proximity to Lake Ray Hubbard.

Thirty minutes later, he arrived at his apartment building and shut down his car. It was quiet at this time of night, the air warm and muggy. Not too bad for May, but soon summer and humidity would have its grip on the Metroplex. Adrian sighed. Hello, high electrical bills.

He took the steps to his apartment two at a time and let himself into the apartment. Throwing his keys on the table in the hallway, Adrian loosened the green tie around his neck and dropped his hockey bag, too exhausted to think of much more, God, he hated dressing up in a sports jacket and tie, but it was one of the mandates from management. When appearing in public, dress like a gentleman.

Yeah, right. Some gentleman he'd been tonight. Sighing, he decided to order some delivery type of food, take a long, hot bath and wash the stink of loser from his body. Maybe things would be better in Eugene. He laughed a little at his optimism. No way would things be better in Oregon. Those guys were killers on their own ice.

Adrian picked up his phone and was ready to dial when he heard a soft knock at the door. For a moment, he was tempted not to answer. Lay low until whoever it was went away. But a voice on the other side of the door made him change his mind.

"It's me, Donelson. And I know you're in there, so open up before I start yelling holy hell and the neighbors start complaining."

An unwilling smile stretched Adrian's lips. If he had to have company tonight—and it looked like company was in the cards for him—he was glad it was his upstairs neighbor, Daria DeCarlo. Daria he could tolerate. Well, more than tolerate. His heart lifted at the sound of his best friend's voice.

He went to the door and opened it. She stood there, topping out maybe at five feet or so, and looked up at him. Dimples flashed briefly in her cheeks as she held out a pizza and six-pack of beer almost like a sacred offering.

"That better not have any of those pukey anchovies on it," he told her.

"Nah, not tonight. You've had a hard enough time. Tempting as it is, I don't want to compound your suffering."

He raised an eyebrow at her. "You don't like hockey. You don't watch it, munchkin. How the hell did you know what kind of night I had?"

Daria brushed by him, heading toward his tiny kitchen. "God, don't you ever turn any lights on in this place, Black Irish? All this darkness gives me the creeps. Anyway, you made the highlight reel on the ten o'clock news. All of Dallas knows of the exploits of the gallant Adrian Donelson, supreme enforcer with the Dallas Blaze. Here, take a piece of this before it gets cold."

Adrian groaned inwardly as he trailed after her, hearing her bang around in the kitchen. It figured they'd replay that damned fight again and again. He had no doubt it would make the front page of the sports section in the morning, too. Score one for the media.

He entered the kitchen, feeling a scowl scrunch his face. Daria pulled a beer off the plastic ring and held it to him silently. He took it, opened it. She opened her own, held it up, and they clinked cans. Adrian took three long chugs, the beer hitting the back of his throat like a cool, wet blessing. Putting the can on the counter, he grabbed a piece of pizza and wolfed it down before snagging another and making short work of that. He hadn't realized he was so hungry. He supposed playoff games complete with bench-clearing brawls would do that to a person.

Adrian turned his attention to the beer again, finished it in three long swallows, and let out a resounding belch. He could do stuff like that in front of Daria. She'd been his best friend—his best *platonic* friend—since college. Besides, she'd grown up with three older brothers who hadn't bothered to practice manners in front of her. Things like belching and chugging beer didn't faze her. Sometimes she even joined in. Daria could belch with the best of them.

Her one-of-the-guys attitude had impressed him when they'd first met in an economics class at Boston University. Adrian was at BU on a hockey scholarship, coming from the moderately well-off Braintree. Daria hailed from the poor side of Roxbury and was at college with help from scholarships and loans. Their personalities were as different as their upbringings. Adrian, the son of a Boston Irish family, was loud, boisterous, always looking for a party and a good time. Daria, who was second-generation Italian, was the shy, studious type, determined to be the first woman in her family to finish college and get a good job.

Despite their differences, they liked each other and began hanging out together, sharing class notes, pizza and beers. They shared each other's shoulders with opposite sex problems. And they were regular escorts for one another in lieu of a date.

The rest of the BU student body, recognizing the nature of their relationship, dubbed them with the unoriginal label of "Brains 'n Brawn," though Adrian was no slouch in the learning department. And Daria, for her height, slenderness and almost delicate features, wasn't a wimp when it came to physical toughness. She had a black belt in karate. Plus her older brothers had taught her how to defend herself from the wolves, which is what she'd called the boys in her childhood neighborhood.

After graduation, Adrian had been drafted by the Blaze's farm team, and lost touch with her. They found one another again in Big D, several years later. She'd snagged a job as an economic analyst with the Dallas Federal Reserve and was living with a guy who was more swagger than substance, in Adrian's opinion. But Daria had turned Adrian on to Rockwall as a great place to live, and he ended up leasing the apartment below hers. When she'd kicked her idiot boyfriend out of her bed and life, Adrian was there to help Daria pick up the pieces. Not that there had been many pieces to collect.

"It makes the decision kind of easy to end a relationship when your boyfriend is screwing another woman in your bed," she'd told him with a resigned smile.

As Adrian pulled his second beer off the plastic ring, popped it open and drank, he reflected how lucky he was to have Daria in his life. She was one of the few people he could trust. Around Daria, he could be Adrian Donelson, human being, rather than A.D., thug defenseman for the Blaze and sometimes an off-ice terror to his teammates.

Appetite tamed, Adrian drank some of his beer, and looked at Daria with true gratitude. "Thanks for the food 'n brew, munchkin. You're a hell of a sight for sore eyes."

She looked at him, concern etching her delicate face, which was framed with long, straight black hair. Then she leaned over and traced his black eye with a gentle finger before shaking her head reprovingly.

"You weren't kidding. Your eye looks sore. That needs ice."

He shook his head, irritated at her fussing. "I'll be fine."

She ignored him—nothing new there—and went to the freezer for an ice pack. She wrapped it in a towel and handed it to him, a sweet smile on her face. He took it from her, grumbling, and held it to his eye. Arguing with her never got him anywhere.

"How'd the other guy come out of it?" Daria asked.

"I thought you saw the highlights."

"I didn't see the score."

Adrian grinned. "I got kicked off the ice, and that set off the whole team. Bench-clearing brawl."

"Who won the game?"

"They did."

Daria shook her head sympathetically. "Tough luck."

"Yup." But he was feeling marginally better, thanks to Daria's presence and the pizza. The beer was doing its job, too, and he welcomed the slight buzz. Adrian put the ice pack on the counter. Ignoring Daria's frown, he stood and, picking up his beer, moved into the living room.

He grimaced as he eased his body onto the sofa, reached for the remote, and turned on the TV, keeping the volume down. God, he was hurting tonight. And, oh joy, he got to do it again in a couple of nights.

"So what do you think?" he asked as she came in with her beer and sat next to him.

"I still think you need more lights in here."

"I like it dark," he said. "The fewer lights, the better. You know that. But you didn't let me finish. Should I retire from hockey?"

Daria looked at him, reprovingly. "You say that every time you lose a playoff game. And I have to spend two or three hours talking you out of it. Reminding you about the glorious time when you skated the Tannen Trophy around the ice."

"Yeah, but I don't remember being so sprung from a game."

"Hmm." She took a ladylike sip from her beer. "So that why there's no blonde entertainment here tonight?"

He snorted at her reference to Tia and Mia. "The only thing I want to snuggle up to tonight was a hot bath and maybe a bottle of bourbon."

"You're losing your touch," she said. "Time was, you could go through a brutal hockey game *and* three girls in the same night and still be fresh for class the next day. Sit up."

He did so, and sighed in pleasure as she began massaging his shoulders. Her touch was impersonal, but friendly and Adrian felt himself relaxing in her presence.

"Oh, wow! Here we go again!" Daria left off the massage as the television showed a highlight of the Greyhound-Blaze game. Namely the non-penalty incurred by Adrian Donelson and the ensuing brawl. Adrian groaned inwardly as he saw himself, reduced in size on the tube, getting into it with Calder. Not that he didn't like fighting; he did it all the time. But this was one of the few times when he hadn't instigated it. He'd still been punished for it, and that fact stuck in his craw.

"Wow." Daria looked at him, her big, brown eyes wide with mock admiration as the highlight ended. "Remind me not to get on the wrong side of you. You have a hell of an upper cut, A.D."

"Leave it, Daria Jane," he said crossly.

"Don't let it get to you, Adrian," she said quietly. She only used his given name when she was concerned about him. She had a whole repertoire of names for him. "Dumb Mick," "Idiot Irish," "Black Irish." Or just "asshole" when she was feeling especially friendly and affectionate toward him.

"That wasn't it," he said, with a sigh. "This time, I actually didn't start that dumb fight. They're not showing *that* on the highlights. Of course. Calder instigated. The crowd saw it. Coach Dick saw it. But *I'm* the one that got tossed. *I'm* the one who made the damned highlight reel. Fucking official."

Daria blew out a rueful breath. "Yeah, but the ref didn't see it. You know that. And they're the ones that count."

"The ref was Jacoby. I swear to God the man has it in for me."

She rolled her eyes. "Criminy, you dumb mick, what ref *doesn't* have it in for you?"

Adrian laughed a little. She had a point there. It was a rare night when he didn't get tossed in the penalty box for some infraction or another. He'd never be up for hockey's Reynolds Award, the one they gave out for gentlemanly behavior in the ice.

"It's not in your makeup to be polite on the ice," Daria was saying.

"You don't know that," he grumped. "You never come to see me play. I keep offering it to you. Great seats, a locker room pass, the works. Worth its weight in gold, Daria Jane. Lots of fans would kill for it. In fact, a lot of my lady friends would cream to see a lot of hard, male bodies dripping with sweat. Especially after a game."

She shook her head, a smile touching her rosebud mouth. Dimples appeared in her cheeks.

"Put a football in those hands of yours, and we'll talk."

Adrian shook his head, wondering why men grunting on the field over a stupid piece of pigskin had more appeal to his friend than the fast-paced, violent-graceful game of hockey.

"Speaking of football, what happened with Eddie Bucher the other night?" he asked.

Bucher, a fullback on the Dallas Steed football team and a golfing buddy of Adrian's, had wanted to take Daria out. Daria had been amenable and even eager to go out with the strapping wide receiver.

But she snorted.

"Talk about a date that was a non-starter. The first half of the night he was mobbed by women of all shapes and sizes for autographs and kisses and even an offer of a blow job, if you can believe it. While I was sitting right there! The second half, all he could talk about was how he was always mobbed by those women when he went out in public and how tired he was of it. But I could tell he was getting off on telling me about it. It was boring. So when another groupie came by for a grope, I slipped out and took a cab home. Watching paint dry is more exciting."

"Have a heart, munchkin. He likes you."

"Wrong, Black Irish. He likes being mobbed. And he likes that his date is seeing it. Plus I'm sure he was looking for me to put out after that. Someone else he can notch on his belt. No thanks. That I don't need. By the way, I never thanked you for not trying that with me."

Adrian considered her comment for a long moment, realizing she was right. "Why haven't we ever made it?" he asked her. "Why haven't you and I ever been to bed together? Seriously. Neither of us are bad-looking—"

"Except for that busted nose of yours."

"Adds character," he promptly said. But part of him was surprised they were having this conversation. Ever since meeting and hanging out with Daria in college, the last thing on his mind had been getting her into bed. The situation seemed the same on her side: She'd never hinted that her interest in him was anything other than platonic.

Now Adrian wondered why. Daria was extremely attractive, slender, with curves in the right places, long hair that flowed over shoulders like dark, rich cocoa, flashing black eyes and a rosebud mouth set in flawless olive skin that was a nod to her Italian ancestry.

The reason why you never tried to make it with her is because you like your lays blonde and stacked. And, oh yeah. Dumb.

No, Daria DeCarlo was one woman he respected too much to screw. But if she wasn't his type, and if he respected her too much to fuck her, why the hell was he getting hard thinking about it?

Didn't take two and two to put it together. A brutal playoff loss, combined with his own bogus penalty, pissed him off. He was semi-buzzed from the beer, but nowhere near ready to go to bed. He needed some kind of release. Preferably sexual. He was momentarily sorry he hadn't taken Tia and Mia up on their offer.

But he realized blonde, dumb and stacked wasn't what he needed tonight. He needed an understanding physical presence. A friendly one.

Who better than his very good friend with the dark, bedroom eyes?

"Character?" she was saying with a smile. "I can tell you what it adds to that mug of yours, but it ain't character."

"I'm serious, Daria Jane. Why haven't we ended up together sexually?"

Daria shrugged and sipped her beer. "Never attracted to one another in that way, I guess. Besides, A.D. I'm not easy to please in bed. And before you open your mouth and some stupid macho bullshit comes out about you being different and giving the woman a good time, let's just leave it at that."

"I've never heard any complaints."

She shook her head. "You just had to do it, didn't you? You had to open your big mouth and say it."

"But you still haven't answered why."

"You're a persistent asshole, you know?"

He just waited, smiling at her. He knew how to wait out people. Players, women, anyone.

Daria finally threw up her hands. "Okay. But don't say I didn't warn you. I like my guys tied up when I make it with them. Another beer?"

In the face of his sudden and stunned silence, she treated him to a sly grin, got to her feet and went to the kitchen. He thought about her comment, his mind working around it incredulously. He'd known this woman for a lot of years. To most people, she was the studious, quiet type, extraordinarily intelligent, only becoming verbal and opinionated among the few people she trusted, himself included.

The last thing he'd expected was that she was into bondage. That she liked her men submissive. It boggled the mind.

Daria came back with two cans of beer and gave him one. Adrian popped it open swigged it, then wiped his mouth. "When did you first do it? I mean dominate?" he asked, trying to keep an open, friendly demeanor. But thoughts of her forcing some hapless male to submit were turning him on. He only hoped she didn't notice the apparent reaction going on between his legs.

Apparently not. Daria sat back next to him and crossed her arms behind her head, a smile lighting her face. "Larry Drager. In college."

"Drager?" Adrian was surprised. Larry Drager had gone to the state championship for wrestling twice, and had even made it to nationals. Definitely the last type of guy he'd figure into bondage, but you never knew.

She laughed, enjoying his surprise. "Believe it or not. We were going at it in his room one night and he could tell I wasn't getting into him. Or what we were doing. So he suggested I tie him up. I thought he was kidding at first. But he encouraged me. And it worked." She shrugged. "Since then, it's what I've liked. But the bindings—they need to be neckties."

Adrian snorted beer out his nose.

"*Neckties?*"

Daria's dimples showed. "It's my fetish, A.D. I make it with men tied with neckties. And sometimes I make it myself *with* neckties. They turn me on. I know it's weird and if you breathe a word of this to anyone…"

"No, no." He mopped spilled beer from his shirt, then shook his head. "I've never heard of such a thing!"

"What, bondage?"

"Don't be a bitch. Neckties?"

She shrugged, drained her beer.

"I hate to say it, Daria Jane. You've piqued my curiosity about you in bed, rather than satisfied it."

"No, Adrian."

"No, what?"

"No, we're not going to do the deed together."

"Why not?"

She looked at him soberly. "Because I don't think you can handle it."

"Yeah?" He grinned at her lazily. "I can handle a lot, munchkin. It's not like I'm some teen-age virgin."

Daria shook her head. "This is different from your experience. And don't look at me like that. Something like this requires being able to let go and trusting that your partner won't hurt you. That she'll give you a good time. It's why I'm never drunk when I do it, and why I insist my partner isn't either."

She looked at the beer can in her hand, and gently placed it on the coffee table. "That's not the case here," she went on. "We've both had a few too many. Besides, I honestly don't see you being able to do it. Letting go and trusting a woman in bed to that extent."

Her calm dismissal of his sexual abilities brought up his competitive streak. He didn't like being challenged, especially when it came to bedroom gymnastics.

"It's not like I haven't—done this before," he said, haltingly. Despite everything, he felt his face turn read. "I've tied women up and—"

"Gave them a few gropes and made them come, right? And I'll bet they were drunk enough to put up with it."

The contempt in her voice made him frown. "And all of this is a problem because—?"

"Because that's not how I like to work things. I'm in it for more than simply a race to an orgasmic finish line. I like the pleasure to be drawn out. Sometimes for hours. To be almost painful for both myself and the guy before I allow us both to let go."

Her face became passionate as she talked and Adrian felt his libido kick up a notch. He'd never seen this side of her and he realized he had to have her. On her terms, if that's what she wanted.

"Do you find me attractive?" he wanted to know.

Since the first time since they'd begun this whacked-out discussion, Daria dropped her eyes and he saw a flush creep along her cheekbones.

"That has nothing to do with it," she said, her voice low.

"Just answer the question, munchkin."

She looked up at him, dark eyes chagrined. "Yeah, I'm attracted to you. I'm attracted to a lot of guys. But not all of them like my thing. Along with the bondage, I like to dole out punishment. Not heavy shit, no drawing blood or anything, but enough to make it interesting. The guy who is able to take it and enjoy it is the one who stays in my life. As a lover."

She grinned and winked at him.

"Don't get mad, Adrian, but I've known you a lot of years. Guys like you don't like your women to take control in the bedroom. And I don't get off unless I have it. Case closed." She stood, stretched and yawned. "I'm exhausted. I'm going to turn in and sleep late. Thank God tomorrow is Saturday. Anyone who wakes me had better have his or her will signed—"

"What if I told you I was willing to try it?"

She looked down at him warily and he enjoyed the surprise on her face. But he'd surprised himself, too, with his comment. She was absolutely right on with him. He *did* like being the boss in bed. Safe to say, his goal was for the woman to have a good time.

Still, he couldn't get the image of his good friend tying his wrists to the bedpost with a green necktie he had...

"This isn't a game to me," she was saying, her dark eyes serious. "And if you're trying to make fun of it—"

He held up his hand to stop her concerns. "Daria Jane, if I'm going to trust any woman, it's you. I know you wouldn't do anything to hurt me."

"Well then, maybe we could try it at some point."

"Tonight."

"Adrian, no."

"Look." He rubbed the back of his neck, feeling the tension there, wondering what he could say to convince her he was serious and not mocking her. "I've had a bitch of a game. I turned down a hot evening with twins, no less, because my ego took a beating. Maybe—maybe what I want tonight is to let someone else take control. For a change. But only if you want to." Adrian took a deep breath and looked at her. "You know me. I'd never coerce you into anything if you weren't willing."

"It isn't a question of willingness," she said, quietly. "It's crossed my mind in the past, to be honest. But it's stayed in my mind, because I'm afraid if we do this, it'll get weird with us. We have such a good friendship going, I don't want to screw it up by becoming lovers."

"Look at it another way, munchkin. Maybe we can take that trust you speak of so well a step further. I'm willing to trust you. Doesn't that count for something?"

She sighed and sat down next to him. "Boy, you're sure a sweet-talker when it comes to getting laid."

"I've had practice," he said dryly.

She laughed. "Yeah. I know. I'm willing to try it, Adrian. But you promise it won't screw up our friendship? If we do this thing, there's stuff about me you'll learn that might change your mind about me as your good friend."

Adrian held up three fingers. "Scout's honor. Nothing about you could make me like you any less."

Daria stared at him for a long moment, as though gauging his sincerity, then nodded.

"Okay," she said. "We need a safe word before we start. One we use if it gets too far on either side. I like to use the words 'stocking run.' It sounds funny in the heat of things and it can stop things if need be. Not that I'm one of those violent dommes, but it's good to know."

Adrian listened, feeling a little uneasy about the sudden direction of the conversation. Safe word? To stop things? He wondered what he was getting himself into.

"Stand up for me." Her voice was low, husky, tickling his nerve endings. A voice he'd never heard from her before. The effect on him was electric, and he felt his groin throb in anticipation.

"Daria—"

"From now on you address me as 'ma'am.'"

"You take this stuff seriously, don't you?"

He smiled at her. Daria's face fell, then a wry grin crossed it and she flung back her hair.

"Never mind, Black Irish. This obviously isn't going to work..."

Adrian stood up. "I'm standing, ma'am," he said, quietly. He felt a little foolish as he waited. Though he couldn't see her reaction, he felt her reluctance, her doubt of him. For a moment, he was convinced she would call the whole thing off. Then he heard her get to her feet. She moved in front of him, her dark eyes intent.

"Strip for me," she told him. "Do it. I want to watch you."

Swallowing his reluctance, Adrian unloosened the green necktie around his neck and took it off, dropping it on the floor.

"Slower," she said, command edging her husky tone. Pressing his lips together, Adrian slowly unbuttoned his dress shirt and slid it off. With hands that barely shook, he undid his belt, unzipped his slacks, and slid them off, along with his underwear. He stood naked before her, while she was still clothed. And the whole thing was turning him on even more.

What now, he wanted to ask. But he remembered her admonition not to say a word and remained silent.

Daria moved around him, her eyes caressing him, her tongue licking her lips almost in anticipation. He remembered one of the blondes doing that same thing earlier, with no reaction from him. But this time, it was different. He found himself growing harder under her hot gaze, his cock straining, yearning to be touched. He trembled for a moment, feeling desire wash through him, and forced himself to stop.

She smiled at him and, reaching out, fondled him. Her hand fisted his shaft, moving up and down slowly, before hefting his balls. He caught his breath at the lust searing through his body, and she chuckled.

"Stay still," she said softly.

Gritting his teeth, Adrian forced himself to remain loose, hands by his side, as her fingers roamed across his hard-on, stroking the underside, then coming back to caress the tip. She came close to him, wrapping her hand around his swollen rod, and her scent came to him. Warm, musky arousal. Daria knelt before him, and he gritted his teeth as she delicately licked around the swollen, purple tip, lapping up his pre-cum with slow, deliberate movements. Her wet tongue was sheer torture as it massaged the sensitive crown of his penis, and he fought against groaning. Much more of this and he was going to explode.

"You might want to think about not coming right away," she told him casually, as though reading his thoughts. "Since you like control so much, let's see if you can hold it for awhile."

Well, that shouldn't be a problem. Given he liked to pace

lovemaking, he could go for hours, if need be. But he wasn't about to tell her that. Give her the impression she had all the power. He could retain his own little secrets now, couldn't he?

Adrian suddenly realized how titillating the domination game could be.

She reached over, picked up the green necktie and wrapped it around his erection, moving it slowly up and down. Despite everything, the cool silk on his engorged cock almost did him in. Trembling, almost unmanned by the excruciating pleasure she was creating, he held on. Barely.

"This should do," she whispered. He shuddered as her hot breath caressed him. Smiling up at him, she handed him the tie and got to her feet. "Take this, go in the bedroom and lie down. I'll be in shortly."

Adrian looked at her, saw the challenge in her eyes. Challenge mixed with lust and desire. The same feelings roared through his body. If nothing else, this would be a night to remember.

Without a word, Adrian turned and went into the bedroom.

CHAPTER 2

Daria examined herself in the mirror for what felt like the umpteenth time. Leather bustier pushing what little cleavage she had into the open. Matching leather thong massaging the tender area between her nether lips. Fishnets, attached by garter straps. And the six-inch pumps.

She was charged up, feeling rowdy. Horny. Putting on this outfit always got her this way. And the object of her desire was downstairs, hopefully waiting for her. She moved a little, catching her breath as the thong pressed gently against her swollen clit. The way she was feeling, it wouldn't take her much to come.

Daria closed her eyes for a moment, telling herself again that this was a rotten idea. Adrian was her friend, her best friend. Had been since their college days. Now they were about to move that friendship into the bedroom. Things could get really, really weird if this didn't work out.

He's had a bad day. He's had too many beers. He's gonna wake up and regret this. You should stop this.

Daria's practical voice was doing its best to stop her. Problem was, the horny, rowdy, charged-up side of her didn't want to. The idea of having Adrian Donelson, thug supreme of the Dallas Blaze, at her mercy was just too tempting to resist. That, combined with the bustier rubbing against her nipples and the thong massaging between her legs, was driving good sense out the window.

"You oughta be horsewhipped, Daria Jane," she muttered to her reflection in the mirror, then grinned. The small, rubber whip she had would be just the thing. That, and the leather cock ring. She wasn't into doling out pain, but sometimes the whip came in handy to drive men into a frenzy. Especially while their sensitive organ was entrapped in soft leather. She sensed that Adrian Donelson, Mr. Control, would need to be taught a lesson. A few lessons. Daria shivered in anticipation as she realized the toys would do the trick.

Still, she'd learned long ago that her particular kick wasn't the usual bondage toys. It was the neckties that did it for her. Nor were neckties only for bedroom play. Sometimes during a meeting at work, she'd focus on a good-looking man's neckwear and fantasize about it. While that good-looking hunk was going on and on about economic times and GDPs and facts and figures, she imagined herself doing a slow striptease in front of the guy, taking his tie, and using it to get herself off while he watched. Hell, while they *all* watched. Often the fantasies were so real she had to take a trip to the ladies' room to relieve the sexual pressure.

But tonight was no fantasy. Daria took a deep breath, feeling the constricting bustier rub her breasts as she did so. Taking a final look at herself, she put on her robe and picked up her toys, slipping a couple of condoms into her pocket for good measure. She could just see the neighbors' response seeing her all decked out like some porno movie star. They all thought of her as Daria DeCarlo, brilliant economic analyst. She wondered what they'd think if they realized this Dallas economist's brain got into necktie bondage in a big way.

Smiling, she went to the floor below, fortunately not meeting anyone. She let herself into Adrian's apartment with the key he'd given her awhile back. All was quiet and for a moment, Daria wondered if he'd chickened out and changed his mind. She'd made him wait for half an hour, on purpose, letting him know who the boss was.

But it might have backfired. He was probably be fast asleep. Probably better, if that was the case. They could laugh it off in the morning and pin it down to the booze. As for her horniness—well, she had the vibrator. It certainly wouldn't be the first time she'd had to use it.

Shrugging, Daria headed for his bedroom, convinced she'd find him asleep. But to her surprise, Adrian was awake, lying on the bed with the green tie next to him, staring at the ceiling. He turned his head and looked toward her, his gray eyes stormy. She could almost hear him screaming the questions.

Where the hell have you been all this time and why were you hanging me out to dry like this?

But he kept silent. Score one for him.

"You follow directions very well," she told him softly. He said nothing, just continued to stare at her. Daria felt a shiver of anticipation worm its way down her spine. He was a beast. A vicious beast. And soon he'd be in her control.

She allowed her eyes to wander over his body. Like most hockey players, he was lean, with an excellent build. Along with his six-feet-two height, Adrian sported well-muscled arms, a sculpted chest with a dusting of dark hair, and strong, defined legs. Between those legs, his penis was flaccid. Well, why not? She hadn't been around, and he was probably pissing angry with her. Neither would boost arousal. But it was a real credit to his determination to see this through that he hadn't told her enough was enough.

Daria noticed a tattoo of an eagle on his left shoulder. She came to him and traced it with a delicate finger, smiling to herself as his flesh jumped under her touch.

"Does that symbolize something?" she said. "You may speak."

"My grandmother was Native American." His voice was hoarse. "The eagle was her guardian. I wanted a tribute to her."

In all the years she'd known him, she hadn't know about that bit of his heritage. Well, that explained his almost bronzed skin and high cheekbones. Not to mention his nut-brown hair. Still, the eagle intrigued her. She'd seen him without his shirt before, at the pool. But this was the first time she'd noticed it.

"It looks sexy on you," she said. "It must be new."

"It is."

She looked at him and he stared back, challengingly. Hmm. Something in her kicked over at that look. A primal urge rose inside her to control. To tame. It was that urge, more than the idea of sex with him that kicked her arousal up another notch.

Daria smiled. "This is the last time you speak to me without permission, unless it's to say the safe words." When he opened his mouth to protest, she held up the small whip, and moved the soft tassels across his chest. Up and down, up and down, caressingly, but in a way that would tell him she knew how to use it. "Next time you open your mouth without permission, you'll feel this."

Adrian looked at her, swallowed, then nodded. He lay still as she ran the whip's tassels around his genitals, which were starting to come to life.

"Think of this as a penalty for some infraction," she continued softly. "Roughing. High-sticking. Unsportsmanlike conduct. But unlike hockey, Black Irish, this penalty will last a hell of a lot longer. And will hopefully bring you a lot more pleasure."

She fancied she could hear him gulp. Deliberately turning her back on him, Daria went into his closet and picked out two ties she'd frequently seen him wear. Just the ticket. She returned to Adrian. His gray eyes sparked questions at her, but he remained silent. Placing the ties on the bed, Daria untied her robe and dropped it, barely restraining a laugh at his sudden intake of breath.

Daria picked up his left wrist and wrapped the red tie around it, before tying it to the bedpost.

"The next time you wear these ties," she said as she repeated her actions with the right wrist and gold tie, "after a hockey game, or during a press conference, I want you to remember this moment. I want to remember how hot you were for me. For it. How much you liked being tied up and submitting. I want you to remember me dressed like this. And I want you getting hard at the memory. I don't care when it happens or were. I want you aroused when you think about this."

Adrian closed his eyes, and Daria saw his cock continue to swell. As she finished tying him, a rush of power jolted through her body. With an effort, Daria fought to slow her breathing and still the trembling of her hands.

Control, Daria. Don't lose control. Not yet.

Taking, slow, even breaths, Daria calmed herself. "Open your eyes," she said softly. He did so, and the ragged desire in them made her weak in the knees. Deftly, she slipped the cock ring around his growing erection and he jumped a little. "Tell me if that starts to hurt. Are you okay now? Speak."

"Yes, ma'am."

"Feel good?"

"Oh, God. Yes."

Daria took the whip and slapped him lightly on the stomach. Though he jumped, Daria saw the reaction she needed. His cock twitched in its leather restraint.

"You're to address me as 'ma'am.' Do so."

"Yes, ma'am." His voice was husky.

"Good." She took the green necktie and caressed his erection and thatch of dark hair between his legs. Gripping the tie by both ends, she moved it across his swollen penis. When Adrian jerked and moaned, she picked up the whip and slapped his stomach.

"Be quiet."

She could see his throat working as he fought against groaning. Lust glazed his eyes and his breathing become faster.

"Good job," she said. "Now. I'm going to play with myself with this tie. You'll watch."

She could see his jaw clench and he closed his eyes briefly, but then opened them again and focused on her. Daria smiled at him, knowing she could drive him crazy by pleasuring herself and he wouldn't be able to do a damn thing about it. He wouldn't be able to touch her—or himself. He'd have to watch in exquisite, erotic torture while she played. Silent torture, knowing the whip was nearby if he so much as groaned.

"Oh, yes," she whispered. In these situations, control and ecstasy fused together, becoming an almost unbearable aphrodisiac for her. Moreso tonight, because of who she was with.

Closing her eyes, Daria felt the heat of his gaze on her body as she caressed herself with the tie, the heavy silk arousing her further. She would take this slow, she decided, touching herself all over with the cloth, bringing herself to a leisurely climax. Making him suffer. Making him burn with an almost uncontrollable need for her. This was what it was all about—controlling the tenor and pace of sex. Controlling the man who was bound before her. Driving him crazy. Making him want it so badly he couldn't think of anything else other than an exquisite, necessary release.

Opening her eyes, Daria undid the stays of her bustier, allowing it to open, revealing her breasts and hardened nipples. She caught his fiery gaze and palmed her breasts, caressing the peaks, then running his tie over her nipples, gasping at the cool sensation on her swollen nubs. Lust spilled through her veins, making her shake, making her weak in the knees.

"This is driving you crazy, isn't it?" she asked softly, moving the tie down her body and sliding it across her belly, biting her lip at the caress of the soft silk on her heated flesh. She dropped her thong, shivering slightly. She was already dripping wet from the pressure of the leather against her sensitive inner folds. Spreading her legs, she touched her herself, catching her breath.

"I'm wet," she confided. "And turned on. Take a good look."

Daria grabbed a chair, placing it near the head of his bed. After laying a towel out on the seat, she sat and spread her legs. Adrian's body jerked as his gaze fell between her legs. Daria smiled and moved the tie to the sensitive skin of her inner thighs, dangling the cloth enticingly along the soft flesh, then wrapping it around her fingers and caressing her outer lips.

"You haven't had the pleasure of tasting me," she told him as she touched her swollen pussy, swallowing a groan at the incredible sensations. "Maybe later I'll give you that treat." She had to pause then, shivering, as she imagined his tongue on her, in her. A spasm of lust held her captive and she suddenly moaned, then got hold of herself.

She was close to coming. Too close. And it wasn't time.

Pausing, taking deep breaths to still the white-hot desire threatening to swamp her, Daria stopped. Adrian's eyes were glued to her silk-wrapped fingers, his body shaking. Knowing he was ready to lose it at her command steadied Daria, and she was able to rein in her lust.

Moving her legs farther apart, Daria spread her nether lips wide with her left hand, giving him a better view. A small sound came from his throat, and he closed his eyes and turned his head away. A moment later, she was on her feet, whip in hand. She slapped him on the stomach and he started at her, gray eyes stormy. He looked ready to attack her, to tear her limb from limb. Only the silken restraints kept him captive. Daria shook again, realizing the power she had over this volatile man.

"No," she said softly. "You have to look. And be silent. Otherwise I'll keep you this way all evening and pleasure myself again. And again. Until you learn your lesson. Your choice, Black Irish."

Adrian clenched his fists, his teeth coming down on his lower lip hard enough to draw a small bead of blood. She leaned over and ran her tongue over his bleeding lip, tasting the salty essence. Then she pressed her lips to his. His tongue came out to touch hers for a long moment, and she almost weakened, wanting to slide on top of him and indulge in more lip and tongue play. Wanting to feel his heat against her sensitive flesh, to feel his hot spear move through her swollen and creamy folds to bury itself deeply inside her...

With an effort, Daria broke the kiss and pulled back, her breath coming hot in her throat. This wasn't good. Something about Adrian was getting to her. Instead of moving the sex at her own pace, she was ready to throw restraint out the window and yield to him with wild abandon.

Control, Daria. Control.

Looking at him, Daria took some comfort in realizing he was in worse shape than she was. His cock was fully extended, straining inside its leather ring. His balls were swollen tight against the lower strap, and Daria couldn't help herself. Leaning over, she ran her tongue slowly across his soft sac, playing with it, caressing it slowly, feeling his testicles tighten further beneath her ministrations. God, he tasted so good. She sucked one ball into her mouth, felt him jump, heard him groan.

In a moment, she was upright, the soft rubber whip striking one thigh, then the other. Somehow, the action of doling out discipline calmed her down. But Adrian suddenly lunged, his eyes wild and bright with a feral, animal desire. Only the restraints held him back, and he growled. The whip came down again on his thighs, harder this time, and he subsided. His lip curled for a moment, and Daria wondered if he was going to bare his teeth at her, like some magnificent, untamed animal. She faced him, unafraid, his almost violent reactions boosting her arousal.

Then he closed his eyes and gritted his teeth. When he opened them again, he seemed to have calmed himself. Daria was impressed. She was convinced that by now he would have been calling the shots. Or trying to.

"Good job," she told him softly. "But keep watching."

Sitting back down, Daria moved the tie between her legs, pushing it into her folds, and groaned. God, the cool, silken feel of the tie against her hot sex was almost more than she could bear. She ran the tie between her legs, forcing it between the sensitive flesh, pressing hard against her clit as she slid the fabric slowly and tantalizingly back and forth between her lips, the fabric darkening with her abundant juices.

But she was burning as Adrian stared at her, feeling control slipping away from her. She would have to do herself, now, or she'd be in trouble. Keeping the tie in place, she pressed it deeply between her inner lips, then slowly rubbed her fingers back and forth with practiced ease. Even through the folds of the tie, Daria could feel her swollen clit, and she lightened her strokes, quickening them, feeling the heat of Adrian's gaze on her as she continued pleasuring herself, feeling pulses of lust flare out from her groin to encompass the rest of her body.

Then, without warning, she was through and shrieking her release, writhing as she continued maneuvering the soaked material around her pussy. She was in such a high state of arousal, she couldn't stop coming and she cried out again as she hit the second pinnacle, her body spasming in almost obscene pleasure..

Finally, when she had enough, she stopped her play and put her head on her knees, breathing heavily. She'd never been so aroused before when playing with herself. Nor had she ever climaxed for so long.

Raising her head and looking at Adrian, Daria realized his much-vaunted control was hanging only by a single thread. His face was flushed, his breath coming in ragged gasps. His cock jerked, almost as though unseen hands were fondling him. Pre-cum oozed freely, spilling down the sides of his erection.

Looking at him got her horny. Yet again. She wasn't ready to release him though, not yet. She still wasn't done.

Smiling sweetly at him, Daria climbed on him, straddling his chest. She rubbed against him, biting her lip as she felt his hot flesh pressed against her swollen folds. He struggled not to groan, and Daria barely restrained a smile. Her desire flared again, as her sensitive genitals moved against his skin. She was tempted to reach an orgasm this way, by rubbing her sex on his chest. But she had a craving to feel his tongue inside her.

Moving up his body, Daria placed her knees on either side of his head, then slowly lowered herself. For a moment, nothing happened. Then she felt his response—a quick flick of his tongue in and out of her lower lips. Then a longer caress. Daria shuddered, remaining in place, and Adrian became bolder, his tongue probing the soft, moist flesh of her engorged and sensitive pussy, eagerly lapping at her cream. Gasping, Daria raised her hips, looked down at him, and smiled. Frustration was clearly outlined on his face. This was her favorite part of sex and she reveled in it. Taunting her lovers. Teasing them. Leaving them hungering for more. Lowering her hips, Daria felt Adrian's tongue move slowly between her legs, working its way around her outer lips, exploring them, tasting her. Before he could go further, she lifted her hips again. Then, after a few agonizing moments, she moved down.

But this time, he was prepared. His tongue attacked her swollen clit, then drew it into his mouth. Keeping the engorged bit of skin captive, he moved his tongue again and again on it, lashing it, caressing it, putting his own form of sensual torture on her. Unprepared for the onslaught of molten lust flowing through her veins, Daria gripped the headboard, threw her head back and moaned, captive to his tongue and lips, unwilling and unable to move as he continued lapping and sucking at her.

By the time he released her clit and moved his tongue slowly through her lower lips, Daria found herself helpless to resist. Seeming to sense her surrender, Adrian tongued her with rough, broad sweeps, licking her again and again, then sucking hard as though he was thirsting for her cream, as though he couldn't get enough of it. Against her will, Daria found herself submitting to the heat caroming throughout her body, wondering with a small part of her mind who was dominating—and who was submitting.

She felt his chuckle on her lower lips and deliberately ground herself on his face. He responded by sliding his tongue into her slick cunt, then bringing it out again before moving in, going deeper. Licking and tasting, Adrian drove her to the edge, then through it, and Daria felt her body convulse in wanton, incredible pleasure. Nor did he release her immediately, but continued playing with her, caressing her clit and pussy in quick, jabbing thrusts, and driving her to the edge again and again.

When Adrian finally stopped, Daria was clinging to the headboard, gasping for air. After a moment, she climbed off him, trying to stem the shaking of her legs. She saw the self-satisfied grin on his face, and her mouth tightened.

"I told you it'd be good," he said.

Daria picked up the whip and slapped him on the belly, harder than she'd intended. He winced and stared at her in surprise and she cursed herself as she dropped the whip. Rule one of the domme was not to become too emotional, or too out of control, otherwise the partner could be hurt. She knew that better than anyone.

She'd never come close to losing control before. Not like this.

Clenching her hands, she willed herself to calm. For a moment, the safe word floated through her brain and she reached for it, about ready to say it.

As though reading her mind, Adrian shook his head, violently. "Don't stop," he whispered. "Don't leave me like this. I'm so hard…I—"

He spoke, and Daria looked at his penis. It was huge, almost purple from its sojourn in the cock ring. She closed her eyes for a moment, in an agony of indecision. Her emotional reaction to him was frightening. She needed to stop. But was it really fair, to take him so far, and not give him some type of release?

Some dommes would do just that, letting their lovers suffer. But she wasn't one of those who believed a lot of pain was necessary for control. It meant nothing to her unless both she and her partner came away from the experience satisfied.

Going to him, Daria removed the ring, seeing he was aroused almost to the point of pain. He was huge and Daria suddenly wanted him inside her. Badly. She touched him gently and heard his intake of breath.

"Seems like you have a little problem here, don't you?" she said, genially. She was glad she felt in control again, but didn't like she'd almost lost it. "Speak."

"Yes, ma'am," he gasped out.

"What do you think we should do about this? Speak."

"I need to come," he said, hoarsely.

"How badly?"

"Badly."

"Badly what?"

"Badly, ma'am."

Daria reached out and rubbed the tip of his swollen cock between her thumb and forefinger, snaring a drop of his pre-cum. She brought the finger to her mouth and inhaled his essence, her nostrils flaring as she took in his scent. Then she tasted him. Adrian clenched his jaw at her actions, and Daria could see him fighting the need to writhe and cry out. But he kept control, breathing heavily, and Daria nodded.

"Beg me for it. Beg me to let you come."

Adrian swallowed, closed his eyes.

"Please," he whispered.

"Please, what?"

"Please. Ma'am. Please let me come."

"I can't hear you. Louder, please."

Adrian gritted his teeth, opened his eyes, and yanked at his bindings.

"Let me come," he growled.

Daria sighed and took up the whip and he quieted down immediately.

"Please," he said, humbly. "Please, ma'am."

Shrugging, Daria leaned over his straining penis, allowing its tip to touch her swollen right nipple. As she moved her hardened peak around his engorged crown, she gasped at the incredible feel of his essence on her sensitive flesh. Then she treated her other nipple to his cock, trembling, almost losing herself in the heat threatening to engulf her.

Adrian writhed in silent agony, the need for his release clear on his face, his body straining and jerking in their restraints. Nothing touched him except the tips of her nipples, which were becoming harder with each pass. Daria kept on, his pre-cum hardening her flesh and spilling over onto her breasts. She stopped at last and stood, trembling, rubbing his juices into her nipples and moaning at the sensation of the wet nubs as the cool air hit them.

"Daria—" Adrian's voice was hoarse, despairing, and she looked at him. He had the look of a man who'd reached his limit, who was ready to go insane at any time. "Oh, God. Please. Stop torturing me. Please. I'll do anything…"

She had him right where she wanted him. But as she slipped a condom on him, she wondered how close she herself was to losing control. She was so hungry for him, she couldn't wait any longer. She simply couldn't drag this out any more.

Daria climbed on him, straddling him, guiding him slowly inside her. Seated on his hips, his cock impaling her and creating a delicious friction against her slick walls, Daria gasped and contracted around him, hearing his groans, his pleas for release. She looked down at him, his burning gray eyes searing into her soul as she slowly rode him, milking him. God he felt good, his hardness pulsing deeply inside her with every movement of her hips.

Then he lost all restraint. His hips rose to meet hers, and he drove himself deeper, fucking her with a frenzy she'd never experienced before in a lover. Helpless before her own uncontrolled passion, suddenly giving him the control she'd withheld during this session, Daria gave into her climax, screaming his name as she came, almost drowning in the heated lust that threatened to undo her. A moment later, she heard his hoarse shout and his hips pistoned wildly as he climaxed, his face worked into a grimace of pain and pleasure.

CHAPTER 3

Adrian started awake, and grunted at the daylight streaming through the window. Normally he was an early riser, but last night must have worn him out. That, and the beer. Maybe last night was a good thing. Instead of torturing himself about the Blaze's loss, he was sexually tortured instead. By his best friend.

Frowning, scrubbing his hand across his face, Adrian glanced at the other side of the bed. Daria was gone. But her essence, her scent, still lingered in the room, and he closed his eyes. Had last night been real? Or had it been some really weird wet dream? No, his groin ached from overstimulation. He hadn't been so hard—nor had he had to wait so long for release—in eons.

Adrian had thought he was an expert in the bedroom. He'd seen it all and done it all, from voyeurism and exhibitionism, to threesomes and orgies. And, as he'd told Daria, he hadn't been adverse to tying up one or two of his lovers and having his way with them.

But last night was a first. Daria DeCarlo had tied him to the bed and had done some amazing things to herself with a necktie. She had toyed with him and played with him, using a whip when he was out of line.

And he'd loved every single moment of it.

Adrian winced a little. He was growing hard at the memory of the night before, and that area was tender. Focusing on the pain and deliberately compartmentalizing Daria, he considered his schedule. The Blaze would be flying out in a few hours to Eugene and no doubt the coach would insist on a practice after last night's debacle. Adrian was surprised he hadn't heard from the powers-that-be at the Blaze about his on-ice performance from last night. Thank goodness for small favors, at least.

Yawning, Adrian climbed out of bed and stepped into the shower. As the warm water sluiced over him and he lathered up, memories kept working their way into his brain. Memories of Daria in that tight leather bustier, cleavage spilling over the top. Memories of her fuck-me pumps, a whip in her hand. Memories of her playing with herself, toying with her clit, touching it, making it grow larger in counterpart to her moans...

Growling to himself, Adrian turned the water to ice-cold and stood under it, until he was shivering. Shivering, but still horribly aroused. Gasping, soaping up his hand, Adrian touched himself, moving his fingers from the tip of his penis to his balls, then back again. He caressed the swollen crown and closed his eyes. He could see Daria on her knees, tonguing him only at the top, then licking the underside up and down, driving him insane. Sucking him gently, fondling his balls, then drawing his entire length into her warm, wet mouth...

With a cry, Adrian climaxed, fisting himself hard, hoping the pain would drive any last vestige of this unwelcome desire from his body and brain. Gasping in the aftermath, he leaned against the shower wall, his softening penis still in his hand. What the hell was happening to him? Normally so controlled, so able to compartmentalize sex and wall it off after it happened, Adrian couldn't stop remembering the night before. Couldn't stop wondering when he could see her again, to have her do him again. And again.

Abruptly he pushed himself from the wall and turned off the shower. Still shaking, but thankfully calm for the moment, Adrian toweled off and, moving into his bedroom, slipped on a pair of sweat pants and a T-shirt and went to the kitchen. When he got there, he saw a freshly brewed pot of coffee and a note in Daria's distinct handwriting.

Hey Stud:

I had to go to work. It's Saturday, but some reports are in, so I need to be, too. Duty calls, as always.

*You have a new nickname now (see above). You also proved
me wrong last night so congrats. Doesn't happen often.*

Daria
P.S. You were terrific, Adrian.

Typical Daria. Except for that last line. *Adrian.* She rarely called
him by his given name. Only if she was emotional about something.

He put the note down and poured himself a cup of coffee, not liking
the implications of her written words. Her concern had been that
moving their friendship to the bedroom might make things a little weird
for them. Might change the dynamics of the friendship, especially
given her fetish for neckties, whips and sex toys. It happened all the
time, he supposed. Friends could become lovers. But could lovers go
back to being just friends?

You were terrific, Adrian.

Going beyond that, what had happened last night had shaken
something in him. Had shown a side of him he'd never seen before.

Adrian had turned total control over to her, allowing her to use him
in whatever way she'd wanted, letting her order him around, command
him, set the tone of their coupling.

And he hadn't minded it, not at all. He'd enjoyed it and was
wondering in the deepest recesses of his mind when they could get
together to do it again. Despite his actions in the shower, his cock
stirred, almost in anticipation of another go-round with Daria the
domme. His body, at least, hungered for her total domination over him,
and his submission to her.

Problem was, his mind was rebelling. He didn't like the idea of a
woman having that kind of power, especially in the bedroom. Stupid
macho bullshit, Daria would have said, and she would have been
absolutely right. The fact he'd allowed himself to lose control, and the
fact they'd both gotten off on that, changed the dynamics of their
relationship, moving it beyond where it was before..

Adrian sighed and stared into space. He'd promised her the night
before that things wouldn't get weird if they ended up in bed. But in the
cold light of the morning after, he realized he couldn't keep that
promise.

He didn't think he could sit across from her and indulge in idle chit-
chat about the day's events without seeing her in that hot leather bustier
with the six-inch spiked fuck-me heels.

He didn't think he could share a pizza with her again without remembering the smell of her cunt as he tongued her, sucking and lapping at her musky cream, feeling her silky walls contract around him as he slipped into her.

He didn't think he could sit next to her calmly as they watched a DVD without thinking about that tender scrap of skin between her succulent nether lips, which became engorged and slick when she was aroused.

And he didn't think he could listen to her talk intelligently about much of anything without hearing that same voice commanding him to do her bidding, without hearing her moans of ecstasy as she approached a climax...

You were terrific, Adrian.

She was terrific, too. A little too terrific, if the truth were known. And while he trusted her implicitly, he couldn't trust any woman with that kind of power. Not just power over him sexually, but emotionally. He'd been burned too much in the past by women who'd been after the fame and fortune of Adrian Donelson, the hockey star. Better to ball 'em and leave 'em, rather than get tied up emotionally with them. Daria DeCarlo included.

Swallowing, Adrian set down the cup on the counter so hard it shattered. He looked down at his hand, seeing a little blood on his finger, from where he cut it. Reflexively, he lifted his finger to his mouth and sucked it. A sudden image of Daria running her tongue on his lower lip where he'd bitten down the night before assaulted his senses, and he groaned.

Shaking, his breath coming almost in gasps, he picked up her note from the counter and crushed it in his hand. He only hoped he could crush memories of her just as easily.

*   *   *

Hours later, when Adrian took the ice for practice at the Eugene Greyhound's arena, he wasn't feeling much better. A plane ride where he lost two hours always took it out of him. Plus he was still sprung. Sprung from last night's hockey game. Not to mention last night's more private game.

Still, he lost himself in the rhythm of the on-ice drills. Point-to-point. Follow the pass. Slot shooting. Though he was a defenseman, an enforcer to protect forwards from the other team, the coach insisted he know how to shoot, too.

But as he worked his muscles on the ice, thoughts of Daria lingered at the back of his brain even as the sweat poured down his body. Daria, the quiet studious brain, with an Italian temper beneath. Daria, his best friend. Daria, the siren, the erotic dominatrix, who was causing his cock to swell despite the punishing practice, despite the restrictive cup he wore…

Adrian stopped by one of the boards and grabbed a water bottle, sluicing himself liberally with it. If only he could dash the cold water on his groin. Having a hard-on under these circumstances wasn't exactly pleasurable. But even the pain wasn't abating his arousal.

As Adrian took a long, deep swig, Blaze head coach Dirk Reneau skated by, gazing at him with a sour expression on his lean and narrow face.

"Now's not the time to indulge in a conditioning program, AD," Reneau said, his slight accent betraying his French Canadian origins.

Great. On top of everything else, he had "The Dick" on his case. Why Corrigan had hired this asshole to coach the team, Adrian couldn't guess.

"Sorry," Adrian said amiably enough. "I got to bed later last night than I intended."

Yep. And sleep wasn't exactly what I did.

Reneau stared him down in disdain. "This is the playoffs. You guys sucked last night. You didn't get enough sleep. Now you're wearing yourself out in practice, and with a time-zone change. This is why we lose games, Donelson. Guys like you who don't respect the playoffs."

The man skated off and Adrian stared after him, fuming. *The reason why we lose games, you jackass, is because of your lousy motivational skills,* he wanted to say. But he didn't. Brian Corrigan had his reasons for bringing Reneau down from Montreal, and it was to rebuild the team. He supposed that kind of stuff worked for youngsters just coming into the league. But at thirty-four years old, Adrian was far from being the twenty-two-year-old rookie who'd been drafted by the Blaze's farm team.

Teammate Joe Friedlander slammed into him, pressing him against the hard wooden boards, just about knocking the breath out of him.

"Shit Freed-o," Adrian grumbled. "That was too damned close to a cross-check."

His friend released him, an unapologetic grin on his face. "How were Tia and Mia?"

Adrian grunted. "I wouldn't know. Last I saw, they were looking to take a wack at Jacobson."

"Sure. Like he'd ever stray from the lovely Jeanne." The other man looked him over, then shook his head. "But something sexy must have happened by your place last night. You sure look like you had some bedroom workout. Must have been some wet dream."

Now he was looking as though he'd been fucked. No wonder The Dick had lectured him. Just what he needed.

"Fuck off, Freed-o," he said wearily, then skated back to the bench. He sensed Friedlander's confusion. Hell, in the past he hadn't hesitated to kiss and tell. That was the goal of locker room talk, after all

But Daria's not a wham-bam-thank-you-ma'am type of girl. She's your good friend. Someone you care about. Someone you trusted enough to let go to the point that you actually enjoyed submitting to her.

Adrian drew a shuddering breath. Before last night, he'd been able to compartmentalize sex. Keep it in its place. Use it for release and not much more. But now sex was spilling over into his game. Into this practice. Because this whole thing with Daria wasn't just about the sex. It was about the fact that, for the first time in a lot of years, he actually cared about the woman he'd made love with.

While losing control had been bad enough, this was infinitely worse. He'd lost his head only once before, in college, over a woman who'd taken him financially and emotionally to the cleaners. Daria, in fact, had helped him pick up the pieces from that abortive affair. And he'd sworn he'd never allow it to happen again. Up until now, he'd succeeded.

But who would help him pick up the pieces this time if it all fell apart? The answer was simple. No one.

Much as he hated to admit it, Daria's concerns had been justified. In moving their relationship into the bedroom, things were getting very weird, very fast. He was just thankful that the next two playoff games were away from Dallas. He wouldn't have to face her for at least another week. Hopefully by the time he arrived back in Dallas, his emotions and cock would have settled down.

Grimly, Adrian knew that The Dick was right about one thing. He needed to get his head in the game if they had any hopes of winning this particular series with the Greyhounds.

CHAPTER 4

Daria was a wreck as she waited outside the Blaze's locker room at Carlyle Arena the following week. She'd finally decided to take advantage of Adrian's offer of game tickets and locker room pass. When she'd called the Blaze's administrative offices, she'd been told that the tickets were on permanent reserve for her, just come on down to will call.

She had, and had sat through the game, though she didn't want to go in and see naked, sweaty bodies as Adrian had sarcastically mentioned to her a week ago.

Though no lover of hockey, Daria had come to the game on a mission; a mission to break the silent treatment she'd been experiencing from Adrian since "the night," as she'd come to call it.

Daria knew that Adrian had been on the road, getting pummeled and pummeling through two very difficult playoff hockey games. The Blaze came home having tied the series. But tonight they'd lost the final, crucial game. No more playoffs for the Dallas team. Series over. Season over.

Normally, Daria would have left the confrontation act until Adrian felt better. Experience told her he'd be furious, criticizing the team and himself over and over again, poking holes in everything, wondering what had gone wrong on the ice to make them lose. He'd get over it, in a few weeks.

If he'd responded to just one of her e-mails or text messages, she would have left the whole thing alone. The man who was always responsive to her communications had shut her off, and Daria knew why.

She'd been afraid things would change for the worse after their evening together. His silence only confirmed her fears.

Now, as she waited for the players to emerge from the locker room, Daria realized that while she'd enjoyed the sex with Adrian, she hated the price she was paying for that night. The loss of her good friend. Her best friend, if the truth were known. She would do anything to get that friend back, even if it meant sitting through a hockey game she loathed.

But what wasn't helping right now was the unwelcome heat stirring in her lower belly at the thought of Adrian in bed. God, he'd been so willing, so pliant in her hands, despite the obvious struggle he'd undergone to cede control to her. The fact that he'd played along with her fetishes had gotten her going to the point that she'd been envisioning more of the same with him. Daria hadn't felt so alive with another man since the first time she'd explored her odd sexual tastes and realized what a turn-on it all was. What had made it special was that she'd shared those fetishes with Adrian, someone she truly cared about. Someone who, until last week, hadn't sat in judgment on her. Who'd been willing to accept her on her own terms, until another side of her had been revealed to him.

Daria closed her eyes on a spasm of pain. She'd blown it, pure and simple. She should have stopped this whole thing before it had started, at least had stalled him until they were both thinking more clearly and were less tired and boozed up. In her experience, men like Adrian never could handle the loss of control in a dominant situation. She knew that.

Well, if I'm so smart about this whole thing, why am I standing here like some stupid groupie, hoping for a glimpse of him?

Because she *wasn't* a stupid groupie. She was Adrian's friend. And friends should be able to talk, to be honest with each other, as they've always been before. But after that night, she'd felt the friendship become something a little more serious. She wanted to talk to Adrian about it. But it's hard to be honest or to talk when the other person won't acknowledge you exist, she thought, resentfully.

Sighing, Daria leaned against the wall, wanting to get this whole thing over with. Then she snorted in some amusement. She'd never been known for her patience. Well, short of bursting into the locker room, there wasn't much she could do. She would just have to cool her heels.

What seemed like eons later, but was likely no more than fifteen minutes or so, reporters began trickling from the locker room, chatting among themselves and comparing notes. A couple of cameramen followed. Daria stood at attention, willing the locker room door to open again. Almost as though her thought process controlled everything, the door opened, disgorging players. Players with faces ranging in emotion from sad resignation to repressed irritation and bitterness. A couple glanced toward her, then did a double-take, clearly wondering if she might be willing to ease the loss somewhat. But after giving them what she'd hoped was a freezing look, they grinned at her and went outside where the more willing hockey females were clustering around.

After a few moments, Adrian strode out, hockey bag over his shoulder, his face dark as a thundercloud. Despite herself, Daria chided herself for the helpless, gut-wrench she experienced at the sight of him. She'd never noticed him physically before—the broad shoulders and chest tapering down to a waist and abs with no ounce of fat on them. She willfully put it all out of her mind; the strong arms, flat stomach and well-muscled legs, as well as the well-muscled cock that rose between those legs...

Daria forced herself to focus on his face, recognizing the pissed-off look in his eyes. She cursed herself for her impatience in coming here tonight, especially after this game. This was no time to harangue him about his silence or about their friendship. She'd get nothing but anger and sarcasm, which was the last thing she wanted or needed right now.

But before she could turn and slip away, he stopped short as he saw her.

They faced each other in silence for a moment. Daria's heart pounded in her chest as embarrassment and anguish darkened his face. Adrian looked tortured, guilt-ridden at her presence. He'd clearly not expected to see her here, and for a moment, she savored the element of surprise.

Then, deciding she was being childish, Daria took a step forward, wanting to go to him, hoping that maybe, against all odds, they could make it better between them once they talked it out.

But then two very blond, very stacked twins oozed their way over to him, putting their hands all over his body in a way that made her blood boil, effectively putting a barrier between herself and Adrian. Tia and Mia. It fucking figured.

"Oh, you got knocked down so much," one purred. "It's awful. Simply awful. We are *so* sorry about those playoffs, Adrian. But we're here. We can make it better for you."

"Tell us where it hurts, and we'll be more than happy to fix it for you," the other cooed.

Adrian hesitated for just a moment, his gray eyes meeting Daria's almost helplessly. Then, deliberately turning his back on her, he offered an arm to both women.

"Ladies?" he said smoothly. "Thank you for your offer. Your place or mine?"

The answer was lost as black rage thrummed through Daria, threatening to overwhelm her. She gazed at his retreating back, wishing her glare was a laser that could cut him down in his tracks. Anger washed over her, making her oblivious to her surroundings. She came back to reality when she felt a tap on her arm. A security officer looked her in the face, curiosity and mistrust mingling on her features.

"You all right, miss?" she wanted to know.

No, I'm not. I just saw the man I've fallen for go off with two blond bimbos. I just realized the guy doesn't care two shits about me. Would you be all right under those circumstances?

Daria took a deep breath, straightened her shoulders and forced a smile on her face.

"Yes," she said.

"Then you need to move on. Locker room's empty, we're about to shut down the building," the other woman said, but her tone was sympathetic.

She probably thinks I'm some groupie who's going home empty-handed, Daria thought in self-disgust. Why the hell do I let a guy do this to me?

Daria hurriedly left the building, the shock of the moist, humid air assaulting her and compressing her lungs after the almost frigid conditions of the Carlyle Arena. Lightning flickered in the west. Storm coming, for sure. A vicious one, by the looks of it.

Daria scowled at the sky, welcoming the pending storm. A violent thunderstorm would suit her mood perfectly. She was ready to scream, to throw something, to hit something.

Finding her car, Daria slid behind the wheel and forced herself to calm down. Last thing she needed was some kind of stupid road accident because of a stupid jerk of a guy. Setting the car in gear, she drove slowly and carefully, resisting the mad impulse to streak down I-30 at one hundred miles per hour. Daria felt charged-up, like the atmosphere, though her cool and analytical side controlled her body, making sure the speedometer hovered just above sixty.

When she arrived home, she glanced up at Adrian's window. Force of habit, something she'd always done since he'd moved in. The dim light in the living room told her he was home. Suddenly Daria wanted a confrontation with him. She badly wanted to get this out in the open. Fuck waiting. It needed to happen now.

With a set, angry smile on her face, Daria shut off her car, preparing to storm into his apartment. Would she find him making it with the twin bimbos? She hoped so. If he was indulging, he'd wait for his pleasure to hear her out. Then she'd leave and he could sink into whatever depravity he wished.

As she climbed out of the car, Daria realized the storm was even closer, threatening to let loose with thunder, lightning and heavy rains. She could smell it on the air—it would be a wild one. But the fury of the coming storm was nothing compared to the fury bubbling inside her. Adrian Donelson. College friend. Confidante. More recently, lover. An unforgettable lover in a night that had seared her and made him unforgettable to her. But apparently that night had been very forgettable for him. So much so that when she'd showed up to talk with him, he'd turned his back on her, preferring to go off instead with two other women. Her anger gave way to a knife-wrench of agony. What had she done to him? Had her control of him driven him out, not only as a lover, but a friend?

Well, she'd find out soon enough. She strode up the stairs to his apartment, but then paused in front of his door, not wanting to know what might be behind it.

Your prize for guessing door number three, group grope with two blondes and a dark-haired stud...

"Screw it," she growled. Raising a fist, she pounded on the wood, then paused for a moment. No answer. She knocked harder and waited. Still no response.

Trembling, Daria pressed her ear against the door, listening. Even with the rolling thunder outside, she heard the radio. If he was getting it off with those groupies and making her stand out here and cool her heels...

"Damn you, Donelson! Open this fucking door. I won't leave until you do! I'll wake up the neighbors!"

She realized for a brief moment that she used the unspoken code between them—*I'll wake the neighbors*. Private ha-ha between them, meaning get the damned door open before I get you in trouble. They'd even laughed about it, in the past. But this time, she meant it. Daria realized she was angry enough to create a scene. And that anger scared her, even as it exhilarated her.

A moment later, the door was flung open. Adrian stood there, dressed in sweats and a plain white T-shirt, a scowl on his face. Daria quailed a moment before the look in his gray eyes, then her determination hardened.

"I hope I'm not interrupting something," she said acidly.

"Just my beauty sleep. And no smart-ass remarks, DeCarlo, about how long I'd have to sleep to get it."

Daria stalked past him, keeping her eyes peeled for the usual signs of sexual play—the frilly underwear, telltale drink glasses and a sated woman. Rather, sated *women* in this case. She'd seen it before with this man. She'd witnessed the aftermaths of some interesting couplings in this very apartment. Had joked about it with him, in fact. And it was okay before. Before she'd become involved with him as more than just a friend. Despite her bravado, if she were to find Tia and Mia here, Daria would die inside.

But to her relief and surprise, his apartment was empty.

"To what do I owe the honor of this visit?" Adrian had stepped up behind her and she jumped. "If you hadn't realized, I'm not exactly in a talking mood right now. We lost the playoffs, if you'd forgotten."

"You wouldn't talk to me," she snarled. "But you had plenty to say to those groupies."

"Jealous?"

"Fuck off." God damn her temper. When it reared up and took control, her language became ugly.

Adrian narrowed his eyes at her. "Get one thing clear, munchkin. I'm single and over twenty-one. I can date and go out with and fuck whoever I like. Just because we spent a night together doesn't mean you own me."

Daria felt her throat clog with tears. Was that all it had meant to him? Just "a night?" God, this whole thing *had* been a mistake from the start. She'd known it. She should have put a stop to it before it ever started.

Struggling to control her treacherous sobs, Daria stood her ground, wanting to move beyond the what-ifs. The room was dim, the way he liked it, but flares of lightning played over the sharp planes of his face, flickering across his high cheekbones, putting in stark relief the slash of his mouth, leaving his eyes in shadow.

"I'm not saying I own you," she said, proud that her voice didn't tremble. "But what I am saying is that when I send you e-mails about something serious, I expect a response. It means when I leave you phone messages, you return the calls. You've always done those things before, even when you're on the road. It means that when I'm outside your locker room after a game because I want to talk to you, that you don't turn your back on me. It does *not* mean you can ignore me."

He let out a short bark of laughter. "You're hard to ignore, munchkin."

"Stop calling me that, asshole."

"It fits."

His smile was condescending and Daria realized, to her wonderment, that he was trying to piss her off. But why?

"What do you call turning your back on me outside the locker room?"

"I call it losing the playoffs and being done for the season. I call it being too pissed to talk about it. Besides, what the hell do you care? You don't even like hockey."

A small part of Daria's mind told her to leave it alone. She knew these black moods of Adrian's. As a sports fan herself, she knew that a playoff loss hurt. Deeply. He was going through five thousand different kinds of hell right now, and all she was doing was giving him more grief. Like some jealous, clingy, insecure girlfriend.

But the image of Adrian willfully turning his back on her and giving those two blondes his easy charm and attention spurred her on unthinkingly.

"It was what happened last week, wasn't it?" she challenged.

"For crying out loud, woman, it was a one-night fuck! Don't make more of it than what it was. We said—"

"What we *said* and what *happened* are two different things." Daria fought the impulse to stamp her foot and throw something at his head. "You were ignoring me. You've never done that before. I've been there through your other playoff losses. Brains 'n brawn, we stick together, remember? Always have. We mourn together. We celebrate together, damn it! But not tonight? Why?"

He turned away, his face sullen. "I don't want to talk about it."

"Well, too bad. *I* do. I want to talk about the fact that maybe you liked that I took control a few nights back. And it's scaring the crap out of you."

The words just slipped out, but his sudden intake of breath and stiffening of his back told Daria she'd hit something and she continued.

"I thought so. For the first time in your life, a woman took control in the bedroom. You liked it, Adrian. And now you're afraid of it."

"Don't go there, Daria Jane."

She ignored the warning in his voice, her fury grabbing hold, making sure she wouldn't back down. "I'll go wherever the hell I want. You *liked* it Adrian. You liked letting go. You liked letting someone dominate in the bedroom. And you liked it was with me."

Adrian whirled suddenly and came close, towering over her, his masculinity almost overpowering in its strength. A flash of lightning, a boom of thunder and Daria flinched.

"Shut up, munchkin," he ground out.

"Don't call me that!"

His sudden smile was pure malice. "I'll call you whatever the hell I want."

Before she could stop herself, Daria slapped him. They stood still for a moment, staring at each other, lightning flickering around them, thunder roaring through the room. Adrian was breathing heavily, and Daria could sense the rage pounding through him in counterpoint to the throbbing in her hand. A small part of herself was stunned at her actions. She'd never before been so driven to violence because of a man.

"You'd better leave," Adrian said. He was clearly controlling himself with some effort, his fists clenched by his side, his face working. "I can't promise what will happen to you if you don't."

"I'm not afraid of you," she said. She meant it. Though Adrian looked mad enough to kill, she had faith in their bond of friendship. She trusted that, though he talked violence, he would never hurt her. But there was something else. Something else that wasn't quite so pure and noble. She was getting turned on by this whole thing. The pulsing anger thrumming through her body was giving way to a hot, sexual need for him. A glance between Adrian's legs showed her she wasn't alone in her sudden and unexpected arousal.

Swallowing, Daria moved toward him. She felt his breath catch as she slid her arms around his neck and deliberately ground her hips against him, moving against his hard-on. He reached up and, pulling her arms from around him, gently pushed her away.

"Don't," he said, gritting his teeth.

"What the hell are you so afraid of? Adrian Donelson. Big man on the ice. Thug supreme for the Dallas Blaze. But can't handle honesty off the ice? Can't handle the fact that you liked being a sub in our little game the other night? And you want more of it?"

"Honesty you want? All right. It was *nothing*—"

She deliberately moved her hand between his legs, feeling his penis throb against her hand, and smiled. "Don't tell me it was nothing, big man. You're hard as a rock."

He flinched a little and gripped her wrist, moving her hand away. "Yeah? So? You turn me on. Big deal."

"So?" She spoke tauntingly. "Before the other night, would you have been so aroused with me standing here?"

Adrian was silent for several heartbeats, continuing to hold her wrist, staring at her. Then before she knew what was happening, he wrapped his hand in her hair, pulling her head back, exposing her neck. He sank his teeth into the soft flesh joining her neck and shoulder and Daria whimpered in combined pain and pleasure.

"You're a first-class bitch, Daria Jane," he ground out against her throat. "God-damned Italian—"

Before he could get out the expletive, Daria broke free of his hold and moved her mouth against his. Their fight, combined with her lust-ridden state and the storm firing outside mixed a potent brew of dark desire inside her. She hungered for Adrian, hungered for him like she hadn't for any man. The way he kissed her back, with a savage, devouring passion, told her the hot, dark need she was experiencing held him captive as well.

"Damn you," he whispered when the kiss broke. "This has gotten us all screwed up—"

"I don't care. Fuck me, Adrian. We both want it."

Daria spoke breathlessly, almost sobbing. He pushed her away violently and she stumbled against the sofa, trying to regain her balance. Before she could, he was on top of her, tearing at her clothes, pulling them off. Then his hands were everywhere, touching her hungry flesh, making her moan, making her hot and wet.

"You're right, damn you," he whispered harshly. "Right about everything. Ever since the other night, all I could think about was us. Was you turning me into your sub. Tied up and at your mercy. And how I liked it. How I wanted to pay you back for it."

He leaned over and took an erect nipple into his mouth, sucking at it hard, laving it brutally with his tongue, then biting it. Daria screamed as the pain boosted her excitement, causing a throbbing to coalesce deep in her belly.

"Adrian," she gasped. "Oh, God. I can't hold out... take me, Black

Irish. Take me hard..."

His hand moved between her legs, and she opened them, begging for his entry. He slid his fingers deeply inside her cunt, finding her soft, sensitive G-spot and pressing hard. Daria bucked against him as tremors shot through her. He pressed again. And again. Driving her to the brink. Pulling her back. Making her go close again. Driving her close to insane.

"I should make you wait for it," he ground out in her ear as his fingers kept moving, pushing her toward the pinnacle, then drawing her back before she could break through. "I should make you want it so badly, you can't stand it. Just like you did to me. But I want to see you come. I want to hear you scream and cry out while I'm making you come. I want that more than anything."

He released her suddenly and she fell back, whimpering, her craving for him so deep, she didn't know what had come over her. She stared up at him, trembling, as he pulled off his T-shirt and sweatpants. Then he stood naked before her, legs braced to take his weight, arms folded.

Quickly, Daria got to her knees, wanting to taste him, wanting his hardness in her mouth. But he forestalled her with a casual push and she tumbled against the sofa. Before she could sit up, Adrian yanked her legs apart and, positioning himself, slid into her. Daria caught her breath, wrapped her legs around him and moved her hips against him, driving him deeper. She closed her eyes as his cock traced a path of fire through her, rubbing against her slick and swollen walls, driving her mad with the need to climax.

"Open your eyes," he commanded. "Keep them open. I want to see you when you come. When you lose it. When you lose control. Do it, Daria Jane."

She gasped and her eyelids flew open as her hands clutched his shoulders, the tattoo of the eagle moving under her touch. Lightning flickered over his face, the stark planes, the flare of almost insane desire in his eyes. Demon lover, brought to her out of lightning and thunder.

"Scream my name. When you come. Scream it."

He was hissing as he thrust deeply into her and Daria felt incredible warmth submerge her, burying her in molten waves. She writhed frantically beneath him, helpless to stop the flow of black heat engulfing her. Feeling those gray eyes pinning her, ripping her soul inside out, turning her to mush. He was still hard inside her and, in a fluid movement, he moved so she was on top and she was riding him with wild abandon. Impaled, she came down on him hard. Then again, moans ripped from her gut as sharp desire seared through her, enslaving her, keeping her captive, keeping her wanting more.

Her climax hit her broadside with a suddenness that left her screaming. Screaming his name as he'd commanded, as he'd ordered. Realizing, as her breaths came out in half-sobs as she came down, that he was still hard, still buried deeply inside her.

He maneuvered her under him again and moved into her violently, brutally, his dark face looming above hers, a snarl on his face.

"Damn you, Daria Jane," he said. "Fucking vixen. Invading my thoughts, my soul, my very life...and you say I ignore you...far from it...you're all I've been able to think about these last few days..."

Before he could say more, he cried out and spasmed. Daria screamed again as she felt the heat of his cum move through her, branding her, causing her to convulse in a wanton ecstasy. As Adrian slid out of her, leaving her a gasping wreck, Daria was marginally aware that the storm had broken, booming thunder in counterpart to the bright lightning flickering around them both. But Adrian's relentless lovemaking had spent the storm inside her, and she collapsed beneath him, gasping for air.

After a moment, he rolled over and gently pulled her toward him. They lay in one another's arms on the floor as the rain lashed the windows, still accompanied by flashing lightning and loud thunder. Daria was exhausted, spent. She felt Adrian shift beside her, and gently touch the wound he'd inflicted on her shoulder. He kissed it softly, and Daria felt her lips stretch into a tired smile.

"Trying to kiss it and make it better?" she asked.

"Is it working?"

The wound still throbbed, and Daria shook her head. They were silent for a moment.

"So you can't get off without bondage?" he asked cryptically.

"Oh, shut up." She was tired and depressed. She, who liked control during sex, had lost it completely to a man who considered her little more than his good buddy.

"I think we need to talk," he went on quietly.

"Great. *Now* the man wants to talk. I wanted to talk at Carlyle, but you couldn't deal with it." Daria realized she was being surly, but couldn't help it.

Adrian was silent for a moment. "I'm sorry," he finally said. The words were stated simply, without artifice. And they reeked of sincerity.

Daria sat up and looked down at him, stunned. He looked back up at her, and gave her a tentative smile.

"You're...sorry?"

"Yeah." He rubbed the back of his neck, the way he did when he was disturbed about something. "I treated you like crap, Daria Jane. You were right. I loved every single minute about the other night. And—and I guess that scared me. It also scared me that you were right about something else. This has changed our friendship. I didn't mean for it to happen, but it did."

She swallowed, realizing the price this proud man was paying to be vulnerable before her.

"I know," she said, her voice faltering. "But there's something more, Adrian. I..I think I've fallen for you. I'm not quite sure how it happened, but there it is."

He reached up with his hand and gently brushed her hair aside. "Yeah. I kind of figured from the note you'd left me after the other night. But it isn't one-sided, munchkin. I think I've fallen for you, too." Adrian laughed a little. "It happens sometimes. Or so I'm told."

Daria sighed and pressed her forehead against her bent legs. "Falling in love screws up things," she told him. "I don't mean with you. Just in general."

"Listen, I'm more gun-shy about this than you are. You know my history. That dumb affair with Roxanne in college. And these days, women coming on to me, right and left, but only for one thing." His face screwed up. "Fame. Fortune. My rock-hard bod."

Daria snorted, and he continued.

"I got tired of it, Daria Jane. It just seemed easier to play hockey, knock a few heads on the ice and ball willing women afterward. Keep my emotions out of it."

"Show them a good time in bed," Daria mimicked Adrian's deep Boston accent and he smiled.

"I didn't hear you complaining."

She sighed. "That's the problem. I like you, Adrian. I always have. I just never thought of you in that way until recently. And it's damned unsettling."

"Why?"

She gestured. "I'm a numbers geek. You know that. I like things compartmentalized. Uncomplicated. Controlled. I guess that's why I like my role as the dominant in bed." She laughed a little and shook her head. "Well, you sure blew that to hell. That night? I'd never been so aroused before. I guess no guy ever moved me like that before like you did. It came as a shock. But I thought it wasn't being returned. You didn't return my e-mails, my phone calls, which is totally unlike you."

"And was totally stupid." Adrian sat up and regarded her seriously. "I know you can't stand hockey, Daria Jane. But I'm going to drag out a hockey example, and don't roll your eyes at me like that. It's like—like when I'm on a penalty kill. You know, a man or two down on the ice, and we have to make sure the puck doesn't get in our goal. We have to change strategy all the time because we never know what's going to happen. Who's going to break away. Who's going to claim the puck. Who's gonna put that slapshot behind the goalie."

He shrugged, and in the dim light, Daria could see a self-deprecating smile. "My job is more than beating up guys on the ice, Daria. It's making sure I can move with the flow and can help the goalie defend the goal. Sometimes the game calls for a fight. Sometimes it doesn't. Sometimes it means that I'm another goalie and I have to block the puck before it gets there. What I'm trying to say is that I can't stay stuck in one place, otherwise I'm toast. Maybe...maybe that's what all of this is about. With the two of us. Change of strategy."

Daria smiled. She'd never heard a relationship put quite in terms like that.

"You love control, though," she said.

"Sure. But I let it go," he pointed out. "On the ice, for my teammates. And for you. Because I trust you."

Daria closed her eyes, feeling the profound truth hit her. Trust. It was a bond she and Adrian had shared for years, one that went deeper than anything else. One that went deeper than any other relationship. It was trust that had made them friends for all these years, despite their differences. Despite her brains and his brawn. And it would be trust that might keep them together as lovers.

"I trust you, too," she whispered. "And I'm sorry if I came across sounding like a jealous bitch a little while ago—"

"I kind of liked that you were jealous," he said somberly. "But I'll tell you one thing, Daria Jane. If I ever find you with some other guy, I'll go to jail for manslaughter. I'm gonna beat the crap out of that guy. Be warned, okay?"

"You're such a romantic, Black Irish." Daria spoke dryly, and he grinned.

187

"Somehow, I don't think a woman who wields a whip and likes to do it with neckties cares much about being a romantic."

"I love you, Adrian."

"I stand corrected," he said, obviously surprised. Then a smile lightened his features, and Daria felt herself relax.

"I love you, too, Daria Jane," he murmured. "Sometimes it takes a knock to the head of the brawn to figure it out, though."

She chuckled as she slid her arms around him. "Just so long as the brawn is ready for action when the brain says it's time."

"Then the brain needs to shut up and start acting," he said as he lowered his mouth to hers.

ERICA DEQUAYA

For more than two and a half decades, Erica DeQuaya has padded her bank account as a freelance journalist, copywriter and scriptwriter.

As an award-winning erotic romance novelist, Erica has penned *Backstage Affair, Double Mitzvah, Mixed Media* (winner of the *Road to Romance's* critic's award) and *Power Play* (a *Road to Romance* "Recommended Read").

Also in Erica's collection of writings is her best-selling "hockey series," including *Penalty Kill, In the Crease* and *Two On One*. She's also at work on *High Stick*, a novel about the clandestine relationship between two male hockey players.

Erica lives in Texas with her husband and soul mate of more than twenty years, her son and two neurotic dogs.

AMBER QUILL PRESS, LLC
THE GOLD STANDARD IN PUBLISHING

QUALITY BOOKS
IN BOTH PRINT AND ELECTRONIC FORMATS

ACTION/ADVENTURE	SUSPENSE/THRILLER
SCIENCE FICTION	DARK FANTASY
MAINSTREAM	ROMANCE
HORROR	EROTICA
FANTASY	GLBT
WESTERN	MYSTERY
PARANORMAL	HISTORICAL
YOUNG ADULT	NON-FICTION

AMBER QUILL PRESS, LLC
http://www.amberquill.com

809921

Made in the USA